Titles in The Crimson Five

THE CRIMSON FIVE

Flip the Silver Switch

Jackie Yeager
Amberjack Publishing
New York | Idaho

Amberjack Publishing
1472 E. Iron Eagle Drive
Eagle, Idaho 83616
http://amberjackpublishing.com

Library of Congress Cataloging-in-Publication Data
Names: Yeager, Jackie, author.
Title: Flip the silver switch / by Jackie Yeager.
Description: Eagle, Idaho : Amberjack Publishing, [2018] | Series: Crimson
    Five ; 2 | Summary: When the Crimson Five travel to Quebec City for the
    Piedmont Global Championships, they are blindsided by a new task and
Kia
    must get them to pull together as pressure builds.
Identifiers: LCCN 2017061618 (print) | LCCN 2018005512 (ebook) | ISBN
    9781944995706 (eBook) | ISBN 9781944995690 (hardcover : alk. paper)
Subjects: | CYAC: Interpersonal relations--Fiction. | Contests--Fiction. |
    Inventors--Fiction. | Qu?ebec (Qu?ebec)--Fiction. | Canada--Fiction. |
    Science fiction.
Classification: LCC PZ7.1.Y434 (ebook) | LCC PZ7.1.Y434 Fli 2018
(print) |
    DDC [Fic]--dc23
LC record available at https://lccn.loc.gov/2017061618

Cover Design and Illustrations: Gabrielle Esposito

For Danielle and Adam, the ones who make my world sparkle.

THE AERO-SCOOTER

I PROBABLY SHOULDN'T sneak out of the house. But if I go now while Mom's buried in her chemistry files, I'll be back home with my suitcase packed before she can panic about me missing the aero-bus. Seriously? Like I would ever miss this trip with my team.

The kitchen door opens without a sound. I peek into her office, and just like I thought, Mom's swimming in papers. Perfect! I run out and grab my aero-scooter from its port and roll it down the driveway. When I get to the street, I push the lift-off button, glide up to the treetops, and let the September wind blow my bangs away from my eyes.

Soon, I see my whole neighborhood below me, including Charlotte's blue house. I wonder for a second what she did all summer while I was away at Camp Piedmont. Did she fly aero-scooters with her new friends? Did she have sleepovers with them? But then I remember that

1

ex-best friends don't wonder about each other, and she's the one who decided I wasn't allowed to go to her stupid sleepovers last year anyway. Whatever. If Charlotte still doesn't think my sixty-seven invention ideas are cool and important, fine. My teammates do. My four awesome teammates who totally get me—and I'm going to hang out with them all day and all night for the next two weeks. It's going to be like one big, amazing sleepover.

I steer toward the sun and my whole body warms up. It's like I just flew into a heat machine.

Hmm, a heat machine.

That could be the best invention ever! It could hang from the sky cables and be shaped like a tunnel. When a person's riding their aero-scooter and they get too cold, they could fly into the heat machine, warm up like toast, and then fly out the other side.

Yes! That would be a really good invention.

The town of Crimson Heights is quiet below with all my classmates back in school. It feels weird to be missing the first day of seventh grade at Crimson Academy, but I don't mind. I have a competition to go to. I leave for the Piedmont Challenge Global Championships in a few hours, and *oh my god* I still can't believe I'm going!

I reach for the medal hanging around my neck. I wear it every day now, just like my teammates do. It's like we're all afraid to take them off, like if we do, we'll wake up and find out we didn't place in the top five at the Piedmont Challenge National Finals, that we aren't going to Québec for Globals soon—that this whole summer has been a dream. But when I feel the metal between my fingers and see *Kia Krumpet* engraved on the front, I know I'm not dreaming at all.

I wonder what it'll be like at Globals. Will we eat scrambled apples in the dining hall and wear matching USA shirts like we did at Camp Piedmont? Will we perform our Ancestor App skit in a classroom like we did for the National Finals? Or will we be presenting it up on a giant stage? Will we have enough time to practice first? Our team preceptor, Seraphina, said we have two weeks until we perform our skit for everyone—two weeks! That's not a lot of time. We might know it backwards and forwards, but what if my teammates forget their lines? What if they've forgotten how to activate the Ancestor App? What if Ander wants to take a million breaks? What if Mare wants to skip practice and take a nap? I can't let any of those things happen.

I steer clear of a sky cable and think back to a few weeks ago at Camp Piedmont. I know exactly what to do. I'll bribe Ander with snacks and jump on Mare if she tries to sleep. That'll work—Jillian and I have done it before. I bet Jax will even help us. I mean, after spending all summer with them, I know my teammates—their good parts *and* their bad parts—and I know for sure they want to win as much as I do, even if they forget what it takes sometimes. So I guess it'll be up to me to hold practice sessions on the aero-bus today. They can thank me later—when we're declared champions of the Piedmont Challenge Global Championships.

Down below, Grandma Kitty is doing her morning exercises in her yard. When she sees me, she waves and rushes to turn off the music. I touch the brake handle and glide onto the grass, careful not to disrupt her perfectly potted plants.

"Sweet Tart! What are you doing here? Shouldn't you be

home packing up your things? Not that I mind a visit, of course!"

"Hi GK, I'm mostly packed."

"Oh, Jelly Bean, of course you are. But what is it then? I know that look on your face."

"What look on my face?"

"You look as skittish as a mouse in a mousetrap."

I take my fingernails out of my mouth. "I'm not nervous."

"You have absolutely nothing to be nervous about. Québec is not that far away. You and those creative teammates of yours are going to have the adventure of a lifetime. Your invention is going to whoop the pants off all the other inventions, and when it wins and gets built, all of us will be better for it. The judges will see how important your discovery is. Mark my words."

I think about that for a second. "But, Grandma, why do *you* think the Ancestor App is so important?"

She looks me right in the eye. "Well, it's very simple, Buttercup. With the Ancestor App, I'll be able to talk to my mother again."

I make a weird face. I know what she means when she says that, but Grandma Kitty's mother is dead, so it sounds strange—even to me—that she might be able to *talk* to her again someday using our invention.

"I was only thirteen years old when she died, not much older than you are right now, and even though I remember her, I wish I could hear her voice again, ask her questions, and listen to her stories. There's still so much I'd like to know."

Grandma Kitty is so old I forget she had parents once too. And then I feel sad. It would be awful if Mom or Dad weren't here anymore.

She wipes her sweaty hands on her stretchy pants. "That's why I *know* your Ancestor App is important. I'm not the only one in this enormous world who wishes they had another chance to communicate with someone they've lost."

"But what if our invention doesn't place in the top three? That means it'll never get built. All those people will be missing out."

"Yes, they will."

"I wish the law about that was different."

"But it isn't, so you just have to focus on things you can control—like this competition. Place in the top three, and the Ancestor App will get built."

I bite the skin around my pinky nail.

"You're not afraid to go on this trip, are you? Winning the Piedmont Challenge has propelled you into this humongous world, with the whole town watching your every move, and I don't want you to be afraid of what's coming next."

I shake my head. "I'm not afraid."

She smiles and her eyes wrinkle. "That's my Lollipop. Now get flying on that fancy scooter. You have a bus to catch."

I start up the motor and she hugs me tight. "I'll see you at the aero-bus station, right Grandma?"

"I wouldn't miss it for the world."

I lift up above her house. I know Grandma Kitty thinks we're going to win, but our team didn't even get first place at the National Finals, and this is Globals. Besides, no United States team has won in ten years. I don't think our chances are very good. My stomach churns thinking about it, and I realize I need inspiration. I need to see the exact place where I won my Golden Light Bulb trophy. Maybe flying over Crimson will help my jitters.

I head for the school yard of Crimson Elementary and hover over the amphitheatre where the Piedmont Challenge began. My stomach stops churning and I think about the trip ahead of me. All we have to do is show our Ancestor App to the judges, just like we've done before. That's all. No big deal. No problem.

I should hurry and get home, but instead I fly across the school yard to Crimson Academy, the school I *would have* gone to for seventh grade today if I hadn't won this medal. With its concrete walls and red edges, it looks identical to Crimson Elementary.

I squeeze the brake and aim for the sidewalk, landing as quietly as I can near a maple tree, hoping no one will hear me, recognize me, or ask me why I'm there. But the motor coughs unexpectedly, so I duck behind the tree trunk and freeze. It's not like I'm trespassing or anything, but after the big deal the whole town has made since we came back from Camp Piedmont, I just want to be here alone—without anyone asking me about our team's invention or what I think of Principal Bermuda's nasty trick.

My helmet presses into the back of my skull and makes my head ache, so I unbuckle the strap. I wish someone would invent a helmet that doesn't squish my ponytail. Oh, never mind, I'll add it to my invention list and make one myself.

I stare at the red school door and grip the handle bars. I can't help it. Most kids like going to a regular school. They like getting programmed into one category, forced to study just one subject for all of seventh and eighth grade—but not me. I'd rather eat mud.

I'm still staring at the school when another aero-scooter zooms up and lands next to me, kicking up stones on the sidewalk. I jump and Ander laughs, flashing his giant grin. "Hey, KK. What's up?"

I smile. It still feels weird to hear him call me by that nickname. I mean, nicknames mean you're someone's best friend, and, well, I just haven't been one in a while.

I shake my head. "Nice landing, *Al-ex-ander*."

"Thanks, you should see me on the rink. I do the same thing in my hockey skates."

I'm not too sure about that. Ander has a way of making everything he does sound bigger and better than it actually is. "Yeah, I bet."

"So what are you doing here? Trying to confront Principal Bermuda, like me? I've been trying to find him ever since we got back from Camp Piedmont, but it's like he's got a force field around him or something."

"After what he what he did to us there—blackmailing Gregor into smashing our project into a million pieces— just so we'd start over again and create a better invention? No, I'm not going to confront him! I don't want to see him ever again." It surprises me how much I still hate him— how much I hate that he was barely punished at all for interfering with the competition.

"What are you doing here then?"

I picture the metal card reader on the wall just inside the red door. I imagine all my classmates who filed in one by one this morning and swiped their student number cards through it. 718, my own number, flashes in my mind like a bolt of lightning. "I wanted to remind myself what I won't be missing when we leave here."

"Like getting programmed?" He picks up a random pebble from the ground, searches for another about the same size, and tries to juggle them.

"Not just getting programmed," I say. "Well, yeah, mostly getting programmed."

"Everyone I know—except our team—is excited about the class they were programmed into. I guess they think it'll be easier to focus on one category."

"That's so crazy, Ander! Art Forms, Communications, Earth and Space, Human history, Math, New Technology—none of them are interesting enough to study for all of seventh and eighth grade."

He drops a pebble. "KK, did you see how high that pebble went? I'm practically a one-man circus act."

I shrug. "But you dropped it."

His hands flail out. "Before that! It soared way up over the flag pole. That's the best I've ever jugged!"

"Jugged? It's called *juggling,* and besides, it's not even juggling when you only use two items."

"Ha! That's where you're wrong. I said jugging. Jugging is the beginner version of juggling—using two props. It says so in the juggling rule book."

"There's no such thing as a juggling rule book."

"Sure there is. I have it at home, and it says right in there that jugging is the way jugglers first learn to juggle. I read up on it when we got home from Camp Piedmont. I figured if I'm going to be Freddie Dinkleweed, the mystical jester in our skit, I should learn to juggle. According to my book, the word juggle comes from the Middle English word *jogelen,* which means to entertain by performing tricks."

Ander knows more random facts than anyone I know.

The red door clicks and creaks open. We freeze. I plant my eyes on the door and hope whoever it is doesn't look over at the tree. A man with hair so slick you could wax your scooter with it, and a belly that's totally trying to escape from his shirt, steps outside.

Ander leans over. "It's him!"

"Shh! I know," I whisper, trying not to move my lips.

Principal Bermuda stops just outside the door, adjusts his belt, and slowly turns toward us. I guess we're not as smart as the whole town thinks—this is a really crappy hiding spot.

His face breaks into a smarmy grin. "Well, if it isn't two of the Crimson Five? To what do we owe this honor? Shouldn't you two be preparing for your trip?"

My voice is stuck. I look at Ander silently pleading him not to confront him. Principal Bermuda's a grown up, and even though he's a bad grown up, he is a *principal*. Who knows what he could do to us if he thinks we don't like him? Just look at what he did to Gregor.

"Uh . . . yes, sir," says Ander. "We are, but we wanted to get one more look at the Crimson schools. First Crimson Elementary, the school that taught us *everything* we know, the school that propelled us to success at Camp Piedmont this summer and led us to the Global Championships. And now we're here stopping at Crimson Academy to remind ourselves of all our former classmates who are counting on us to do great things at the Global Championships."

Whoa. Where did that come from?

"I see, Mr. Yates. That's very nice to hear, but it's getting close to lift-off. I suggest you and Miss Krumpet fly back home now. You wouldn't want to be late for your *first task* now, would you?"

"No, sir."

Principal Bermuda tugs at his suit jacket and waddles his way to wherever it is that he's going. Ander and I hop on our scooters and kick them into gear. *What's wrong with me?* I couldn't even answer his question. I should have told him what I thought of his nasty trick at Camp Piedmont, but I couldn't even speak. I'm such a coward. Even if he is a principal, I should have told him that what he did to us— and to Gregor—wasn't right. But I couldn't say anything at all.

Wait, what did he mean by our "first task"? We don't have another task to solve. We already solved one—a big one—to get to the Global Championships. I look at Ander and I think he's wondering the same thing—but we don't dare say anything out loud. Principal Bermuda probably has listening bugs wired into the trees. And after what he pulled at Camp Piedmont, I wouldn't be surprised.

THE BLINKING LIGHT

WE ARRIVE AT the aero-bus terminal with only minutes to spare, which is not how Mom likes it. She hurries us out of the car, and I look around the parking lot for Grandma Kitty. Dad pulls my suitcase and backpack out of the trunk and glances at me. "Don't worry, Kia. Grandma Kitty will be here."

"I hope so."

He crouches down to talk to me face to face. "So, Little Bear, are you ready for this? I mean, really ready?" He waits for me to respond, but when I only let out a breath, he smiles. "Never mind. I know you are."

My fourteen-year-old sister Malin jumps in front of me. "Okay, Kia, now listen. This summer was a major fail for you. You may have won second place in the competition or whatever, but you didn't come home with any good stories."

"What? I had a million good stories!"

"Oh, Kia. Kia, Kia, Kia . . . not those stories. I don't care about floating playgrounds, Nacho Cheese Ball, or robotic monkeys. I'm talking about the hotness factor of the boys at Camp Piedmont. When I get to Québec in two weeks to watch you in the competition, I'll be expecting you to provide me with *actual* stories. Good stories. Stories about boys. Got it?"

I shake my head. As usual, my sister doesn't get it at all.

We walk through the parking lot toward the Sapphire Terminal, the one that houses our special aero-bus. My little brother Ryne races ahead but soon sprints back to us with his arms wide open.

"Where are all the people? The whole town was here when you came home from Camp Piedmont."

We turn the corner and see a small group gathered around the egg-shaped bus. Mom hurries him along. "Principal Bermuda assured us this will be a private send-off this time."

"I hope so. I'm not sure I like people asking me questions about our invention every time I see them—every time I go to the store or sit on our front porch."

"I bet he's afraid that people will ask him more questions about what he did to your project," Dad replies. "And he should be. That bit he said to your team when you got home last month was a load of crap."

That day was horrible.

All I wanted to do when he "welcomed" us off the bus was punch him in his nasty face. All of us did. But we all did the same thing. *Nothing.* Nothing at all. We stood there like statues. Even Mare. Like we forgave him or didn't mind that he wrecked our whole project because it forced us to make an even better one. Yeah sure, it worked, but we didn't forgive him. Not one bit.

We get closer to the crowd of people, and Ander breaks through, bouncing a tennis ball. "KK, what took you so long? You missed me entertaining the audience with my juggling skills."

Mare rolls her eyes. "Yeah, they were entertained all right." She looks at me and smiles. It's not a huge grin like Ander always gives me, but it's definitely a smile. For Mare and me, that's progress.

"Hi guys," I say. "Did I miss anything else? Besides the Ander show?"

Ander grins, obviously proud that I would call his "juggling" a show.

"Nope," says Mare. "We're just waiting for Jillian and Jax." She nods in the direction of the bus. "Here comes Jax. Let's see how long it takes for his face to turn red."

"Mare, don't be mean," I say. "His face doesn't turn red all the time—well, not anymore anyway."

"Yeah, we'll see." She smiles her intimidating smile, the one that still comes out every once in a while.

Jax walks over with the best posture of any kid I've ever seen.

"Big Guy!" Ander calls. "Glad you made it. Our team is not a team until every teammate is here."

Jax's face doesn't even turn red. "Uh, thanks, I guess."

"Where's Jillian?" I ask. "She's not here yet?"

Ander laughs. "Well, if you mean Jillian and her two-ton suitcase, I think that's her."

We turn around and Jillian is dragging her oversized suitcase behind her. It's probably five times the size of mine. Instead of wearing shorts like Mare and me, she's wearing a skirt and boots, looking like she stepped off a Paris runway. Her hair is curled to perfection, and her jacket even matches her backpack.

"Darlings! I missed you all so much. Are you ready for our international adventure? Glad to see you all dressed up for the occasion."

I shake my head. Leave it to Jillian to turn on the drama before we even get on the bus!

Jax looks down at his shirt, and his face turns the shade of red we're all used to. "Were we supposed to dress up?"

Ander bounces the ball and pats Jax on the back. "We look great, Jax—as usual. Khaki shorts and collared shirts are the perfect attire for traveling internationally, if I do say so myself."

I look up at Jax and smile. "Seraphina's probably going to give us shirts to change into when we get there anyway."

"True," says Jillian. "But that's after we arrive. I like to travel in style."

"Since when?" asks Mare tucking her straight blond hair behind her ear.

Jillian shrugs. "Oh look, girls, you have matching Converse sneakers!"

Mare looks at her feet and then at mine. "Oh, goody."

I place my foot next to hers. "We do, Mare. See, we're twinning!"

"Just what I want—more matching. Like we won't be wearing the exact same shirts for the next two weeks again."

Jillian links her arms through mine and Mare's. "This is going to be the best trip ever—I just know it is."

I smile because I hope she's right. I hope this will be the best trip ever.

Soon a motor whirs and sputters overhead. I should have known—Grandma Kitty! She circles above us on an aero-scooter with red, white, and blue streamers trailing behind her. She waves, hovers above us for a second, and spins in a circle. Our mouths hang open as she lands on the pavement in a not-so-graceful plunk.

She brushes herself off and grins. "Hello, Lemon Drop! I told you I'd make it."

"That was awesome!" says Ander. "KK, your grandma's cool."

She cuts the motor, takes off her helmet, and the red sparkles in her hair pop out from underneath.

"Grandma Kitty! Where'd you get the aero-scooter?"

"This was a present to me from me. I figure if riding on an aero-scooter fuels your creativity, it has to be able to re-fuel mine too. A lady's got to do more with her time than make fancy earrings. I'm thinking of switching to sparkly scooter goggles instead. They'd be real useful riding in the air all day. I may even fly this thing to Québec later this month—if I can figure out how to navigate the birds."

"You should! Then you can take me for a ride through the university campus."

Mare peeks inside the aero-bus. "The bus driver's in there. What's the holdup? I thought Principal Backstabber was supposed to be here to send us off or something."

Before we can answer, an aero-cart zooms over and three men hop out—one with a television camera, one with a microphone, and one with slicked back hair and a bulging belly.

Ander drops the tennis ball. It bounces under the bus.

Our families quickly gather around us in a pack. Principal Bermuda waddles over. "Hello there, everyone. Glad to see you're on time."

"What's the TV camera for?" asks Ander. "I thought you

wanted our send-off to be private."

"Private *in person*. You don't think the town wants to miss out on your grand departure, or watching you solve your send-off task, do you?"

"Our send-off task?" I ask.

"That's not even a thing," says Mare.

"Yeah," Ander replies. "We got a letter from the Piedmont people about what's happening today. There is no Piedmont send-off task."

"You're a smart boy, Mr. Yates. There isn't a *Piedmont* task but there is a *Crimson* task."

Grandma Kitty shoulders her way toward the front of the group. "What for?"

"To show the people of Crimson just how smart and creative all these kids are, to generate more buzz about their travels."

"I think you've generated enough buzz about their travels, don't you?" Mom says with more *Mare* tone than I thought she had in her.

"Ah, Mrs. Krumpet, one can never generate too much buzz. Your daughter and her teammates are making history as we speak. I plan to document it all."

"With all due respect, Principal Bermuda, because of your *involvement* with the project these kids created during their time at Camp Piedmont, it's my understanding that you are to have no contact or interaction with the Piedmont competition."

"And I intend to fully cooperate with the Piedmont Organization's decision. While these kids may be both representatives of New York State and the United States of America at the Global Championships, they are also representatives of the town of Crimson Heights and the

Crimson Central School District. It is within my rights to give this community what they desire—a glimpse into the adventure these amazing kids are about to embark on."

What does that even mean?

"You don't object to interviewing the kids before they leave—asking them a few questions?"

"Well," Mom replies, "I think we should ask the kids."

Principal Bermuda licks his lips. "Kids, what do you say? Take one for the team, the team that supported you back home? Answer a few questions for the cameras?"

I'm not sure what to say. All this attention feels really weird. My teammates and I look at each other. I'm not sure we're allowed to tell him no though, and the camera man is waiting. "I guess that's fine," I say.

Principal Bermuda claps his hands. "Okay Larry, let's roll 'em." He pulls a wrinkled piece of paper out of his coat pocket. "Parents? Do you mind stepping away from the cameras, please? Kids, stand right here next to me in front of this spectacular aero-bus."

We shuffle over and the man with the microphone steps toward us. He motions to the camera man, and the tiny blinking light on his camera flashes. "In a continuation of our on-going story, we're here live with the kids from Crimson Elementary who placed second in the Piedmont Challenge National Finals and have since become known in our community as The Crimson Five. With the Piedmont Global Championships just a few weeks away, they're packed and ready to take off on the aero-bus right behind them for Québec City. I'm joined today by Kia, Ander, Mare, Jax, Jillian, and their school principal, Blake Bermuda."

"Kids, we've said it before, but we'll say it again. Your

accomplishment is inspiring. We wish you luck in global competition. Now, Kia, we've learned that you'll present your solution to the judges once again in this competition. How is it different from your last competition?"

The red light blinks at me angrily. My heart pounds, but I resist the urge to bite my pinky nail. "Well, sir, last time we were competing against other American teams for a chance to compete at the Global Championships and a chance to enroll at PIPS—the Piedmont Inventors Prep School. This time, we're competing against teams from all over the world to have our invention chosen."

The reporter nods and looks at Jax. "Chosen for what? Jax, can you tell us?"

Jax stands up even straighter than he already is. "The top inventions will be built at PIPS, or the other creativity schools at the teams' respective countries—they will become more than a prototype and eventually be used by people all over the world."

"Ander, the solution you created for the National Finals has been kept under wraps. Is there anything you can tell us about it?"

Oh no! I think back to when Ander let it slip to nasty Witch Girl from Michigan that we were doing a skit to explain our task solution and invention—something no other team had done before.

Ander leans toward the microphone. "No, I'm sorry, but I can't. According to the rules, our solution needs to be kept a secret until we present it in Québec."

The reporter turns to Mare. "Okay then. Mare, can you at least tell us how you came up with it? Whose idea was it?"

Mare shrugs. "We all came up with it together."

"Well, it had to have originally come from one person, right Jillian?"

"No," Jillian says. "It came from all of us—all our small ideas turned into one big idea."

He looks around at each of us. "I see—then your solution is even more impressive. I like the teamwork. You certainly seem to have that skill perfected."

I stare at the red blinking light. None of us say anything; we just smile.

"Now, Principal Bermuda, what do *you* think it is about these kids that makes them special—that got them this far in the competition?"

"Well, that's easy. The education they received at Crimson was top notch."

The reporter nods. "You told me earlier that you have a question you want to ask the kids."

Principal Bermuda grabs the microphone with his plump hand. "Yes, I do. This competition began with a series of tasks. I'd like the kids to solve a task right here for our viewers."

What?

Ander's eyes get big. "Right here?"

"Sure. I bet our viewers would like the opportunity to watch you solve a quick-thinking task—one like each of you solved in your Swirl and Spark Recall. So, here's a quick one for you: Starting with Mare, in thirty seconds or less, name one thing that bothers you about the teammate to your left—and go!"

Mare looks at Jillian and then at each of us.

"The timer is ticking," he says.

"Um, well, I don't know. She's kind of messy, I guess."

"Next!" Principal Bermuda says.

Jillian looks at Ander. "Well, if I had to say something, I guess I'd say Ander can be bossy."

"Next!" he says again.

Ander looks at Jax. "Well, Jax doesn't say much. He could loosen up a little."

"Next!"

Jax turns to me. "Um."

Principal Bermuda taps his watch.

Jax's face turns crimson. "Um, Kia's kind of intense."

Intense? How?

"Next!"

I look at Mare and then at the blinking light. "Mare can be . . . outspoken."

She glares at me.

"Time! And that's how quickly these kids can think on their feet without even knowing ahead of time what they will be asked."

"Wait a minute," says Mare. "I have a response to add about you, Principal Bermuda. Principal Bermuda can be—"

"Cut!" calls Principal Bermuda.

The light on the camera disappears. "Larry, please cut Mare's last remark."

The reporter nods and heads back to the cart with the camera man.

Grandma Kitty stomps over to us dragging her scooter alongside her. "Principal Bermuda, what on Earth was that?"

He straightens his tie, a fat one with weasels printed all over it. "I told you, a chance for our viewers to see these kids think on their feet."

"With a question like that—designed to tear them apart? The Piedmont judges would never ask them a question like that."

"Well, well, I think we have all we need for our commentary on the Crimson Five. It's time for lift-off. Say your goodbyes, kids—and remember the whole town of Crimson will be watching you. Make us proud. Make me proud!"

Ick. I'd rather choke him with that stupid weasel tie.

My dad wraps me up in a hug, and my stomach drops. Québec is even farther away than Maryland, where Camp Piedmont was held. I wish that was where we were going now, back to our star bed, to the spinning food flowers, to the air purification sparkles, to Mable, to Meeting Room Twelve, and even to Swissa. I know what to expect there. At the university in Québec, I don't know anything at all.

"Bye Kia!" says Ryne.

"Remember what I told you," says Malin. "I want *stories.* Good ones."

Mom kisses me on the side of the head. "See you soon, Baby Girl. Be safe."

I catch the tears running down her face even as she fumbles for a tissue to hide them.

Dad wraps his arms around us both. "We'll see you in two weeks, Little Bear. It won't be as long as last time. You can show us all around the university when we get there—I have a feeling there'll be a lot to see."

I hug them tight then make my way toward the aero-bus. Grandma Kitty is standing guard by the doorway with a serious look on her face. "You have fun, Sugar Plum. Show those global teams what the Crimson Five are really made of! That invention of yours is spectacular—it'll win, I just know it. Mark my words."

I hope she's right. If the Ancestor App gets picked, then

everyone can talk to their ancestors like we did. Besides, somebody's invention has to win. I pick ours.

THE SKIT MIXER GAME

I FOLLOW MY teammates up the steps to the aero-bus and the door closes behind me. The driver smiles as we pass by. My breath catches when I see the sparkly walls and all the red couch seats. This time though, the couches aren't arranged in rows; they're situated along the sides of the bus. We set our luggage in a cupboard and each claim our spots.

Ander plops into his couch. "I like this new arrangement."

Mare grins. "Now this is the life. I'll see you guys in nine hours. Wake me up when we get there."

Jillian heads to a table in the back where a red box awaits. "Look, guys, it's a present."

Mare sits up. "Who's it for?"

She flips open the tag. "All of us."

We scurry for seats around the table. I head to the only seat that's left in between Jillian and Jax. Jillian pats the seat. "Here, Kia, sit next to me."

Mare looks at her. "Where else would she sit? It's the only chair left."

"I know," says Jillian. "I was trying to be polite. Have you forgotten your manners? It's proper etiquette to welcome a newcomer to the table, especially if they're the last to approach it."

Mare's left eyebrow shoots up.

"What? I'm just practicing for when we're in Québec. The French people have perfect manners, and I want to fit right in."

"Well," says Ander. "That will be real useful for when you go to France. Newsflash: Québec City is in Canada—the people are *Canadian*."

"I know that, but the people speak French there too."

"Merci bou coup!" he replies.

I laugh. "That was the worst French accent ever."

Mare reaches across the table for the box. "Well, what are we waiting for?" She opens the envelope as Jillian peeks over her shoulder.

> *Hey Crimson Kids,*
> *I can't wait to see you in Québec. To help you pass the time on the aero-bus (not that you need help doing that) and also to help prepare you for the Global Championships, I've left a game for you to play. Have fun. See you soon!*
> *Seraphina*

"Awesome," I say. "We have nine hours on this aero-bus. Lots of time to play."

Mare looks at me with her Mare-ish scowl. "Are you crazy? I'm not playing this game for nine hours—no matter how great it is. I know you're all about team bonding and everything, but we're already bonded, practically for life." She waves the medal around her neck as proof. "So I'll play, but then I'm taking a nap. It would be stupid to waste the couches."

"Fine," I say. I know from spending the whole summer with her that there's no point arguing with Mare. I have to fight the important battles, and let her win the small ones. "Okay, so who wants to read the directions?"

Ander jumps up, opens the box, and grabs a note taped to a smaller box inside.

> *Hey team . . .*
> *Inside this box you'll find my preceptor project, a game called SKIT MIXERS. I'll be presenting it to the Piedmont Committee at the Global Championships. You're my test subjects—lucky you! But don't be worried. You'll like it. Just remember our team mantra as you play:*
> *Be Curious. Be Creative. Be Collaborative. Be Colorful. Be Courageous.*
> *Seraphina*

I twist the silver band on my wrist, the one with the same message engraved on it, and see my teammates are all doing the same thing.

"Okay," says Ander. "Here's the sheet that goes with the game."

> *SKIT MIXERS is an activity kit designed for kids who like to act out imaginary tales. It contains everything needed to create a short play, complete with characters, settings, and problems to solve. With hundreds of card combinations to mix and match, the skit possibilities are endless. SKIT MIXERS is a fun way for kids to portray characters, work as a team, brainstorm ideas, creatively*

solve unique problems, and perform for an audience!

Kit includes: 25 character cards, 25 descriptor cards, 25 setting cards, 25 problem cards, instructions, planning pages, and script pages

Instructions:

• *Gather your friends and siblings! SKIT MIXERS can be played with 2 or more performers.*

• *Mix up the green (character) cards and scatter face down. Each performer chooses one card. This card indicates what character he or she will portray.*

• *Mix up the purple (descriptor) cards and scatter face down. Each performer chooses one card. This card gives a description of the performer's character.*

• *Mix up the red (setting) cards and scatter face down. One performer in the group chooses a card. This is the setting for the group's skit.*

• *Mix up the blue (problem) cards and scatter face down. Another performer chooses a card. This is the problem the group will solve in their skit.*

• *Next, the group must work as a team to create a short story (in the form of a skit) that demonstrates the setting, descriptions of each character, the problem they face together, and the solution they create together.*

• *Use the planning pages to plan it out.*

• *Use the script pages to record each character's lines.*

• *Practice and perform!*

Ander sets down the instruction sheet. "Wow, Seraphina's game sounds professional."

I feel a smile breaking across my whole face. "I like this game already!"

"I wish we could make costumes for it," says Jillian. "Maybe supplies are hidden on the aero-bus someplace."

"I doubt it," says Mare. "Let's just play it like Seraphina's instructions say."

Jax opens the box and pulls out the four decks of cards. But in a flash, our chairs move us away from the table. The table spins and grows to the height of a tall counter top. The chairs tip forward and pop us out of them. The floor opens and the chairs get sucked somewhere below the aero-bus.

What just happened?

"What the—" says Ander.

"Okay . . .?" says Mare.

We stand against the round counter, our elbows propped on top. "This is weird," I say.

"I guess no lounging for you, Ander," says Jillian.

"I don't care," he replies. "I do my best thinking while I'm standing anyway."

"While standing on chairs, you mean," adds Jax.

"Why yes, Jax. Yes, I do."

Jax shakes his head and laughs.

"Break out the character cards," says Mare, twisting her hair into a bun. "I don't want to stand all day."

I shuffle the green and purple cards and place them face down on the table. "Okay, everybody choose one of each." We take turns picking our character cards and descriptor cards. I look at mine. "Hmm, I'm a fairy who has x-ray vision."

Jillian pouts. "I'm a clown who hiccups while she talks."

"I guess I'm a superhero who snaps her fingers all the time," says Mare.

"Well," says Ander. "I'm a pirate who crawls instead of walks."

Jax frowns. "At least you're not a farmer who picks things up with your elbows."

I laugh and shuffle the red cards. "Okay, someone pick a setting card."

Mare reaches over and chooses one. "In a dance studio."

Ander rolls his eyes. "Great, our skit takes place in a dance studio."

I shuffle the light blue cards. "Now someone choose a problem card."

Jax turns over a card and shows it to the rest of us. "The crayons have come to life."

Mare flips over her cards. "So what do we do now? Make up a play about a bunch of characters who go into a dance studio and see a box of crayons come to life?"

"Yup," says Ander, tapping his fingers on the table. "But I'm starving. I think we should eat before we start."

"Where?" asks Jax.

Ander points to a tin box high above the table. A sign in block letters reads: SNACK CHOOSER.

"How did you notice that?" Jillian asks.

"I always notice snacks. So KK, since you were the last one to get to the table, you have to pick the snacks."

I start to reach up to the Snack Chooser, but then I realize how stupid his request is.

"Seriously?"

"Yup."

"You're just as close to the Snack Chooser as I am."

"But you choose better snacks than I do."

"You've got to be the laziest person on the planet."

Ander grins and leans back in his seat.

I jump to pull down a tin container suspended above the middle of the table. It spins in a circle, flashing pictures of pastries, crackers, cheese, and fruit.

"Pick something good," says Mare.

I turn the knob to chocolate covered cookie dough in honor of Seraphina. It's only been three weeks since we left Camp Piedmont, but I miss her already—especially her platform shoes, purple nail polish, *and* chocolate snacks.

I touch the button, the tin box flies back up, and the snack tray pops up from an opening in the center of the table.

"What the heck?" says Ander. "That was cool."

Jillian adjusts one of the upside-down cookie dough pieces. "There, that's better."

When we're done devouring the cookie dough pieces, we break out the planning pages and scribble down ideas.

"What if one of us is a dance instructor for a class full of unusual characters, not real dancers?" suggests Mare.

"Okay," says Ander. "And since I don't walk, I only crawl on my hands and knees. The instructor hates me."

"Me too," says Jax. "Because I pick up everything with my elbows."

"And she's mad at me too," says Jillian. "Because I keep hiccupping during class."

"That's good," I say. "And what if I'm the one who notices a box of crayons in the corner of the room? Since I have x-ray vision, I can see inside the box. I warn everyone that the crayons are coming to life and planning to escape their box."

Ander jumps on the couch. "Yes! And when they leap onto the floor, Jax and I surround them—with me crawling and him trapping them with his elbows."

I turn to Mare. "Why don't you be the superhero dance instructor?"

"Yeah," says Jillian. "And once the crayons are surrounded, I can scare them into surrendering with my hiccups."

"Right into my cape," says Mare. "I'll snap, scoop them up, and force them into their box."

"I like it," says Ander. "Are we all on board?"

Jax nods. Mare stands there stone-faced with her arms crossed in front of her.

Are you kidding me?

"What, Mare? You don't like it? It's not like anyone's going to watch us perform it."

Mare laughs. "You're so paranoid, Kia. Let's write our lines."

"Oh, sorry," I say. "I'm just used to you—"

"What? Not liking your idea?"

"I didn't say that."

"You did say I was *outspoken*."

I bite my lip. "That reporter made me say that. I had to say something."

"So now I know your true feelings about me. Why didn't you just call me bratty? That's what you really meant."

I point to Jax. "Well *he* said I was intense."

His face burns up. "I just meant to say that you're kind of energetic—in a good way."

"Energetic?"

Jillian steps in between us. "Why are you guys picking a fight? Mare said I was messy. So what? I am messy. Most creative people are."

"And I'm good at being in charge," says Ander. "If that means I'm bossy, I don't care. And Jax doesn't say much, but that means he's a deep thinker. That's not news."

Jax stares at Ander. I look at Mare. She stares at me. None of us says anything for way too long. This is not good. If we start fighting, no one will want to practice for the competition.

Mare shakes her head. "Principal Bermuda is an idiot."

"He was totally trying to make us fight or something," says Jillian.

I let out a breath. "Well, it's not going to work."

"Nope," says Ander.

"Okay," I reply. "Let's start writing our lines."

We sink onto the couches and brainstorm our lines. When we've finished, we toss our pencils and pages back into the box.

"Can we practice it later, like after lunch?" asks Mare. "I'm hungry again."

"Yeah," says Ander. "I definitely need a break."

Jax pulls down the tin box, but instead of seeing the snack choices, we somehow drop through the floor.

THE HOT AIR BALLOON

WE LAND WITH a plop onto red, white, and blue chairs inside a restaurant decorated like the American Flag. The walls are lined with red and white stripes and blue stars, and our table is covered with pictures of important people from American history—most of them we learned about in Human history, the most boring category in the world. But if I could learn about them by hanging out here, maybe that category wouldn't be so bad.

"It feels like the Fourth of July in here," says Jillian.

A small robotic creature zooms out from behind a counter. It looks sort of like a monkey, and then I realize what it is—our robotic monkey assistant from Camp Piedmont!

"Mabel!" I call. She stops next to my chair, and her dress lights up.

"Aww," says Jillian. "She's dressed up like the American flag."

I lean down to pet her, and when I do, a voice projects from her robotic ear:

Mabel has been programmed to tell you that your lunch will be ready shortly. Mabel believes you will each be eating a hot dog with a bun, macaroni and cheese, a garden salad, and a slice of warm apple pie. Mabel will also bring you a tall glass of lemonade. Mabel is happy to see you. Mabel will be right back.

"She's our waitress!" I exclaim.

Ander leans back in his chair. "Awesome, I'm starving."

Mabel rolls away but soon returns pulling a cart behind her loaded with our trays. We take them as another voice message blasts from her ear:

Hi girls, it's Swissa. I'm back at school now. No more room cleaning or flower deliveries from me! But I wanted to send a message to you and the boys, and Mabel helped me do it.

Ander leans over to me. "Wasn't Swissa your chambermaid at Camp Piedmont?"

"Yes," I say. "She was so nice."

Mare looks at me like daisies just popped out of my throat.

"Well maybe she wasn't so nice at first, but after a while she was."

Congratulations on getting to the Global Championships. I heard that despicable principal of yours isn't allowed to have any interaction with the Piedmont Organization. Good! What kind of person forces another to destroy the hard work of kids? He sounds like a monster. But here's the thing. He stopped at my Art Forms High School today and pulled me out of my theatre class. He asked a lot of questions about your team—he said it was for the news coverage. I just wanted to let you know that you're going to be a big deal in this state and maybe everywhere. He's making sure of it. So I don't know what you think about that, but I thought you should know I didn't give him any dirt about the three of you . . . like how messy Jillian was, or how Mare pretended to hate me, or that Kia was secretly nice to me. Anyway, good luck in the competition. I know you'll be great!

Mare shakes her head. "I wasn't pretending to hate her. I did hate her."

"But did you hear what she said? It's like Principal Bermuda is stalking us," I say.

"He *is* stalking us," says Ander.

"We shouldn't worry about him," says Jax. "He's back home and we're headed out of the country. He can't do anything to us anymore."

"I don't know," I say. "I bet he's sitting in his office dreaming up ways to cause trouble."

"But he wants us to win," says Jillian. "What could he even do?"

"He wanted us to win last time and look what he did."

Ander takes a giant bite of apple pie, leaving apple mush on his chin. "Relax, KK, and have some pie. This is almost as good as scrambled apples."

My teammates aren't that worried about Principal Bermuda, so maybe I shouldn't be either. "Fine, let's finish eating and then practice our Skit Mixers skit. Seraphina may want to see it when we get off the bus. We'll still have time after that to rehearse our real skit for the competition."

"I think we should explore first," says Ander. "We don't even know what else is on this bus. There was a movie theatre last time. Remember?"

"Yeah, I remember. Okay, but then we have to work on our skits."

Mare rolls her eyes at me, but that's nothing new. I kind of expect it now so I just smile back. It's like our special game.

When we're finished eating, we realize we don't know how to get back up to the main part of the bus. But as we step away from the table, the floor lifts us back upstairs. None of us can figure out how it happened, but we've pretty much learned not to question *everything*. Anything's possible when it comes to this competition—even secret passageways, I guess.

Ander looks around. "This stinks. I wanted to explore."

"I guess there's nowhere else to go on this aero-bus," says Jillian.

"Well," says Mare, "if we're going to practice, we better do it now—then I'm napping." She stands up, faces the rest of us with her feet in a first position ballet stance, and places her hands in a circle in front of her. She looks so perfect, like she really could be a ballerina. "Good afternoon, class. My name is Madam Bratty. Please take your places at the barre."

Jillian (Messy the Clown) skips over to an imaginary bar next to the couch. I follow her and smile wide at Madam Bratty. "I'm Lightning the Fairy. I've never taken a ballet class before."

"Wonderful," snarls Madam Bratty.

"Arg! I'm ready," calls Ander. "I'm Bossy the Pirate. I'll take my turn first."

"Only if you stand at the barre with the rest of the class."

"I won't, Madam Bratty, and neither will my first mate,

Brainy Farmer here. Crawling is the new walking."

Madam Bratty snaps her fingers. "Oh get up. Both of you."

"I'll stand up, Ma'am, but if something falls on the ground, I'll be fixin' to pick it up with my elbows. It's the law of the land," says Jax.

"That's a stupid law."

"That's not—hiccup—stupid," says Jillian. "That's just the way he does things."

"Whatever," says Madam Bratty. "We'll start with a releve and pas de bourree."

"Wait! Madam Bratty, we have a problem," I say.

"What now?"

"The crayons—they're planning to escape from their box. I can see it with my x-ray vision."

"No!" she snaps. "That will not do. We cannot hold class if the crayons are coming!"

"But what—hiccup—can we do?"

"Oh swashbucklers!" shouts Ander. "It's too late. Here they come now!"

Ander crawls toward the imaginary crayons rolling in a pack. Jax scoots down and pretends to trap them with his elbows.

"Madam Bratty, hurry!" says Ander. "Scoop them up with your cape. You must save the day!"

"I'm on it!" She snaps her fingers, pretends to scoop them up, and forces them back into their box.

"Now we can—hiccup—get back to the barre," says Jillian.

"She saved the day! She saved the day!" I cry, twirling around the room.

"Arg! That was the best dance class I ever took!" says

Ander. "The End!"

We burst out laughing and fall onto the couches. "That was fun," I finally say. "But that was the worst skit ever."

Jillian nods. "I think we should stick to the one we made at Camp Piedmont."

Mare turns over on her side. "Well, if we're done here, I'm taking a nap."

I shake my head. "I thought we were going to practice our real skit first." But Mare is already in prime sleep position. "Fine, we can take a quick break, but there's no way I'm going to sleep. I'm going to rehearse my lines instead. The Global Championships are in just two weeks, and I'm going to make every second count. I'll wake you all up in a few minutes."

We settle in on the couches, and I stare out the window, but instead of saying my lines in my head, I spin my wristband.

Be Curious. Be Creative. Be Collaborative. Be Colorful. Be Courageous.

Seraphina's words helped our team a lot at Camp Piedmont, and now we have an awesome invention. But we still have to be totally prepared when we present the Ancestor App to the judges at this competition. We have to show them it's better than all the other inventions in the whole world—and that's a lot of inventions.

I stare at the bright sky and watch the clouds morph into a lollipop. The swirl spins around and around, then opens up into a skinny pathway. My eyes flicker, feeling heavy, and I wonder where the path leads. The pathways at Camp Piedmont were bumpy and full of pebbles. I wonder if the pathways in Québec will be bumpy too. I wonder if our rooms will be filled with inventions like the ones inside our bed chambers—or if we'll have a chambermaid like Swissa. I wonder if we'll all remember our lines and be able to make our Ancestor App work. I wonder if we can pull off another miracle and place in the top three. I wonder if the Global Championships in Québec will be anything like Camp Piedmont at all.

The aero-bus lands in Québec City, the capitol city of the Canadian province of Québec. None of my teammates wanted to practice our real skit and I'm not happy about that, but I guess we do have two weeks, so it'll probably be fine. Besides, now that we're here, I can't wait to see what Québec City is like. I step off the aero-bus and expect to see the university where we're staying, the sprawling grounds with all the buildings, but I don't see it anywhere. All that's here is one concrete garage. My teammates and I look at each other. The bus driver obviously dropped us off at the wrong place. I make a move to step back onto the bus, but the door slides shut in my face. The driver nods and looks away.

"Wait!" I yell, knocking on the door.

Ander pushes up next to me. "Don't go!" he calls. "This isn't the right place!"

Mare pounds the door harder. "Open up! We need to get back on."

The driver doesn't change his expression at all. Instead, he points to the sky behind us, lifts the aero-bus off the ground, and flies away.

I turn around, but all I see is a sign above the concrete building written in French. I have no idea what it says! "What do we do now?" My heart starts beating like the drums in Art Forms class.

Jillian squeals. "Oh my god! He's leaving us here."

"Look!" Ander says. I turn around again and see what the bus driver was really pointing at—a miniature hot air balloon floating toward us. It gets closer and closer and soon lands at our feet. The colorful stripes are filled with words written in English: Think, Imagine, Solve, and Fly. We peek inside the basket but it's empty—except for a message written on the floor.

Greetings, New York Team!
Follow me to the Piedmont Global Championships . . .

The wind picks up and the balloon floats just out of our reach.

"What if it's a trap?" says Ander. "What if it's really a spy balloon, leading us into enemy territory?"

Jax shakes his head. "Or it could actually be sent from the Piedmont people."

"Come on," I say. "Let's follow it."

"What about our bags?" Jillian asks. She nods in the direction of our suitcases lying in the spot where the aero-bus used to be. I grab mine and start chasing the balloon. Ander catches up to me first. "This is crazy! Where are we going?"

"I guess it's leading us to our bed chambers, or the sign-in building—just like at Camp Piedmont." I check over my shoulder. Mare is right behind us but Jillian is fumbling with her giant suitcase. "Come on, you guys, the balloon is getting away!" Jax grabs her suitcase and they race to catch up.

The hot air balloon disappears behind the concrete building. We round the corner and it stops at a set of stairs that look like they lead to an underground subway terminal. It heads down the stairs, bouncing on each step as it descends.

"I'm not going down there." Mare plants herself firmly on top of her suitcase.

"Yeah, it looks creepy," Jillian agrees.

"What else are we supposed to do?" asks Jax. "If we want to get to the Global Championships, we have to follow it. Maybe there's a hallway down there that leads to the check-in building."

I bite my ring nail and then tuck it into my fist. "Jax is probably right. The campus is probably on the other side."

"Okay, Buddy, but I'm not going first," says Ander. "You lead the way."

Jax shrugs. "Fine, follow me."

The balloon dips further into the stairwell. We stay as close as we can to it, but soon I have to cover my face. Swirls of dust gather around my nose. This place is so creepy I have chills on my arms.

"Yuck! It stinks down here," says Mare. "And it's getting dark."

The stairs wind around and around and around—the lower we walk, the dizzier I feel. I grab a hold of the railing with one hand, trying to hold onto my suitcase with the other, just as a light appears along the steps.

"That's a little better." Jillian sounds relieved. "Where do you think we're going?"

"I don't know," says Ander. "But I hope we get there soon. This place is freaking me out."

We reach the bottom of the stairs but all that we find there is a small metal door—our only option. The balloon hovers next to the handle and flashes.

"I think it wants us to open the door," I say.

"Yeah. Open it, I guess," Mare replies.

I turn the handle, and the balloon dips into a concrete room. The floor is empty except for five cots lined up against the walls. Shelves are scattered everywhere holding about a million books, toys, and other stuff—so much stuff that I can't even count it all.

Ander eyes the place with suspicion. "This looks like a jail cell."

"You've got to be kidding me," says Mare. "This can't be where we're supposed to go."

The balloon spins in a circle and drops to the center of the floor. The basket lights up again and we step closer to see the new message:

> *To reach the Global Championships you*
> *must complete the following task:*

> *Using the white paper and duct tape provided, cover the items in the room that begin with a letter of the alphabet. Then place the remaining items in the balloon basket. Upon completion of the task, the pathway to the university will be revealed.*

"What the heck?" says Mare. "I thought there weren't going to be any more tasks."

Jillian lets out a huge sigh. "We're going to be here all night. There are a million objects in this room. There're like a hundred paperclips on that shelf and look—there's a bucket of tennis balls."

"Cool, I'll practice my juggling while I'm in here."

I let out a breath. "Ander, will you please focus?"

"What? I'm just saying—it looks like we're going to be here for a while." He nods toward the cots.

"I don't get it," I say, picking up the pile of paper. "We need to check into our rooms today. We can't if we're stuck in here."

"Then we better work fast," says Jax.

"But we only have this much paper. We don't even have enough to cover all this stuff."

"But we don't have to cover all of it," says Jillian. "Only the ones that begin with a letter of the alphabet. The rest can go in the basket."

We stare at Jillian and then she gets it. "Oh, right. Every single thing starts with a letter of the alphabet."

"This task doesn't make sense. We'll be here all night."

"Look, there's food on this shelf," says Ander. "We won't starve . . . grapes, granola bars, and bread."

"This is stupid," says Mare. "I say we go back."

"Back where?" I ask.

"Back upstairs to the garage. We can talk to someone there and they can send for the aero-bus."

"I say we go back too," says Jillian. She pulls on the door but it doesn't budge. "Oh my gosh, we're trapped in here!"

"We're not trapped," says Jax. "The balloon said that the pathway to the Global Championship will be revealed once we solve the task. And Ander's right. We do have food and cots to sleep on tonight."

My head starts to pound. "Hold on. We're supposed to be there soon. I think the cots are here to throw us off, to make us think the task will take us all night."

"Hey, you may be right, KK. Maybe this task is easy to solve, we're just looking at it in the obvious way."

"What do you mean?" asks Jax.

"We all think we have to wrap every single item in the room in this white paper in order to get out of here, right?" he asks.

"Right," says Jillian.

"But we don't have that much paper."

"Right," says Mare.

"So there must be a way to cover all the stuff in paper that isn't so obvious. We must be overthinking it."

"Or not thinking the right way," I say.

"So how should we be thinking?" asks Jillian.

Ander falls onto one of the cots. "I don't know. I thought of that part. You guys can take it from here."

Mare pulls him off the cot. "Oh no, you don't. If I don't sleep—and I am *not* sleeping on that thing tonight—then no one does. We have to figure this out—now."

I sit down cross-legged in front of the balloon. My teammates follow suit, and we form a circle around it. I bite my pointer nail. "So what do we know so far?"

"We have to cover every object that begins with a letter of the alphabet with white paper," says Jax.

"And the ones that don't begin with a letter from the alphabet have to fit in the balloon basket," says Jillian.

"Well, we already said that none of the items go in there," says Mare.

"I know. I'm just stating what we know."

Ander stands up and grabs the clump of grapes from the shelf. "If we eat these grapes, that's one less item we have to cover." He pulls off a branch and tosses the rest to Jax.

Mare nods. "Good thinking. I'm starving."

"So let's eat the rest of the food too," says Jillian.

"That's a good start," I say. "But look at this pile of paper. We have to consolidate somehow. We don't have that much to use, and even if we did have more, it would take us forever to cover every single object with it."

Ander tosses me a handful of grapes. "Maybe it's easier

than it looks. The Piedmont people are all about secret clues and all that."

My brain feels squished. "The task could be easier than it looks. If the hard part is covering all these pieces with paper, and if it *is* easier than it looks, maybe that means we do have enough paper, and it won't take that long for us to cover everything up."

"But we do have to cover all the objects," Mare insists.

"But we don't have to cover them individually, do we?" asks Jax.

"That's it," says Ander, his grin huge and eyes shining.

"What's 'it'?" asks Mare. "What did I miss?"

My brain un-squishes, and I think I know what Ander has in mind.

He jumps up on one of the cots. "We can put some of the objects inside each other, stick the little objects inside the big ones, and then cover the big ones with the paper and duct tape."

"That's what I was thinking too," says Jax.

Ander nods. "Jax and I will grab the big objects. You girls get the small ones."

The girls and I scurry around, placing each tiny item inside something a little bigger. I take the paper clips and place them inside a bowl, then I place the bowl inside a jewelry box. Ander tosses a granola bar to each of us. *Of course* he's still taking care of the snacks. Jax finds two barrels and drags them over. We fill one of them with as many books and toys as we can. We do the same with a bucket, a large pot, and a vase, then drag them to the second barrel, and place them all inside.

"Perfect," says Mare. "We can cover the two barrels with the paper easily, and we'll still have a little leftover."

"I'll rip the duct tape into pieces and hand it to you guys," says Ander. "It'll be faster that way."

"Wait," says Jax. "What about the cots?"

I look at the empty room. The shelves are bare but the cots still line the walls.

Jillian groans.

"Crap," says Mare. "We forgot about those."

"I have an idea," says Jax. "Maybe we can put the barrels under a cot and cover that instead."

"Then what about the other cots?" I ask.

Ander places one on top of another. "They stack!"

"Awesome," I say. "That should work."

Mare and Jillian pick up one of the cots and place it on top of the barrels. Ander carries the others and stacks them on top of the first. "Okay, I'll start ripping the tape."

It takes us only a few minutes to cover the structure completely. When we're done, we stand up and wait. Nothing happens.

"What the heck?" Mare asks.

"We followed the directions," says Jillian. "Everything's covered in paper."

I look over at Ander tossing the roll of duct tape in the air. "Everything but the duct tape."

Ander drops it like it's on fire. "We forgot about the tape."

"Geez, guys, do I have to think of everything?" Mare picks up the tape, walks calmly over to the structure, tips it back, and slides it under. As soon as she tips it back down, the balloon springs up from the floor. A panel in the wall opens, and we follow the balloon right through.

THE TREE SUITE

WE PILE OUT of the room dragging our suitcases behind us and enter a forest with trees taller than any in Crimson Heights. Summer Tanagers, small red birds singing strange notes, surround the balloon. *Tipi-tuck-i-tuck. Tipi-tuck-i-tuck.* We follow them along a brick pathway, but with so many twists and turns, I soon lose my bearings and have no idea which way we're going. *I hope they all know where they're going, because we are so lost if not.*

Luckily, before long, we emerge from the forest. A grassy clearing stands before us, and in the very center is a shimmering pool glistening in the sunlight. It looks like it could hold a thousand kids! At least one hundred silver cottages line the perimeter of the square. We walk along the pathway toward them, and as we get closer, the cottages get bigger and bigger. The balloon stops and dances in front of one of them, and I realize it's not a cottage at all. It's the most amazing treehouse-looking thing I've ever seen! Except I'm not actually sure that it's a treehouse either. It's not made of pine or oak or any other kind of wood that treehouses are usually made from. The stairs, the bridge, and the house itself are all made of metal and built into giant branches. The sign staked into the ground reads:

THE UNITED STATES OF AMERICA
The Team from New York
Marianna Barillian, Kia Krumpet, Jax Lapidary, Jillian Vervain, Alexander Yates
Preceptors: Seraphina Swing and Gregor Axel

"Holy cow!" Ander exclaims. "Is this where we're staying?"

A side door flies open, and Seraphina runs down the staircase with her purple platform heels tap, tap, tapping on the metal. "My Crimson Kids, you're here! We were wondering when you'd arrive!"

"Seraphina!" I call. She opens her arms wide and scoops me into a hug before embracing everyone else too.

"Actually, I knew you'd figure out that paper task pretty quickly. Gregor wasn't so sure."

Gregor strolls out the door right after her. "I see Seraphina is making me look bad already."

We charge to the top of the stairs. "Gregor!"

He pulls away from our hug and adjusts his shirt. His mouth breaks into a slight smile though. "Hello team. It's good to see you all again."

Seraphina is still grinning at us. "How was your ride on the aero-bus?"

"It was good," I say. "Your game was really fun."

Ander leaps from the top step to the bottom. "Yeah, I was a pirate who crawls. You should have seen me!"

Gregor nods. "I'm sure you were outstanding, young Ander."

"Oh, I was."

"How was your break?" Seraphina asks. "I heard your town is making a big deal of you."

"Yeah," says Jax. "We were interviewed by a TV reporter before we left."

"Wait until you get started here in Québec. Then they'll really have something to talk about back in Crimson Heights."

Why does everyone need to keep talking about us? I mean, I want everyone to know about our invention, but I bet some people—like Charlotte, will think this whole thing is weird, so I'd rather Principal Bermuda just keep his big mouth shut.

"Is this really where we're staying?" asks Jillian.

"Yes!"

"All of us—together?" asks Mare.

"Yes," Gregor replies. "You'll stay together this time as a team. Come this way and we'll show you."

He leads us across a bridge made of swaying metal boards. I grab onto the ropes to steady myself, and as I step across, each board turns into a different color and words flash across them: *Be Curious. Be Creative. Be Collaborative. Be Colorful;. Be Courageous.*

"Our team mantra," Ander calls, hopping off the bridge.

"Of course," says Seraphina with a laugh. "It will be even more important here at the Global Championships."

Each of us step off the bridge and see that the door is

above our heads—way above our heads.

"What are we supposed to do now?" asks Jillian.

"Remember, Jillian: physical fitness promotes creativity," says Gregor.

"So we'll climb up to the door. Follow me." Seraphina slips off her heels and pushes the doorbell. Small rubber ledges pop out of the wall. She shimmies up to the top, one foothold at a time, with no problem at all. Ander jumps onto the first foothold next, and one-by-one we follow her up. But when we step inside the treehouse, I gasp. It's nothing like I was expecting. In the center of the room is the floating playground from Camp Piedmont!

Ander's looks at me, grinning. "The bouncing blobs are here!"

Seraphina flashes a purple lipstick smile. "Go on, have at it."

Ander and I race for the blobs. I get yellow, he gets blue. They bounce us throughout the room as high as the ceiling—up and down, up and down.

Jillian climbs a winding ladder and steps onto a carpet. It shimmies for a second and then floats around the room above our heads. "Guys, look! I'm riding on a flying carpet!"

Mare and Jax race on the obstacle course, climbing through airborne tires, up a floating rope wall, and over a spinning log. Jax attempts to climb up the slippery pole but slides back down. Mare pulls herself up easily and reaches the finish line first.

I jump off my blob and climb up to the clouds. They toss me around like I'm in a tub of marshmallows. I peek over the edge, and Gregor is standing in the corner with his hands on his hips, as usual—only his crabby grimace has been replaced with the tiniest smile.

"Well?" asks Seraphina. "What do you think?" She stuffs her hands in her pockets and walks over to the bottom of the winding ladder.

We hurry over to her, all of us huffing and puffing and red in the face.

"This is awesome!" says Ander. "How did you get this stuff here?"

"Ah, the magic of science, young Ander. Nothing is impossible if you use the right tools."

"Oh, like hammers and nails."

"Not always. Sometimes you need your imagination."

"Well, yeah, I know that, but didn't you just box up the playground from Meeting Room Twelve and ship it here?"

Seraphina laughs. "What fun would that be? We recreated it all, right here by ourselves. If you remember, the items back in Meeting Room Twelve were made mostly of materials found in the Piedmont Pantry. This floating playground is made mostly of duct tape, commercial strength fishing line, and super glue."

Jax looks underneath the floating carpet. "But how did you get the carpets to fly?"

"Hover gel . . . just like the substance you pour into your aero-scooters. We didn't need to use fuel though, since they don't go far."

We scurry like mice to get a closer look at the playground. I can't believe it. The flying carpet, the clouds, the obstacle course—all of it is made of duct tape—probably like a thousand rolls!

"You guys are fabulous," squeals Jillian.

"Thanks! Why should you guys get to do all the awesome stuff? We figured once the competition starts, we can't help you at all, so we may as well get our creative fingers moving while we can."

"Do all the teams stay in treehouses like this?" asks Mare.

"They're staying in tree suites similar to this. But it was up to the preceptors to fill them with items they believed would help their teams be successful in the Global Championships."

"And you filled ours with the floating playground?" I ask.

"Not just that," said Gregor. "I believe you'll want to see what's upstairs. Follow me."

We follow Gregor and Seraphina to a fluffy staircase behind the floating playground, a stark contrast to the metal and shininess of the main floor. We reach the top and look over the railing at the playground below.

"As you can see, the railing prevents you from falling to the floor, but if you think you can climb on top of it and make a swan dive for the floating clouds from up here, you would be mistaken. Plexiglas has been installed right on top of the railing. That way you won't be tempted to turn the railing into a diving board."

"Aw, man," says Ander. "That would be awesome."

Gregor turns away from the Plexiglas. "This floor has two large rooms: the Work Room and the Inspiration Room. This one is the Inspiration Room."

We peek into a long space filled with the sound of rushing water. "It's divided into sections. This end, with the waterfall, is called the Quiet Area. It's full of pillows, books, and windows that look out into the forest. If you need a quiet place to read, think, or brainstorm, this is the area to find it."

"Can I take a nap in there if I want to?" ask Mare.

I roll my eyes. "We're not going to have time for naps,

Mare. We have a competition to win, remember?"

She scowls at me, but I don't care. *How can she think we have time for naps?*

"The area at the other end, separated by soundproof Plexiglas, is the Harmony Area. Some of you may do your best thinking when music is playing in the background. Musical instruments are at your disposal, but there is also recorded music—if you'd rather listen than play."

"Oh, cool, they have a saxophone," says Jax.

"You play the sax?" asks Ander.

Jax nods. "Yeah, I do."

"Cool, I did, too, for a while."

We walk to the Work Room. "Inside the Work Room," says Gregor, "you'll find the tech area. It's filled with air screens, desks, and wall-sized monitors. It's set up to handle any research you may want to do."

"I know where Jax will be hanging out," Mare mutters.

"We may all have to hang out in here to work on our Ancestor App," I say.

"True, I'm just saying that I won't spend my free time in here; I'll be napping in the other room."

"Stop talking about naps! We're only here for two weeks! How much free time do you think we're going to have?"

Mare looks right at me. "I see you haven't gotten less uptight lately."

I huff out a breath and whisper to Ander. "I might have to invent a stay-awake machine for Mare. That way she won't need sleep." He tries his best to stifle his laugh.

Seraphina leads us to the other end of the Work Room—a colorful area with a long table full of fabrics and crafting materials. "Okay, now this is heaven!" squeals

Jillian.

"It's like a mini Piedmont Pantry," explains Seraphina. "All the materials you need are here. I know you already have costumes, but if you need a quick fix, supplies are available."

"But wait," says Jillian. "Can we be in these rooms even if we don't have a particular reason to be? Like can we just come in here to make stuff?"

"Of course," she answers. "This tree suite is designed with imagination and inspiration in mind."

Jillian smiles so big, I can see every tooth in her mouth. Oh my god, if she has her way, she'll spend the whole two weeks making dresses or something. Now I have to worry about Mare taking naps *and* Jillian going sew-crazy.

Gregor heads to the door. "Do you want to see where you'll be sleeping?"

"Um, yeah!" says Mare excitedly.

"Alright," says Seraphina. "Up to your tree chambers we go." We walk to the center of the tree suite in between the two rooms and climb another set of steps colored in pink, yellow, dark blue, light blue, and green. Our team mantra phrases are written across them just like they were on the wiggly bridge. We reach the top, and a tall window looks out into the forest.

"Before we split up into the girls' tree chamber and the boys' tree chamber, I want to give you these." Seraphina reaches into her pocket and pulls out five watches, all in different colors. "These are your Piedmont Watches. Gregor and I have them too. They allow us to see where each of you are at all times, within a matter of inches, so you'll never get lost. You can give the number to your families too in case they want to call or message you."

She hands me a yellow watch, and I put it on my wrist.

"Yay, pink!" says Jillian. "Thank you."

Mare gets light blue, Ander gets dark blue, and Jax gets green. Gregor's is gray and Seraphina's, of course, is purple.

"Make sure you wear them at all times. They're waterproof."

"Can we play games on them?" says Ander.

"No," Gregor replies. "These watches do not have that capability. Besides, if they did, you'd most likely spend your time playing games instead of interacting with your teammates and other kids here at Globals."

Good. Our team doesn't need any distractions!

"This is where we split up," Seraphina continues and leads Jillian, Mare, and me to the Girls Tree Chamber on the left as Gregor leads the boys to the Boys Tree Chamber on the right.

Seraphina practically skips down the hallway. "The bathroom is here on the left. It's like the one at Camp Piedmont with three of everything, except the shower. You'll have to share that. And across from it are your cubbies, a section for each of you."

Mare nods. "So even Jillian should be able to fit her clothes neatly."

Jillian shrugs. She doesn't seem to mind at all that she can't keep her clothes neat or that Mare is ribbing her about it.

Seraphina continues. "And you'll each have your own sleeping eggs."

"Do you mean sleeping bags?" I ask, trying to catch up to her.

"No," she laughs. "I mean *sleeping eggs.*"

"Here at the end of the hall is your nest, complete with

sleeping eggs—where the best ideas are hatched!" Three colorful egg-shaped beds, arranged like a U, are built into twig-lined walls.

"We're like baby birds!" says Jillian.

"Birds who invent things," I say.

Mare climbs into the one in the center. "Um no, maybe birds who sleep all day."

"Not so fast," says Seraphina. "But I do hope you like them."

"I've always wanted a treehouse," I say.

"So, your tree suite is close enough?"

I laugh. "Definitely!"

"Good. I've left dresses in your cubbies—for the Piedmont Gala."

"Wait, what?" I ask. "What do you mean—Piedmont Gala?"

Jillian looks at her, wide-eyed.

"Well, this is the Global Championships, and you're about to meet kids from all over the world, so don't you think it makes sense that we'd have a gala to attend? I'll meet you downstairs in thirty minutes. Oh wait, one more thing. Next to your wall of cubbies is a mini elevator—for items, not for people. If you open it up you'll find your travel cases, got it?"

"Got it," says Mare.

Jillian is spinning in front of the sleeping eggs. "First a craft room, and now a gala? Can you believe it? I didn't think this could be any better than Camp Piedmont!"

I open up the elevator and pull out my suitcase. "I thought we were here to showcase our invention—to do our skit. The information packet about the Global Championships didn't say anything about going to a gala. What do you do at a gala?"

Jillian grabs her suitcase out next. "Don't be such a worrier, Kia. I don't know what we do at a gala either, but I hope we get to dance."

Mare pulls her pillow close. "I hope we get to take a quick nap before we go."

"Ugh," I tug at the zipper on my suitcase. "I just hope we have time to practice when we get back."

THE PIEDMONT GALA

FOR THE GALA, we're all supposed to dress in our country's traditional clothing. So I swish down the hall of our tree chamber in a yellow dress, adjusting the puffy sleeves. Mare and Jillian swish down after me in dresses just like mine, except that Mare's is light blue and Jillian's is pink. It feels weird not wearing our normal matching t-shirts and shorts, and I can't imagine that American girls in the 1700s wore giant dresses like this.

"Kia," Jillian calls. "You forgot your bow."

I take the yellow ribbon from her and twist it around in my fingers, but when I fumble with it for too long, she grabs it back from me. "Never mind, I'll do it."

She pulls the sides of my hair up into a half ponytail and secures it with a band. Then she wraps the ribbon around it and turns it into a bow.

Mare fluffs out the bottom of her dress. "I told you we'd all be dressed the same."

"But we're so fabulous, Mare. Look at us!" says Jillian. She grabs us by the hands and spins us around in circles. Mare resists for a second, but soon she laughs with me as we spin along the tree chamber hallway.

"I feel like Martha Washington," she says.

"All the kids are going to be dressed in their country's traditional clothing," Jillian reminds her. "I can't wait to see what they're wearing."

"Everyone else will probably be wearing shorts, and we'll be the only ones dressed up like this," says Mare. "If that happens, I'm out of there."

We hear voices, so we open the door to the main hallway. Ander and Jax appear in front of the window wearing old-fashioned suits—Jax in green and Ander in blue. "Just call me Thomas Jefferson," says Ander. "Like our breeches and waist coasts?"

"What's with the shoes?" asks Mare.

I laugh. "Buckles?"

"Yup," he replies. "Revolutionary shoes with buckles. Would any of you ladies care for an escort down the stairs?"

Mare gives him the stink eye. "No, thanks. I can walk by myself." She grabs the railing and swishes her way down.

I think about my giant puffy dress and the chance that I'll roll all the way down to the bottom. "I would."

Ander nods and holds his elbow out toward me. I grab onto it, and together we follow Mare.

"Well, I guess that just leaves you and me," Jillian says to Jax in a mock-Southern accent. She swishes behind me, and all I can do is hope she doesn't trip and send me rolling all the way down to the first floor.

Seraphina and Gregor appear from behind the floating playground. Seraphina looks like a movie star in her bright purple dress with her hair piled up on top of her head.

Ander whistles. "Wow, Seraphina. Now that's what I'm talking about."

She laughs. "I think that's a compliment, so I guess I'll just say, *Thank you, kind sir.*"

Gregor, wearing a gray suit, walks to the door and opens it wide. "Gentlemen, I'm glad to see you know how to dress yourselves. Ladies, you look lovely. Shall we proceed to the gala?"

My butterflies stir as I walk through the door. An aero-cart, almost like the one we rode in on the way to Piedmont Pantry, is parked outside. Gregor opens the cart door for Seraphina while the boys hop into the back row. Then he holds the middle door open as the girls and I scoot into the second row, stuffing our dresses in as well as we can. As much as I hate to waste time at this gala, I do like riding there in style.

Gregor drives the cart along the uneven bricks. Soon, we lift above the trees and soar over the other tree suites. Instead of feeling excited like I usually feel when flying through the air, my stomach suddenly feels sick. I'm not too sure about this gala. *What am I supposed to do there?*

We're barely out of sight of the tree suite colony when I feel a tap on my shoulder. "Hey KK, look!"

Our aero-cart descends and just ahead is a cluster of buildings—fancy white buildings with tall peaks. Seraphina spins around. "Welcome, Crimson Kids, to le Universite de Creativite!"

I scan the massive campus before us. *This place is incredible!*

Gregor lands the cart, we pile out, and Seraphina gathers us around. "Impressive, huh?"

I can't look away, even for a second.

"When we get inside the Imagination Centre you'll see the other teams that are here for the Championship. This is a really great chance for you to meet kids from all over the world, including the other teams from the Unites States. Be sure to be say hello to them. They'll be dressed just like you, so they should be easy to find."

"Where are the other American teams from? I forgot," asks Jillian.

"Pennsylvania, Texas, Idaho, and Maryland."

"As long as that nasty team from Michigan isn't here, I'm happy." I picture Witch Girl whipping her braid around at us.

"You're safe, Kia. The Michigan team didn't place in the top five at the National Finals to qualify."

"What do we do at this gala?" asks Jax.

"That much we'll find out when we get inside. Everybody ready?"

"Yup," says Ander. "We're ready."

We proceed up a long sidewalk lined with low brick walls and lamp posts as the twilight sky emerges, and the lights flicker to life. A man in a suit pulls open a heavy door for us. "Good evening, New York team. Welcome to the Piedmont gala."

We enter the Imagination Centre, and it feels like we've stepped into another country—only I'm not sure which one. "Ander, this ceiling must be a thousand feet high!"

"Imagine the juggling I could do in here."

"There must be a thousand kids here," I reply. Girls walk by wearing Indian saris and Japanese kimonos. Boys joke around in languages I don't understand, some wearing Mexican sombreros and others wearing German lederhosen. Kids just like us, but not quite like us at all.

We walk cautiously around the room, nodding and smiling. Not all the kids speak English, so we won't be able to talk to some of them. Part of me wishes we could talk to everyone here at this gala, but then I remember we're competing against them. Only three of the inventions will get chosen. That's not a lot. So I smile at everyone I see but decide that I won't become friends with any of them. It's never smart to underestimate the competition or let your guard down.

For the next hour, we walk around, eating food on tiny plates. The perimeter of the room is filled with the same spinning food flowers we saw at Camp Piedmont. They're constantly spinning and changing the foods we can sample—all from different countries, like sushi, egg rolls, quesadillas, hot dogs, and chocolate cream puffs.

Soon Seraphina drags us away from the dessert table to meet some of the other teams.

While I'm wiping the cream from the side of my face, Jillian elbows me in the side. Heading toward us are five kids dressed just like us—except there are four girls and one boy—obviously one of the other American teams. The boy waves to us. "Hi y'all! We're the Texas team. We're here to say hello. I'm Colton."

"Well, hi there," Jillian purrs. "I'm Jillian, and we're the team from New York."

"It seems weird to be dressed all the same," says a girl in the same blue dress as Mare. "I'm Becca."

Mare looks her up and down. "Great, even more people dressed just like us."

I may not want to be friends with these kids, but I don't want to be rude either. "Hi, this is Mare, and I'm Kia."

"And I'm Ander, and this is Jax. We are *very* pleased to meet you."

Becca blushes. "This is the rest of my team . . . Annalia, Penelope, and Dawn."

"Maybe we'll see you around the tree suite colony," says Colton. "Like at the pool."

"Okay," says Mare, trying not to smile.

Before I have a chance to remind both of them that the Texas team is our competition, an older girl runs over to Seraphina, and they both start hugging and squealing, piercing my eardrums. She has dark hair and a very big smile.

Seraphina squeals. "Mathilde! What are you doing here?"

Mathilde laughs. "My silly American friend, the same as you, of course!"

Seraphina smiles, and they hug and jump around and around. I stare at them, not sure what to make of this girl with a French accent.

"Mathilde, I can't believe you're a preceptor too! I had no idea."

"It has been too long since we have spoken!" She turns toward us. "Is this your team?"

Seraphina's face lights up like she suddenly remembers we are standing next to her. "Yes, it is! Let me introduce you to them. This is my other preceptor, Gregor . . . and this is Kia, Ander, Mare, Jax, and Jillian. Team, this is my French pen pal and exchange student. Her name is Mathilde, and she is one of my best friends in the world—literally!"

We shake hands with Mathilde, and I listen closely as

she speaks. Her words sound like butter melting on a warm piece of toast. "You have a wonderful preceptor, you know. Seraphina is one of my most favorite people in the world."

"I can't believe you're here too. I hope we're able to spend some time together. But where is your team?"

"Oh, they shall be along shortly, I am sure . . . oh, yes, here they are. Please do allow me to introduce you to them." She calmly shuffles her team over to us, and I suddenly feel starstruck. I've never met anyone from France before.

"Children, I would like you to meet my very good American friend, Seraphina Swing. She and I were pen pals and exchange students several years ago. And these are my new American friends, her team from New York." She smiles as she tries to remember our names.

Seraphina holds her hand up. "Here, let me help you. This is Kia, Ander, Mare, Jax, and Jillian. And I'm Seraphina, and this is Gregor."

We nod and say our hellos, and Mathilde turns to her team. "And here is my team, all from many different beautiful areas in Brittany, France: Maelle, Gwyndol, Danielle, Zoe, and Stephan."

Maelle reaches her hand out to shake mine. She is small, like me, with light brown hair and brown eyes. "Hello," she says. "Your dress is quite, how do you say? Beautiful."

"Thank you, I mean, *merci*. I don't know French, but you speak English really well."

"Thank you. At my school, we learn to speak English when we are very young."

Soon the lights dim, and Seraphina motions for us to follow her. "The ceremony is about to begin. We should head over to the theatre."

I say goodbye to Maelle and hurry with the rest of my

team through the doors into an octagonal next to the ballroom. We take our seats and two familiar figures step onto the stage: Master Freeman and Andora Appleonia. Dressed in regal clothing, they look like a king and queen. All that's missing are their crowns.

"Welcome, children, to the Piedmont Global Championships!" He speaks in English and then follows it with languages I don't understand. Confetti falls from the ceiling and the room goes dark—except for the eight walls. Each one lights up in a different color and displays inspirational words: *Dream. Believe. Create. Imagine. Inspire. Solve. Think. Fly.* My butterflies hiccup, and I sit on my hands.

"We wish to congratulate you on your achievement in reaching this phase of the competition, and as you can see on the walls, we are honored to have representatives from all over the world." The walls quickly change to display the countries that are represented: Canada, France, USA, Mexico, England, Ireland, Germany, Greece, Switzerland, China, Japan, Norway, Morocco, Dubai, Russia, Spain, Italy, Brazil, Thailand, India, South Africa, Australia, and more.

"Over the summer, national competitions were held all over the world, and at those competitions, each team solved a task which included the creation of an invention. The results were outstanding. Now we have the pleasure of witnessing the great talent that you possess. Each team will be given the opportunity to showcase their inventions to our judges and to the teams represented from around the globe. But there's much more to this competition than that. This is a global event where your minds will be expanded, connections created, and friendships made."

"We have many extraordinary activities planned and much for you to be excited about! The Global Championships will kick off with a big day tomorrow. During the daytime, you'll participate in the Piedmont Showcase Festival—where your inventions will be judged."

Tomorrow?

"The festival will be held in the gala ballroom inside the Imagination Centre, which will be transformed into a showcase of your achievements. Each team will have its own booth where they'll demonstrate their invention to our distinguished guests and judges. You will be notified of your judging time, and during your off time, you'll be free to roam the Imagination Centre and experience all of the other inventions showcased by your peers."

"This is bad," I whisper to Ander. "I thought judging wasn't for another two weeks. We just got here. We haven't even practiced!"

He swallows hard. "I know."

"Tomorrow night, we will direct our attention to the university grounds for the Sport and Game Festival. There, representatives will be demonstrating a game or sport that was invented in their own country. You are encouraged to explore the campus and sign up for whichever activities you like. The more interactions you have with children from other cultures, the more fulfilling your experience at the Global Championships will be."

Ander whispers again, "We get to meet kids from all these countries and play their sports, too!"

"But we're competing against them, remember?"

"KK, we already know we get to go to PIPS when we get back home. That was our goal, right? To go to a school where we get to build these awesome inventions."

"Yeah, but I want our invention to place in the top three so *it* can be built. It *has* to be picked. I want it to be *real!*"

"Me too, but even if it doesn't win, it's okay. We never thought we'd even get this far."

"I did," I whisper, but I don't think he hears me.

Master Freeman continues, "After our day full of showcases and games tomorrow, our competition will officially begin. The scores from your presentation to the judges will be added to the other two scores you get while here at the Global Championships—the scores you receive in Swirl and Spark Recall and your new Global Task."

The crowd goes silent.

Wait, what? More tasks?

"Details of the Swirl and Spark Recall task will be given to your preceptors, but at this time, I will introduce to you Andora Appleonia, who will present this year's Piedmont Global Task!"

The Imagination Centre erupts into applause. The butterflies in my stomach freak out.

This is not happening.

Andora steps to the center of the stage, and a task illuminates on the wall behind her. Her voice crackles through the speakers.

"The world is full of life-changing inventions. Your task is to take an invention commonly used by people today and re-imagine it. It must continue its current function but also yield a new, life-changing function. Your task solution must be created using skills from all six categories, take no more than twelve minutes to present, and include lyrics to a song."

What? Two more tasks?

Ander slides down in his seat. "This task is harder than the one at Camp Piedmont."

"And we only have two weeks to solve it!"

Master Freeman continues, "And now for the Piedmont Surprise!"

I look at Ander. His eyes get huge.

"This year, there will be an extra incentive for the teams who place in the top three at these Global Championships. Not only will *both* the inventions by those teams be brought to life when you return to your own countries, but the top three teams in this competition will participate in the year-long Swirl and Spark Tour put on by the Piedmont Organization.

"Those three teams will travel around the world, show-casing their inventions to schools in cities across the globe, teaching younger children all that is possible when you work hard, think more, and dream big. They'll travel with their preceptors by aero-bus and experience cultures they've only ever dreamed of!"

I look at my teammates, and we all exchange glances.

Oh my gosh. A tour with my team?

And before I can think any more about the possibility of that, balloons fall from the ceiling, and just like at Camp Piedmont, as I catch one in my hand, it pops and everyone else's does too. It's like fireworks with all the pop, pop, popping! When mine pops, instead of seeing the broken balloon in my hand though, I'm holding a slip of paper, a message that I know from my time at Camp Piedmont is meant just for me:

Our true dreams are sometimes different than what we wish for. Have the courage to make your true dream come true.

I fold the slip of paper inside my fist and commit it to memory. I wonder what it could mean, except that I already know what I'm wishing for—to have the Ancestor App become a real thing. I want to build it with my teammates at PIPS, the Piedmont Inventor's Prep School, when we get back home. That's my dream, and it's never going to change—not even if this piece of paper thinks it might.

Moments later, the Piedmont gala is over, and my teammates and I follow Seraphina and Gregor out of the Imagination Centre. My mind swirls as I think about what just happened. I don't understand it. I thought we just had to present our Ancestor App to the judges at this competition. That's it. That was supposed to be our chance to get it built at PIPS. But now we have this new, really hard task to solve too, plus another one at Swirl and Spark Recall. I feel so confused right now, like my head is going to spin off.

We ride back to the tree suite colony in silence, and I stare out at the sky. Just when I think I know what to expect, I realize that I don't know what to expect at all. All I wanted to do was show everyone our invention. I thought it would win for sure. But now that's not enough. The Ancestor App alone won't be enough.

Gregor stops the aero-cart at the pool in the center of Colony Square. The lights in the trees cast a glow all around it. "Hop out, kids," says Seraphina. "We want to show you something." We step out and swish along the brick.

Gregor looks out at the sparkling water. "You may congregate here in the Creativity Pool any time you like, with any of the other teams. Feel free to dive from the Thinking Pad, swim in the rejuvenating water, swing on the Idea Swings, or climb across the water using the problem-solving bars. A computerized life guarding monitor system has been installed and is working here at all times."

Ander jumps on the ledge surrounding the water. "This

is so cool!"

"I can totally wear my new bathing suit," says Jillian.

"But what about our new task?" I ask. "Don't we need to be working on that?"

"Indeed you do, but if I know this team, I imagine you'll need breaks as well." He looks at Ander and grins.

"I have no shame," Ander replies. "I definitely need breaks."

"But why would we hang out with the kids from the other teams?" I ask. "We're competing against them."

Seraphina smiles. "It's true that you're in a competition with the other teams, but you can still do good work and be friendly too. That's all part of the experience."

"But if we can take breaks whenever we want, how do we stay focused? Aren't you going to give us a schedule?"

"We'll assist you in the same ways we did at Camp Piedmont," says Gregor. "But this isn't Camp Piedmont. This is le Universite de Creativite. There is much here that's meant to inspire you, and that includes new friends from around the world. Seraphina and I will be staying in suites in the lower level of the tree house. Hers is directly below the girls' and mine is directly below the boys'. We will certainly be close enough to keep you on track."

I climb back inside the cart. I don't understand how any of this is supposed to work.

We hear the whirl of a motor, and soon another aero-cart drives toward us. Three boys dressed just like Ander and Jax pile out and race to the edge of the pool. A red-haired boy picks up a rock and chucks it at the idea swing. It lands several feet away with a plop. He yells to his teammate, "Beat that, Simpson, or are your fingers glued to your computer?" He glances at another boy still sitting in the aero-cart.

Simpson looks up from his computer for a second, but then looks back down at the screen. A girl, wearing a yellow dress just like mine, walks toward us. Her long black hair is pulled back into a ponytail . . . no, a braid—and she has a harsh scowl on her face.

Jillian whispers, "Is that Witch Girl from Michigan?"

What? No!

She stops at our cart and smirks. "Wow, I'm surprised the famous New York team isn't off writing another Broadway play."

Ander looks at the boys by the pool and then back to her. "What are you doing here? Your team didn't make it to the Global Championships."

"Actually, we did. The Maryland team was disqualified. Their original language turned out to be not original after all, and we slid right into their fifth place spot. So here we are, ready for world domination."

Mare scowls. "Yeah right, your team won't be dominating anything."

"Oh yeah? Well, as you can see, Simpson is already busy at work on our new task. If my calculations are correct, which they usually are, he should be finished with it by morning."

"How can you make him do everything?" asks Jillian. "That's not fair."

"Being part of a team means passing out jobs that best fit each team member. Simpson is a wizard on the computer. The rest of us are good at watching him work. And if his idea is terrible, the rest of us let him know, and he gets back to work."

"That's really unfair," says Jax.

"Maybe, but our invention won't be. Anyway, I'm here to say hi. We're supposed to meet all the other teams, so here I am doing the right thing."

I force myself to say, "Hi."

She twists her braid. "I'm Martina."

Jax clears his throat. "I'm Jax."

Ander and I look at each other. "I'm Kia," I say. "And this is Ander."

Jillian follows my lead. "I'm Jillian, and this is Mare."

"Cool," says Martina. "The one in the cart is Simpson, and the rest of them over there are Drake, JT, and Fletcher." She turns to the boys by the pool. "Guys, this is the NY team."

They nod and go back to throwing rocks in the pool.

"Well, I better go see what fantastic invention Simpson has thought of. He's determined to come in first place this time, so no matter what you think up, it won't be anything like his."

She spins around and stomps back to her cart.

This is so unfair.

Mare's eyes are practically bulging. "I can't believe that stupid team is here now too."

"Seraphina, why didn't you tell us? I thought you said they wouldn't be here."

She shakes her head. "I had no idea. The Piedmont Committee must have realized the error at the last minute. But it doesn't matter. You have the same number of teams to compete against and you're going to create a wonderful solution. Don't worry about them."

"But what if we don't want to come up with another wonderful solution?" asks Jax.

I look at him like he just spoke like an alien. "Why not?"

"Well, like what if we don't want to win after all?"

I stare at Jax. His face is turning red but probably not redder than mine.

"Why wouldn't you want to win?" Jillian asks.

"I don't know."

"Yes, you do," I say. "You wouldn't say it if it wasn't true."

He doesn't say anything.

"Jax!" I say.

"I know why," says Ander. "You don't want to go on the Swirl and Spark Tour, do you?"

Jillian shrieks. "Why not? Didn't you hear what Master Freeman said? We'd get to travel all over the world!"

"Stop making him feel bad," says Ander.

I'm so confused. I don't understand why he wouldn't want to go.

Seraphina places a hand on Jax's shoulder. "Listen everyone. Let's go back to our tree suites. It's been a very long day. We can figure this out tomorrow."

This competition is not off to a good start.

I climb into my sleeping egg and draw the blankets up to my face. Mare turns off the light, and the whole room looks like the outdoors. Stars twinkle overhead through a skylight, and a cool breeze fills the room. A speaker startles me. "*Germ eliminator in progress.*" I peek out of the blankets and see millions of tiny eggs zooming in the air. They get bigger and bigger and when they get to be the size of actual eggs, they disappear through an opening in the skylight.

"Yikes," says Jillian. "They're germ-eating eggs. This has to be an invention from one of the past teams. How did they think up that?"

"I liked the air purification sparkles better." I throw the covers over my head. Germ-eating eggs? Whatever. I don't care about the amazing germ-eating eggs. I'd rather be sick.

THE SHOWCASE FESTIVAL

I WAKE UP to a knock at the door and climb out of my egg bed to open it. But no one is there. I turn around, and Jillian sits up. Mare looks like she could be dead. I push my bangs away from my eyes and hear the knocking again. It's coming from a tiny square cupboard near the bathroom. I open it and Ander's face appears on a screen.

"Hey KK, hurry up. Get dressed. We're starving! Meet us downstairs in five minutes." His face disappears, and I'm not sure where it went.

"What the heck was that?"

Jillian rubs her eyes. "That was Ander."

"Yeah, I know, but like, where is he?"

"I don't know. Downstairs someplace."

Jillian and I stare at Mare, dead to the world. We both know how this is going to go. If we try to wake her up nicely, she'll just lay there and yell at us to leave her alone.

On the other hand, if we drag her out of bed, she'll give us the stink eye *and* yell at us to leave her alone, but at least she'll be out of bed.

I shrug, and Jillian and I each grab one of her arms.

She tries to squirm away. "What are you guys doing? Let go. I'm sleeping!"

I strengthen my grip "We have to meet the boys for breakfast. Come on."

We pull her onto the floor, and she lands with a thump. Jillian and I try really hard not to laugh. She glares at us and huffs off to the bathroom.

Ten minutes later, we're all wearing our American flag t-shirts and walking along the brick path. We pass the Texas and Idaho tree suites and keep wandering, looking for a building marked *le Cantine de Universite*.

When we get in between a Canadian tree suite and a Chinese tree suite, we see the sign and take the brick pathway that cuts through the forest. Soon, the trees thin out and we come to a clearing at the edge of the university campus. Beyond the grass, *le Universite de Creativite* shimmers in the distance. With the sun shining over it, it looks like a sparkling palace.

The largest building is full of tall peaks with deep sloping rooftops. The surrounding buildings are smaller but still regal-looking. We cross the clearing, and I feel the magic of this place pulling me in. On the side of one small building is the entrance we're looking for. When we finally walk through the door of le Cantine, we're bombarded with the sounds of voices and clanking silverware. There must be a thousand kids in here. It's not exactly magical, but it's definitely spectacular. We pick up our trays and get in line.

The dining hall is full of foods from all over the world.

I pass by the stuff I don't recognize and fill my tray with pancakes. I wish I could find the warm peppermint-y scrambled apples from Camp Piedmont, but they don't seem to be anywhere. I quickly realize my teammates and I have been separated. I search for signs of them, but all I see are signs written in languages of countries I've never been to. Everyone seems to know everyone, and my stomach flips over. How could my teammates leave me? Where are they? I walk in circles but don't see them anywhere.

I stop at the beverage station, relieved to see Maelle, a girl from the French team. "Hello, Kia. How are you today?" She's wearing a shirt with the French flag on it.

"Hi, Maelle. I'm fine. How are you?"

"Mm, good. We are sitting over there. Is your table close by to us?"

I smile because I suddenly see Ander waving from the corner. "Yeah, it's just over there." I look down at the croissant on her tray. "Is that all you're going to eat?"

She laughs. "Well, yes, there's chocolate inside."

"You're having chocolate for breakfast?"

"Mm, yes. I always have chocolate for breakfast. I should go to my table and eat now. I will see you another time, alright?"

"Sure, see you later." I carry my tray to the table marked with our sign. Seraphina and Gregor have just started eating, but the rest of my team is almost finished.

"Morning, Kia," says Seraphina.

"Did you get lost?" asks Ander.

"Yes! But then I was talking to Maelle from the French team. Hi, Seraphina. Do you know what time we present to the judges?"

"Our report time is nine o'clock. Your team will be

presenting at 9:45 a.m."

I bite my thumb nail. "But we need to practice."

"You need nourishment," says Gregor.

I nod and quickly eat my pancakes while Seraphina continues.

"The Showcase Festival will also be open to the distinguished guests of Québec. After judging, your job will be to answer their questions about your invention."

"Who are the distinguished guests?" asks Jax.

"Many are teachers, some are engineers, and some are scientists. They come from several countries and could be the people turning these inventions into real items one day. We'd like you to stay in the New York booth for a while after you compete to answer questions from these guests or from kids on the other teams. Gregor and I will be there to help you."

I wipe my face with a napkin. "Okay, so can we go now? We have to practice. The judges will be coming soon!"

"Kia, we can't even get into your booth yet."

"But I'm not ready! We didn't even practice on the aero-bus."

"I don't feel ready either," says Jillian. "Is there somewhere we can practice?"

"Yeah, can we?" asks Ander. "We rehearsed right before Pre-Judging at Camp Piedmont, and then again before the National Finals, but it's been three weeks since then."

Mare stands up. "What if we forget what we're supposed to say? I don't want to look like an idiot in front of the judges and the distinguished guests, or whoever they are."

"But aren't our props over at our booth?" asks Jax.

"Yes," Gregor responds. "Perhaps you can practice

without them. There is enough time."

Seraphina stands up. "Okay, come on, guys. I have a place we can go."

We clear our trays and scurry out of le Cantine. Seraphina and Gregor lead us back across the clearing towardthe tree suite colony. Before we get as far as any of the tree suites, we stop at an area in the forest, full of tall, gnarled trees. Most are tangled so badly it's hard to tell which one is which, but we do find two large limbs lying on the ground.

"Perfect!" says Seraphina. "We can sit here. Why don't you run through your lines first to make sure you haven't forgotten them? After that, you can act out the entire skit in this clearing."

We spend the next forty-five minutes rehearsing the skit that goes along with our Ancestor App invention. Crimson Catropolis slowly comes back to life—sort of. Each of us messes up our lines at least once. No matter how many times we try, we can't get it quite right.

"We're never going to get it," I say. "And we're running out of time."

"This is just great," says Mare. "I said right from the beginning at Camp Piedmont that I didn't want to do a play, and now we have to do it for international judges and make total fools of ourselves."

"You're the one who wanted to take a nap on the bus instead of rehearsing," I remind her.

"We were supposed to have two weeks here to practice!"

"She's right, KK. None of us knew we'd be judged today. Don't worry. Maybe we just need to be in the right environment."

"You may be right, Ander," says Seraphina. "This isn't

working, but it's not as bad as you think. You have *most* of it down. Maybe you *do* need the props and costumes to perform your best. Let's head over to the Imagination Centre. The doors should be open soon. We'll have just enough time to set up before the judges arrive."

The butterflies in my stomach wake right up as soon as Seraphina says that, but I take a deep breath and start walking with the rest of my team. It takes hardly any time at all to get to the Imagination Centre, or maybe it just seems like that because I don't feel like we're ready at all. I hope Seraphina's right. Maybe once our costumes are on and we're standing with the Circle Spinner, we'll be okay.

We enter the building, and I'm surprised at the sight. The Imagination Centre doesn't look like the gala room at all. Last night it was full of food and kids in fancy clothing, but now it's full of partitioned booths and kids unpacking boxes. Hundreds of booths are set up, one for each team, marked with the flag from their country. That's when it hits me. This is the Showcase Festival—where the greatest inventions will be on display from kids all over the world, just like us, but not like us at all. I'm not sure if I love or hate being around all these amazing inventions—inventions that may be better than ours.

"This is awesome," says Ander, bouncing on his toes. "I can't wait to see all the cool stuff!"

We walk up and down the aisles looking for our booth and finally reach it. An American flag banner hangs above the back wall with a New York sign underneath it. The booth itself is empty except for our boxes, each sealed with tape. Some are small—probably containing our costumes. One is very large. It holds the Circle Spinner, the metal holder containing my Golden Light Bulb, where we project the Ancestor App.

Seraphina looks over them all. "Why don't each of you take a box? Be careful when you open them up. We don't want to have any disasters."

I pick a small box and open it slowly. Inside is the air screen that controls the Ancestor App. I carefully unwrap it from its cocoon. The box holding the Ancestor App is lying flat on the floor. Seraphina grabs hold of the cardboard corners and carefully pulls the box away as Gregor holds it in place. The Golden Light Bulb is still secure and the metal stand is in one piece, but scattered on the floor are pieces of wood that used to be glued to the front as decoration. Now our invention looks broken.

"Oh no!" says Jillian. "Some of the pieces fell off!"

"But it's not that bad," says Ander.

"But it doesn't look good. Does it even still spin?" she asks.

"Don't spin it," says Jax. "More pieces may fall off. They probably loosened during transport."

"Where's the toolbox? Did that make the trip?" asks Mare. "We need glue."

"Yes!" says Jillian. "We packed it in one of the costume boxes. Glue was definitely in there."

Ander pulls it out of the box. "I'll do it."

"Wait," I say. "The judges will be here in twenty minutes and we still have to change into our costumes. There's no time for the glue to dry."

"Great," says Mare. "Our invention is going to look like we slapped it together in five minutes."

I rifle through the toolbox. "Not if we use this." I hold up a roll of duct tape.

"Perfect!" Ander gives us the thumbs up. "I'll cut the

pieces. You guys stick them on the wood."

We get to work rolling the duct tape into tiny pieces and sticking them to the backs of the broken wood pieces. We press them onto the Circle Spinner and it starts to look better, but still, it doesn't look perfect.

"It's going to have to do," says Seraphina. You only have eight minutes until the judges arrive."

This is horrible!

We grab our costume bags and race past invention after invention on the way to the bathroom. While I'm running, I pull my hair into two pigtails. We find a bathroom just around the corner and slip inside. I've never changed so fast in my life! While I buckle my overall shorts, I think about my talk with Grandma Kitty yesterday morning when I was at her house. She wants to be able to communicate with her dead mother again. Winning is the only way to make that happen, so we just have to ace this presentation.

We take two seconds to make sure we all look okay and race back to our booth. The boys arrive after us, which is so typical, and they don't even have to worry about their hair! Ander jumps into the booth with his jester costume on inside out. "Freddy Dinkleweed, at your service!"

"Oh my god, Ander."

"What?" he asks.

Jillian gasps. "Your costume is inside out!"

I see the look of panic on his face, and I should tell him it's fine, but no way. If we lose because he can't figure out how to put his clothes on like everyone else, then I'll never forgive him.

"Don't worry," Seraphina assures us. "Freddy Dinkle-weed would definitely wear his clothes inside out."

I look at Ander again, and yeah, I guess she does have

a point. Seraphina glances down the aisle. "They should be here any minute." We scurry to take our places in front of our props. Seraphina and Gregor take their places at the front corners of the booth and keep watch. Seraphina nods. "You've got this, my Crimson Kids. Ready to show 'em what you've got?"

And just as the judges appear in front of our booth we chant, "Yup de dup dup dup. We're ready to show you our team's circle!"

But my heart is thumping out of my chest. I'm not sure I'll be able to say my lines. Two men and one woman in matching gold shirts laugh. The woman, wearing a flowered hat, laughs the loudest. "Well, we certainly are ready to see it."

"Do you have the proper paperwork?" asks one of the male judges.

"Yes, of course," Gregor responds, and hands a packet of papers to him.

While the two male judges read through it, the female judge walks over to us, "You aren't nervous, are you?"

Ander tugs on his inside out shirt. "Nope, we're not."

"Because I don't want you to be nervous. This is only one small portion of the competition. The real hard part comes next when you attempt to solve the Global Task."

Don't remind me.

"But in case you are nervous—like if you feel like you may faint or throw up—just take all that imaginary garbage out of your head and pretend to hand it to me." She holds her hand out to each of us. "Now just place those nervous, sick-feeling thoughts right in my hand, and I'll throw them all away."

Is she crazy? I didn't have major sick-feeling thoughts

before, but now I do.

Her palm is cupped in front of me. "What are you waiting for?" she asks.

I look at the rest of my team. Jillian shrugs.

This is really weird.

I pretend to place something in her hand. She places my pretend something in her pocket.

The rest of the team does the same thing, and she walks to the front of the booth and pretends to empty the contents of her pocket onto the floor.

Are you serious?

"New York Team from the United States of America," says one of the men. "We're ready for you. You may begin whenever you like."

We stand there, frozen.

Seraphina seems to realize we need someone to start us. She quickly says again, "Team, are you ready?"

"Yup de dup dup dup, we're ready to show you our team circle!"

And just by saying those words, the magical world of Crimson Catropolis slowly comes to life. Our voices boom, and I'm sure the judges can hear us over the noise of the people walking in the aisles. It's hard to perform our play in such a small space, but we adjust for the difference, trying to stay out of each other's way. As we skip around the space, I notice a crowd gathering around our booth. Other kids and distinguished guests are watching our skit. But it doesn't make me nervous—not like the lady in the hat did—it makes me feel like a star. Jax flairs his cape. Mare snaps her gum. Jillian spins the spinner. Ander activates the Ancestor App. When Ander's great-great-grandpa Jim appears from the smoky swirl and begins answering Ander's questions, the crowd gasps—just like the audience at Camp Piedmont did.

At the end of the twelve minutes, the crowd is clapping for us, and I feel like I'm floating on a cloud. But the judges don't cheer one bit. They write their notes, enter stuff into their portable air screens, and off they go. No smile, no "good job." No nothing. Not until the lady judge says to Ander, "Did you know your costume was inside out?"

Without hesitation, he replies, "Yup, I knew."

"Impressive. It definitely added to the quirkiness of your character."

She walks away, and Ander tries not to smile.

"Nice save on that one," says Mare.

He nods. "Yeah, I planned it all along."

Before we can ask Seraphina and Gregor how we did, we're bombarded with questions from the crowd. "How did you think of that?" asks a man in a suit. "How many hours did it take you to assemble it?" asks a woman in a skirt. "Do you know what this will mean for people?" asks another.

We do our best to answer their questions, and it's fun at first, but then it gets tiring and I wish they would go away. A group of kids dressed in matching outfits depicting the red, white, and blue colors of the French flag walk up to the booth. We quickly realize it's our new French friends.

"Hello," says Gwyndol. "We just heard a large group of people talking about the American invention from the New York team."

"Mm, yes," says Maelle. "They said it was very good."

"Your costumes are so very nice too," says Danielle. She smiles and her whole face lights up. Her hair is long and wavy with a small clip on the side.

"Thanks," says Jillian. "It took us forever to make them."

"What are you supposed to be?" asks Stephan.

Ander starts to answer, but then he looks at me. I nod at him to let him know he can tell them. "We dress up like pretend characters to show our invention to the judges."

"You are finished with judging, yes?" asks Zoe. Her dark curls bounce as she talks.

"Oh yeah," I say. "We were judged a little while ago."

"Were you nervous?" asks Maelle.

"No, not too bad," I say. "It was weird when the crowd started getting bigger."

"The crowd?" she asks.

I realize she may not know what that word means. "Yes, all the people. A lot of people came to watch."

"Is that allowed?" asks Zoe. "Don't the judges watch in private?"

"No," says Ander. "It's a showcase. Anyone can watch."

"I must not have understood that correctly," says Maelle. "We have not been judged yet. I think I will be nervous."

"It wasn't bad," says Jillian. "It's like being on stage!" She tosses her feather boa over her shoulder. Gwyndol laughs as he throws his scarf over his shoulder too.

"Do you want to see it now?" asks Ander. "We're supposed to show anyone who asks."

"Oh yes!" says Maelle. "I would."

"We're not doing our whole play, right?" asks Mare.

I think about that for a second. Even though the French team seems really nice, I don't want them to see our whole play. "No," I say. "Just the Ancestor App."

Ander walks over to the Circle Spinner with the remote in his hand. He pulls out the air screen and programs in the information. After a minute or two, the French team is watching with their eyes wide. "How did you make up that invention?" asks Gwyndol. "That's good."

"Thanks," says Ander. "We sort of figured it out together."

"Well," says Maelle. "I like it very much."

Danielle smiles. "We are judged at two-thirty. You may come to see our invention before then if you like."

"Okay, sure! We'll come as soon as we can."

But we spend forever explaining the Ancestor App to the people visiting our booth. At times, there are so many people that Seraphina and Gregor answer questions too. I feel like a celebrity. I had no idea the distinguished guests and other teams would be this excited about our invention.

In the back of the crowd I see Witch Girl—I mean Martina. She's watching us with her arms crossed in front of her. When she catches me looking at her, she runs away, probably because she's spying on us. This is not good.

THE INVENTIONS

LATER, WHEN THE people have cleared out of our booth, Seraphina calls us over. "Look, my Crimson Kids, the Showcase Festival is almost over, and you haven't seen any of the other teams' inventions. Gregor and I will pack up your materials. It's time for you to walk around and see the amazing work out there."

"What time is it?" I ask.

"Four o'clock. The festival closes in an hour."

"Oh no!" I exclaim. "We told the French team we'd stop at their booth before they were judged, but that was a while ago. I hope they're not mad."

We race through the aisles, not sure where to find the French team, and pass some really cool-looking inventions along the way. We wave hello to several teams but keep a fast pace as we search for the French flag.

"Don't worry about stopping to see our invention," a

voice calls from behind us. I spin around and Martina is standing in her booth with the rest of the Michigan team. The boys are huddled around a computer.

"Sorry," I call without looking back. My team is already ahead of me, and I don't want to see her invention anyway.

Finally, we find the French kids standing outside a booth halfway down the row. Jillian runs up to Gwyndol. "We're so sorry we didn't come sooner. We had a lot of people in our booth. We couldn't leave at all!"

Gwyndol smiles. "That is alright. We have been very busy too."

"How did judging go?" I ask.

"It went very well. The judges were kind and nice," says Maelle.

"Except for the judge who would tell us to not be so, how you say, anxious?" says Zoe.

"Yes," says Danielle. "She was the one who made us so anxious."

Ander shakes his head. "I know! What's up with that? I wasn't even nervous before she said that stupid stuff about feeling like we're going to throw up."

Mare makes her voice sound like the lady. "Here, children, put those nervous feelings in my hand. All your worries will float away like pixie dust."

Maelle and I laugh. What an idiot that judge was. I thought all the Piedmont people were so smart. Why would she try to make all of us nervous on purpose?

"Can we see your invention?" Ander asks.

"Yes, of course," says Zoe.

Stephan steps up to a long table. Situated on top of it is a pitcher of water and a small container. "The task in our country was to create a food or drink that begins as one type and turns into a new food or drink that will improve our society in some way. We chose a pitcher of water."

Zoe steps up to the table. "You can see it is a pitcher of water, yes?"

I nod. "Yes."

Stephan continues, "We developed a formula for increasing a person's honesty, which would definitely improve our society. It is here, in this small container."

Danielle opens the container and smiles. Inside are tiny silver gel packs shimmering under the fluorescent lights. "These are the honesty gels."

"When we add them to the water, the water is no longer regular drinking water, it is now honesty water," says Gwyndol.

"And most importantly," says Stephan, "we have invented something that will help our society be more honest."

"Wow!" says Ander. "That's cool."

"Does it really make a person more honest?" I ask. "Just by drinking a glass of it?"

"If it does, it would be a really important invention," says Jax.

Maybe even more important than the Ancestor App.

"Definitely," says Jillian.

"We think it works," says Gwyndol. "We have conducted hundreds of tests. We are almost certain the government will agree with our formula."

I bite my ring nail. "Wow, I bet the judges really liked it."

Maelle frowns. "We are not sure. They have such serious faces. It is very hard to tell."

"We know what you mean," I say. "The judges were very

serious with us too."

"Well hello, my New York friends!" Their preceptor Mathilde calls as she approaches the booth. "I am happy you were able to stop by to see us."

"Hello, Mathilde," says Jillian. "Your team's invention is really good."

"Why *merci*! I'm sure yours is quite good as well."

Maelle smiles. "Oh Mathilde, you should see it. They invented an object that has capability for people to communicate with their relatives who have died many, many years ago!"

"That's an impressive invention," she replies. "I would have liked to see it."

"Seraphina has probably already packed it away," says Mare.

"Maybe soon it will become a real invention, not just a prototype, and I will see it then."

"I hope so," I say.

"We should get going," says Jax.

"Yeah." Ander is already walking off. "I want to see if we can catch a few more inventions before all the booths close down."

We say goodbye and hurry away. In the far row of booths, we see that a team from Mexico is still showcasing their invention.

We stand there quietly while they explain it to a man in tan pants. When he leaves, one of their team members looks over. "Your outfits are . . . different."

I look down at my yellow overall shorts, and Ander adjusts his jester hat. I had forgotten about our costumes. We must look like idiots.

"Oh, these?" laughs Jillian, tossing the feather boa over

her shoulder. "We haven't changed back out of our judging clothes."

"You guys must be the team from New York. Everyone is talking about your play."

Ander grins. "Everyone?"

"Well, maybe not everyone."

Mare smiles at him. "Can we see your invention?"

"Sure. We made a parachute suit. We had to design an object that would improve an already existing item that we use. We hate carrying parachute packs on our aero-scooters. They're too heavy. So we built one into this suit. You wear it over your clothes. It saves you from getting splashed with bird crap while you're flying too."

"Hmm." Ander gives it a once over. "I would wear it."

Jillian reaches out to touch the fabric. "Are there other colors?"

Mare shakes her head. "This isn't a store, Jillian."

The boy smiles. "Yeah, fashion isn't really my specialty."

We thank the boy and continue down the aisle. The rest of the booths are deserted now, except for one that's close to ours. It belongs to the team from Switzerland, and when we walk up, two boys are placing a cover on a large box.

"Hello," says one of them. "We were just about to pack up."

"Sorry," I say. "We're kind of late getting around. We're from New York, in the USA."

"I'm Finn," says the other boy. "And this is my team-mate, Lars."

"What's your invention?" asks Jillian.

"It's a Thought Translation Box," says Finn.

"A what?"

Finn laughs. "A Thought Translation Box."

"What does it do?" asks Jax.

"It decodes thoughts in your brain and puts them into words up on the screen inside."

"Whoa! So it's like a mind reader?" asks Ander.

"Sort of. It's designed for people to make sense of an idea—an idea that's stuck in their mind. When you sit inside the box, the sensors all around you will extract what you're thinking from your entire body. If the thought is in the very forefront of your brain, it will take only a second or two. If the thought is buried and working its way to the forefront, it will take a little longer, but the Thought Translator will eventually help you decode it."

"Wow," Jax says in complete awe.

"Can I try?" asks Ander.

"Sure," says Lars. "Just take your shoes off. Lasers will be sensing your feet too. When the thought translator is done figuring out your thought, it will flash it on the screen up there."

Ander crawls inside the box. Finn closes the door, and Ander waves at us like a circus clown. Immediately, laser beams fill the walls around him. Within seconds, Ander is pointing at the screen. He pushes the door open. "It worked! Did you guys see that? It said, 'This is the coolest invention ever!' and that's what I was thinking!"

I can't believe they invented a mind reader.

"Yeah, I was trying to think of what I was going to think, but before I could, the screen flashed that message, and it was right."

"That's amazing," says Jillian.

"Thanks for showing us," says Jax.

We walk away, and I feel sick to my stomach. That's totally better than the Ancestor App. I wish we never saw any of these other inventions.

By the time we get back to our booth, Seraphina and Gregor are sitting on our pile of boxes. "Did you get to see any inventions?" she asks.

"Yeah," says Mare. "Some were really good."

"I thought they would be. It's inspiring to see all the great ideas."

Yeah, and demoralizing.

"But now you better change so we can head over to le Cantine for dinner. The Sport and Game Festival is tonight, and you won't want to miss that."

THE SPORT AND GAME FESTIVAL

AFTER DINNER, SERAPHINA and Gregor lead us out of le Cantine to the fields behind the university building complex. Twenty flags, one from each country, are staked into the ground. Kids are running around everywhere, scattered like bugs.

"Okay," says Seraphina. "Here's the deal. Each country is going to be showcasing their own local sport or game. It'll be demonstrated by a group of preceptors chosen by the Piedmont Organization."

"Are you and Gregor going to be demonstrating for the United States?" asks Jillian.

"No, we already have jobs here, silly! The preceptors chosen were from teams who didn't qualify to compete here."

"Oh, that makes sense."

"What sport is our country showcasing?" I ask.

"Nacho Cheese Ball, of course!"

"Awesome!" Ander exclaims. "Will we get to play?"

"That depends," Gregor replies. "The showcase is a chance for you to learn about the different games and sports originated in each country. Once you've learned about as many as you can, you'll be allowed to sign up to participate in the activities of your choice."

"Could we sign up for Nacho Cheese Ball?" asks Jax.

"You could, if that's what you all decide. But I would remain open to playing the other games or sports as well."

"Okay," says Mare. "When do we start?"

"Master Freeman has a brief welcome message, and the games will start shortly after. Let's go find a spot on the grass to sit and listen."

The night is warm even though the sun is low in the sky. Music plays loudly from hidden speakers. When we arrived, the song that was playing was in English, but the one playing now sounds like it's in Spanish. We walk past kids from all over the world—some that I recognize from the gala last night and the Showcase Festival earlier today, and many more that I don't. I recognize some words as I weave through the crowded field, but mostly I hear languages I don't understand at all. I suddenly wish that I had learned another language, or maybe even two. At Crimson Elementary, we only learn English in our Communications class. I wonder if that's one more thing that's against the rules of our country now. That never bothered me before, but now it kind of does.

We find a spot on a hill not too far from where Master Freeman will be speaking. The stage is decorated with the Piedmont Crest and purple, gold, and white streamers. Two women dressed in purple dresses with ribbons woven through their hair stand tall on either end of the stage. They smile brightly as they hold silver harps.

Master Freeman steps up to the microphone, and the music fades away. "Welcome, children, to the Piedmont Game and Sport Festival! As you know, here at the Piedmont Organization, we believe in the power of imaginative play and healthy competition. Tonight, you will see a plethora of each. This is creativity at its very best, showcased by some of the very best minds and bodies from around the world."

He raises his arm. "And now, let the fun begin!" He blows a whistle and the preceptors run out from the crowd to take their places on the fields behind him.

Hundreds of kids scramble to their feet and race to watch. "Where should we go first?" I ask.

"I don't know," says Mare. "Let's watch the Swiss game. Those boys yesterday were cute. Maybe they'll be there watching too."

We start looking for a red flag with a white plus sign in the middle and find it at the far end of the field. Next to the Switzerland flag, a banner is staked into the ground: *The Swiss Chocolate Game.*

"Ooh, this looks fun—and yummy," says Jillian.

We stand against the ropes, ready to watch the game begin. Ten Swiss preceptors walk up to a long white table in the center of the field—five on either side, half wearing red shirts and half wearing white. Kids from other teams crowd around us, and soon there are about twenty other kids watching too.

A preceptor, a teen boy of about eighteen years old, turns toward the crowd. "Hello everyone, you are just in time! We are about to demonstrate to you how one of our traditional birthday party games is played—for both children and adults. It is called the Swiss Chocolate Game and is very fun. Over the years it has evolved and has now become a popular backyard team sport.

"On this table, you will see in front of each team: an oversized pair of dice, a wool hat, a long knitted scarf, a pair of very large gloves, a knife, a fork, and a delicious chocolate bar—of course made from the finest Swiss chocolate. When the whistle blows, a player from each team will take turns rolling the dice. When a set of doubles is rolled, that player will put on the hat, scarf, and gloves, unwrap the chocolate, and attempt to cut it with a knife and fork. Whatever is cut must be eaten. The other players will take turns rolling the dice until he or she rolls a double. At that time the hat, scarf, and gloves will be removed and passed along with the knife, fork, and chocolate to the player who rolled the double. He will then proceed to cut and eat the chocolate. The game continues until each player on the team has rolled a double, worn the clothes, and therefore cut and eaten chocolate. In order to win, the last player on the team must cut the remaining piece in two and eat both halves. The first team to do this and finish the whole chocolate bar is declared the winner. Please stay and watch, and if you like, please sign up to play with your team later this evening."

"This looks funny," says Jax.

The whistle blows. The preceptors begin frantically rolling the dice on each side of the table. This continues for several minutes before someone finally rolls a double.

"A pair of fives from the white team!" yells a referee standing at the head of the table.

A boy in white quickly ties the scarf around his neck,

puts the hat on his head, and pulls the gloves on. "Hurry!" calls his teammate as she hands him the fork and knife. He does his best to cut the chocolate, but it slides away from him and only a small piece slivers off. Meanwhile the red team keeps rolling, but they have no luck. They begin chanting, "Double, double, double!" when suddenly a small blonde girl finally gets one.

"A pair of twos for the red team!" calls the referee.

She quickly puts the hat on, throws the scarf over her shoulder, and pulls the man-sized gloves onto her tiny hands. She fumbles with the chocolate, desperately trying to unwrap it while the white team rolls another double.

"A pair of fours from the white team!"

The boy slides the chocolate, knife, and fork down to a girl at the end, and pulls off the hat, scarf, and gloves. His hair is standing up from static, and the whole table laughs. His teammate grabs the pile of clothing and tosses it to her. While she gets dressed in the clothing, the referee calls out again, "Another pair of fours, now from the red team. It looks like the game is tied!"

I watch, mesmerized by the rolling dice and flying pieces of chocolate. Cutting the chocolate must be harder than it looks. Soon the preceptors are rolling the dice faster and faster, and the gloves and scarves and hats are thrown from one person to the other. Another blond boy's hair is full of static, and the whole bunch of them are laughing.

The chaos continues, and the referee yells, "A double three for red!" The clothes fly, and a girl pops a piece of chocolate into her mouth. And soon, "Another double for red, this time a pair of ones!" The last boy quickly puts the clothes on, cuts the rest of the chocolate bar in half, and shoves both in his mouth. As soon as he does, the referee exclaims, "The win goes to red!" Their team jumps into a heap on the ground and the white team is left shaking their heads.

A preceptor at the bottom of the pile eventually emerges with a huge grin. Both teams shake hands, stand in a row in front of us, and bow. "Thank you for watching the Swiss Chocolate Game. We hope you'll come back soon!"

Ander looks at me and exclaims, "That was awesome! Do you think they have extra chocolate?" Before I can tell him not to be so rude, the preceptors step over the ropes and pass out pieces of chocolate to the crowd.

I pop the small square into my mouth and let it melt. "I think this is the best chocolate I've ever tasted."

"Come on, guys," says Mare. "I don't see the Switzerland boys here. They must be watching another game. Let's try to find them."

"Maybe we could watch another game," Jax suggests.

"Well, yeah," she responds. "But if we *happen* to see them watching a game, then we may as well watch with them, right?"

Jax doesn't answer her, so I pull his arm and drag him along behind me. We come up to another red flag with a picture in the center. A banner with the word *Dinifri* is stuck into the ground next to it.

"What country is this?" asks Jillian.

"I don't know," I reply.

"I think it's Morocco," says Jax.

"It looks like we missed the rules, but it might be cool," says Ander. "Let's watch for a second."

We find a close spot on the grass. The square field has been marked off with paint and four smaller squares are painted inside it, one in each corner. Another square is also painted in the center. Four objects are piled up in the center square, maybe rocks. The referee is holding a baton type object. It looks like it might be a piece of cardboard rolled up with string.

Two teams with five players each are standing on opposite sides of the field. One is dressed in yellow and one in red. The referee blows the whistle, and the two teams take turns trying to knock over the pile of rocks in the center by tossing the baton. It takes several tries, but once the yellow team knocks them over, chaos erupts. It looks like now the yellow team is trying to pick up all the rocks in the center and put one on each of the four corner squares. But the red team is throwing the baton at them. This must be how they play defense, because each time someone on the yellow team gets hit with it, they're out. And every time it happens, the game pauses. The red team dances and chants something that sounds like, "Chi, chi, ka, kahh," in celebration for several seconds. Then the action suddenly starts back up. By now the yellow team has lost all their players except one. Three of the rocks are in a corner square, but one remains inside the yellow player's hand. He races for the empty corner and a red player throws the baton his way. The yellow player dives under it, crawls on the ground, and quickly places the rock inside the final square.

The referee shouts something we don't understand and then announces in English, "The yellow team is victorious!" The yellow team cheers and walks over to the red team to shake hands and pat their opponents on their backs.

Both teams approach the large crowd. A tall boy cups his hands to his mouth so he can be heard above the noise. "Thank you so very much for watching. *Dinifri* is a very competitive game that we love in Morocco. Feel free to sign your team up for a game as well."

We look at each other and grin. "I want to try that one," I say.

"I'm in," Ander replies. "What about you guys? Should we sign up?"

"Maybe," says Jillian. "Let's watch some more, and then we can decide, okay?"

We continue walking around the campus checking out as many games as we can and come across *Queimada* from Brazil and *Bocce* from Italy. When we get to the United States field, we see a large crowd has gathered to watch Nacho Cheese Ball.

Witch Girl—I mean Martina—from Michigan walks up to Mare and me. "Wow, it looks like the crowd is here to watch Nacho Cheese Ball, not the amazing team from New York for a change. How is that possible?"

Mare glares at her. "What are you talking about?"

"Oh please. Don't tell me you didn't notice all the people watching you at the Showcase Festival earlier."

I look at her confused. "Well, yeah, but I'm sure they were watching everyone else's inventions too."

"You think so?"

"Um, yeah."

"Well, I walked around the whole day, and all the other booths had small crowds. Of course, our booth did great, but we would've had even more people if they didn't get stuck watching your play."

Mare shrugs. "Oh well. It's not like we asked them to come."

"Sure you did."

"What do you mean?" I ask.

"In the media blast."

"What media blast?"

"The one sent by your principal, telling the whole world about your invention."

"What?" I ask. "He told the whole world about our invention? He doesn't even know what it is."

"He didn't actually say what the invention was, but he basically told anyone with eyes and ears that you created this breakthrough invention that's going to change the world."

"Oh my gosh," says Mare. "No wonder our crowds were so big."

My stomach suddenly feels sick. "Why did he do that?"

Martina turns around and walks away. But before she's out of earshot, she says, "Beats me. But I'm not sure that's allowed. I wonder what Master Freeman would say."

Mare and I stand there frozen.

"What are we going to do?" I say. "What if we get disqualified? We have to tell Seraphina and Gregor!" I grab Jillian and yell for Ander and Jax. "Come on, guys, we have to go!"

"But I was just watching Nacho Cheese Ball," Ander replies. "Haven't you been watching these guys? They really know how to play!"

"No, I wasn't watching, but don't argue with me. We have to go!"

Mare shoots dagger eyes at him. "Now, Ander!"

"Okay, okay." He sprints to catch up with me. "What's going on?"

"I'll tell you when we find Seraphina and Gregor." We race to the hill where they were sitting with us before, but they aren't there anymore. "I have no idea where they are!" I twist my head in every direction to find them.

"I'll just track them on my watch," says Jax.

"Good idea," says Jillian.

He taps his watch a few times and sees that they're over by the Canadian field. We race toward it, cutting through the crowd of kids. "Excuse me," I say.

"Sorry!" yells Ander.

"Excuse *moi*!" yells Jillian.

I look at her over my shoulder.

"What? Can't I at least pretend to be French for a few minutes?"

"I don't care what language you speak as long as you keep running!"

We find them along the ropes of the Canadian field watching curling, a game played on ice with brooms and a big rock shaped thing. "Awesome! Let's watch this!" says Ander.

"Ander, can you focus, please?"

"Sorry, I forgot."

We skid to a stop next to Gregor and Seraphina.

Seraphina sees us first. "Oh hi, guys, what's up?"

"Well," says Ander. "We really want to stay and watch curling, but we have something big to tell you. I don't know what it is because Mare and Kia wouldn't tell us until we found you."

Gregor's expression looks worried. "What is it, girls?" I grab both of them and drag them away from the ropes.

"Tell him, Mare," I urge.

"Okay, so remember Martina, the girl from Michigan?"

"Yes, I remember," says Seraphina.

"Well, we just saw her and she said that Principal Bermuda sent out a media blast about our team. He told them all about our amazing invention. That's why so many people came to our booth. They all heard about it and wanted to see it."

"I never heard anything about the media blast," says Seraphina.

"But are we going to get disqualified?" I ask.

"Did the blast say what your invention was?" asks Gregor.

"No," I say. "Martina said he didn't say what it was, just that it was super cool and will change the world and it's the best kept secret of the week."

"Hmm," says Gregor. "It's sounds like he's building up interest in your invention in case it wins. Very smart I must say."

"But is that against the rules or not?" asks Ander.

"I don't think so, but I don't know for certain."

"And can't he get in trouble for interfering with the competition?" asks Jillian.

"Well, he didn't directly interfere with the competition."

"Yeah, but why is he telling all these people about us?" I ask. "Why is he doing all these TV interviews and media blasts? Why can't he just leave us alone?"

Seraphina shakes her head. "Don't worry. He can't do anything more to your team. He can't hurt any of you anymore."

My head knows she's probably right, but the rest of me has a hard time believing that. Besides, he's trying to make us famous or something, and I don't like it. I don't like anything that he does. Not one bit.

Seraphina looks at her watch and bites her lip. "Oh no."

Gregor frowns. "What?"

"I have a message from Andora. She wants to see me in her chambers immediately."

Oh no. The media blast.

Gregor's face turns serious. "I'll stay here with the team. Please let me know what she says."

"This is bad," I say. "What if we get disqualified?"

Mare huffs. "If we get disqualified because Principal Backstabber is the biggest jerk ever—"

"Don't panic yet. Let's wait to hear what Andora says. In the meantime, I suggest you direct your attention back to the games and choose what activities you'd like to sign up for."

We huddle together and I force myself not to think about what Andora and Seraphina are talking about. I try not to think about Martina or Principal Bermuda either. But this could be the end for us. No sports, no games, no competition. No making Grandma Kitty's dream of talking to her mother a reality. Nothing.

"Kia, are you listening? What do you want to do?" Jillian is staring at me.

"Oh, sorry. Whatever you decide is fine."

In the end, we pick Nacho Cheese Ball, The Swiss Chocolate Game, and Queimada, so we head over to the sign-up table.

We play Queimada against Brazil first, and then the Swiss Chocolate Game against Italy. At first it's hard not to worry about Seraphina's meeting, but the games help me push it out of my head temporarily. I decide I shouldn't worry because Grandma Kitty always says that worrying is just imagining the worst possible outcome, and I definitely don't want to do that.

Next we move over to the Nacho Cheese Ball field.

"We need a strategy this time," says Ander. "Like we need to have an actual offense and defense planned. Last time at Camp Piedmont we didn't know what we were doing. We're lucky we got as far in the tournament as we did. But there's bragging rights at stake here. This is an American game. I want to be sure that no one beats us, especially no one from another country. What do you think? Should we make an actual game plan?"

"Sure," I say. "I'll play offense or defense. It doesn't matter to me."

"Me either," says Jillian.

"Alright, then since I'm the only one with any real sports experience, I'll be the captain. I think we should start with positions. Jax, no offense, but you're pretty slow, so it wouldn't make sense to have you running for the target on offense. But you *are* big, so that would make you intimidating, meaning you'd be awesome at defense. Okay?"

"I'm good with that."

"Okay, great. And, KK, since you're fast like me, I think we should be offense."

"Okay."

"Then Mare, since you can be intimidating too, why don't you be defense with Jax? And Jillian, you could be a floater. You could do both defense and offense depending on where the action is."

Jillian makes a face. "I don't want to be a floater. I'd rather have one position all the time."

"I'll play floater," says Mare. "I'll get more action that way."

"Okay, perfect," says Ander. "Those are the positions."

We get our equipment and find out that Nacho Cheese Ball is shorter here than normal, so the games are capped at 100 points. The first team to reach that scores wins. We face India in the first game and then Ireland in the second.

We win against both teams and as we race off the field still wearing our silver suits and covered in cheese, a news reporter comes racing toward us. He escorts us to a quiet place away from the action, pulls down an air screen from absolutely nowhere, and shoves a microphone in my face.

"Hi Kia, I'm Steven Sanford from Nightly News Tonight. We're broadcasting live on the events of today's Sport and Game Festival at these Piedmont Global Championships. Much has been said about your team, the Crimson Five, as you're now known. Our viewers are interested to hear about your experience so far. I see you've just finished playing Nacho Cheese Ball, the game invented in the USA. How did it go today?"

I'm stuck for what to say at first, wondering why anyone would care how we're doing in Nacho Cheese Ball. "It was a good match, I think. A little messy, but fun."

Ander leans in toward the microphone. "We won both games, one against the team from India and one from against the team from Ireland. They were worthy opponents though and gave us a challenge."

Soon after, the man from the news show leaves, and Seraphina finds us. "Good news, my Crimson Kids. You're not disqualified."

"We're not?" I ask.

"No. Andora had a question about my Preceptor Project."

"You mean, the game from the aero-bus?"

"Yes."

"And she didn't say anything about Principal Bermuda?"

"Oh, she had plenty to say about him, but he didn't break any rules—this time."

I let out a breath. I hate Principal Bermuda.

After the festivities wind down, we head back to the tree suites. The lengthening shadows follow us along the brick path. If I wasn't here with my whole team, this walk might feel creepy, but maybe it just feels this way because Principal Bermuda keeps popping into my brain. I just don't trust him. I thought we could get away from his tricks here, but I have this awful feeling he has more planned.

THE TASKS

AFTER BREAKFAST THE next morning, we meet with Seraphina and Gregor in the forest behind our tree suite. We shuffle through the leaves and branches and gather around a birch tree. Pinned to it is a copy of the Global Task. We gather close to read it, but it's hard with so many fallen tree branches in the way.

The world is full of life-changing inventions.

Your task is to take an invention commonly used by people today and re-imagine it. It must continue its current function but also yield a new, life-changing function. Your task solution must be created using skills from all six categories, take no more than twelve minutes to present, and include lyrics to a song.

Seraphina crunches the branches with her purple sneakers. "We've brought you back here so that you can get started on the Global Task. Here is where you'll think about possible ways to solve it."

"Where?" asks Ander. "Aren't we going to brainstorm?"

She smiles. "We're not brainstorming yet. You haven't had time for your brains to process the task."

"So where do we do that?" I ask. "Is there a place like Meeting Room Twelve for us to meet in?"

"Not exactly," she replies. "But there will be."

"Where?" asks Mare.

"Right here!"

I look around at the forest surrounding us.

"Here?" says Jillian. "We can't work here."

"Why not?" asks Seraphina. "Is there a problem with it?"

"Um, yeah," says Mare. "It's gross. There's, like, no place to sit and there are leaves and twigs everywhere."

Gregor strolls over with a cartful of stuff. "Then I suggest you solve this problem. Your task is to make your new work space un-gross. You have forty-five minutes to complete it."

"What do you mean?" I ask

"What is all that stuff?" asks Ander.

"This, young Ander, is a set of old-fashioned garden tools. Long before yards cleaned themselves up, people did the work manually."

Jillian coughs. "Manually?"

"Yes, Jillian, manually."

"But why doesn't this area have a garden cleaning mechanism built in?" asks Jax.

"We requested the yard cleaning feature be turned off."

"Why?" asks Mare. "This area could be the perfect spot to meet in just a few minutes."

"That's true, Mare," Gregor replies. "But nature has a way of bringing out creativity. This will be your thinking time before we brainstorm. And I would suggest you get busy. Last month for the Piedmont National Finals you had six weeks to solve the task. Solving the Global Task in two weeks will not be for the faint of heart."

"You heard him!" I say. "We have forty-five minutes. Let's go!"

Ander grabs a long pole with several prongs sticking out of it. Jax grabs a cart with two wheels. They stare at the objects like they're from another planet. Gregor looks at the boys in disbelief. "Don't tell me. You don't know what to do with these?"

"Nope," says Ander. "Not really."

Gregor shakes his head. "I thought you kids were supposed to be smart."

"On second thought," says Ander. "I know what mine does. You take it and whack it at the branches on the ground—to smash them into small pieces."

Gregor shakes his head. "No, not even close. This is a rake. The prongs are used to rake up the leaves. You turn it over this way to gather them up. You can also use it to smooth the dirt. Jax, your cart is actually called a wheelbarrow."

Ander shrugs. "Okay, maybe I'm not smart about everything."

I take the other rake like Ander's and the girls grab the buckets. "Okay," says Ander. "Let's make a plan. Let's pick up all the big branches first and put them in Jax's wheelbarrow and then he can dump them over there. We can put the small sticks in the buckets and toss them over there too. Now, let's see how fast we can do this."

"But wait!" I say. "This is our thinking time so no talking. Just think about ways to solve the task. Got it?"

Mare rolls her eyes. "Got it."

Jillian wipes her hands on her shorts. "Do we have gloves or something?"

"Sorry, Jillian," says Gregor. "No gloves."

"Wait! I can run back inside to the craft room and make some real quick—for all of us!"

"Jillian, no!" I say. "We don't have time for that, and we don't need them anyway. Let's just get to work, okay?"

She frowns and looks at the ground full of branches. "Okay."

For the first few minutes, we scurry around picking up the big branches. Jax dumps them someplace in the forest with his wheelbarrow. Then we gather the small twigs, branches, and leaves, place them in the buckets, and dump those too. We don't say a word, but I'm not sure anyone is thinking about how to solve the task. Every time Mare looks at Ander, she laughs. I'm not sure why. I shush her to make her keep working. Jax makes several trips to the edge of the clearing, and every once in a while, I hear Jillian humming. Ander climbs a nearby tree to get a bird's-eye view of the area, or so he says. Jax walks back from dumping the wheelbarrow and stops to read the task. I drag a large branch over to the pile and on the way back, I re-read it myself.

Now that we can see the dirt that was underneath the mess, Ander and I use the rakes to smooth it out and collect the tiny leaves. Mare motions for Jax to help her move a fallen log. They can't lift it by themselves, so the rest of us run over to help them. We move it to the cleared-out area, then search around the forest for more, and find three additional logs. Together we drag them over too. We stand there for a few seconds and Ander makes the shape of a square in the dirt. Then he sits down and leans back against one of the logs. He motions me next to him to do the same. That's when we all get what he's trying to do with the heavy branches. We form them into a square, large enough for us all to sit inside with our feet extended, and lean back against the logs. The tall trees around us form a canopy overhead.

We have six minutes left, so we walk up to the tree and re-read the task. Then we find our places in our newly-created clubhouse and sit in silence. I think for a few minutes about how to solve the task, and an idea comes to my mind, but it's lame so I keep trying. Hopefully my teammates are thinking up something better—or anything at all.

Seraphina and Gregor reappear. "Wow," Seraphina says. "This place looks great. And you solved this task with a few minutes to spare."

"It's like our own secret clubhouse," I say. "No one will even know we're back here."

"Yes, this will certainly work as a meeting room. Well done, team."

"We didn't talk or anything!" Ander exclaims.

"We did hum a little, but that's it," I say. Jillian turns pink, probably thinking no one could hear her.

"It's perfect," says Seraphina. "Except for maybe one thing that will make you more comfortable." She turns to the metal wall of the tree suite and pushes a button. I feel tingling on my bare legs and then scratching. I bend my knees. "What the heck?" The ground below us is growing grass!

"I thought you turned off the yard maintenance," Mare says.

"We did, all but the grass feature. We had a feeling it

might come in handy."

I run my hand along the soft green blades. "This is way better!"

"Are you guys ready to brainstorm now?" she asks.

"Yes!" I reply. "Very ready."

"But I don't get it," says Ander. "Why did we go to all this trouble? Why aren't we just brainstorming in the Inspiration Room?"

Gregor grins. "You'll have plenty of chances to use that room. But nothing fuels creativity like the great outdoors."

Ander shrugs, and we make room for them in the square. Gregor raises his arm and makes a motion with his fingers. An air screen drops down, a red board appears, and just like that, it feels like we're back in Meeting Room Twelve at Camp Piedmont.

"Whoa!" says Ander. "I didn't know those could work outside."

Seraphina smiles. "Anything's possible, Ander. Remember that." She pulls the red board closer to her. "Okay, you guys know the drill. Call out as many ideas as you can. The red board will record them, but remember to be respectful of your teammates' ideas. There are no bad ideas. All ideas are useful and may lead to an even better one. At this point, it doesn't matter whose idea it is, only that we have as many ideas to work with as we can. Also, remember that Gregor and I cannot help you. This solution must be created entirely by all of you as a team—and no one else. Understand?"

We nod, and the brainstorming session begins. I try to think of something cool to say, to tell my team all about my brilliant idea, but I don't actually have one. The red board records an idea from Ander and one from Jillian, but they aren't very good, and it's still pretty empty—and Mare, Jax, and I haven't added any ideas at all.

"These ideas are okay, but I can't see how either of them can work. What do you guys think?" asks Jillian.

Mare leans her head back on the log. "I don't know."

Ander does the same. "I'm hungry."

Seraphina looks at her watch. "I thought you might be. It's lunchtime anyway. Run over to le Cantine. We can meet back here after."

We take the path through the forest passing several different teams, but I don't recognize any of them. We make our way across the clearing, and of course Martina and her team are walking out of the dining hall just as we walk in. She pushes her team aside and says, "Watch out, boys, make way for the famous New York team. They want to eat, so by all means, let them through."

"Whatever," says one of her teammates, and together they keep walking.

Mare makes a start to run after her, but Ander grabs her arm before she can.

She lets out an angry sigh. "I don't get what her problem is. What did we ever do to her?"

"I don't know," I say, "but she really doesn't like our team."

"She thinks we're famous," says Jillian.

"Yeah, she does," Jax agrees.

When we get inside le Cantine, it's almost empty. I guess most of the teams must have eaten already. We load our trays with chicken sandwiches, celery, and some mushy thing with grapes, and I decide I don't care what Martina thinks. She's our competition, and I'm not here to be friends with her anyway.

After we eat, we race back to our clubhouse, where Seraphina and Gregor are waiting for us to continue brainstorming. But all of our ideas seem to be stuck in our brains, and the afternoon session turns out to be just as bad as the morning. After working the whole day, all we have to show for it is a homemade clubhouse. And yeah, that was more fun than I thought it would be, but the calendar pages are flipping, and we need to think up an idea.

Later that night, we climb into our sleeping eggs, and Andora's voice rings out through the tree suite speakers. "Good evening boys and girls. We hope you had a productive first day working on your Global Task. But now we encourage you to get your rest. Tomorrow is Swirl and Spark Training Day! Good night and remember . . . Think more. Work hard. Dream big!"

I drop my head onto the pillow. *Great. Another lost day. When are we going to have time to solve this stupid task?*

Early in the morning, we head to the Imagination Centre training facility, where we have practice for the Swirl and Spark Recall task. This is the part of the competition where we'll solve a task that we're not given ahead of time. It tests our ability to think quickly and creatively. None of us know what type of task we will get. It could just be a question we need to answer or we could be instructed to do something. We just won't know until we enter the room.

It's good we're getting practice time on these tasks, but we're wasting a day we could be working on the big Global task, and we don't have that much time to begin with. I feel like dragging my team to a secret spot so we can brainstorm again, but instead, I walk into the training facility.

The facility is like a big gymnasium with stations. Each

station is set up with a different five-minute task—like the ones we could be asked to solve on competition day. Seraphina leads us to the first one where there's a rope hanging from the ceiling. This must be a physical challenge.

A voice projects from speakers all around us. "At the top of the rope is a bucket of cotton balls. Each team member must grab a handful of cotton. Before time is up, the cotton must be placed in the box next to the door. Press the red button when you have finished. You have five minutes to complete this task and will receive bonus points for speed. You may begin now."

Seraphina and Gregor step aside.

"Okay guys, who should climb first?" asks Ander.

"Can you climb that high?" asks Jax. "I can't."

"Well, someone needs to try first," says Mare.

"I don't think I can," says Jillian. "I'm afraid of heights."

"Come on, you guys! We only have five minutes," says Ander.

I grab the rope. "I'll go." I place my hands around the rope and try to shimmy my way up. But then it burns, and my hands start to slip.

"Don't look at me," says Jax.

"But we all have to climb," says Ander.

I look up at the bucket of cotton. "Hold on, no we don't. The voice didn't say that. We each have to grab a handful of cotton, but only one of us has to get the cotton."

"Oh, yeah," says Jillian. "Can any of you do it?"

"These chicken arms?" says Ander. "Um, no."

Mare grabs the rope, one hand after the other, to hoist her body up to the top. She tips the bucket over and we catch the cotton balls as they fall to the ground. "Wow, Mare, awesome!"

We each grab handfuls and place them in the box next to the door. Jillian hits the red button and our time flashes on the box. *Three minutes, twenty-four seconds.*

Gregor steps into the center of the station. "Well done, team. Well done."

Seraphina beams. "That was good! Let's try another one."

We move to a station filled with small puzzle pieces that have been scattered on a table. The voice calls through the speaker. "This puzzle can be used to tell a story. You have five minutes to use every piece to tell an original story of your making."

"What? That's impossible!" says Ander. "There are hundreds of puzzle pieces here. We don't know what it's a picture of."

"Yeah," says Mare. "We'll never have time to put them all together."

"Well, we have to try," says Jillian, searching for matching pieces.

"Wait, hold on," says Jax. "The instructions didn't say we had to put the puzzle together. It just says we have to use it to tell a story."

I feel a smile come over my face. "Okay then . . . I've got this. Once upon a time there was a little girl in Crimson Catropolis walking through a meadow."

Jillian smiles. "On her walk, she picked hundreds of little flowers."

"They were such odd shapes," Mare continues. "They almost looked like puzzle pieces."

"They even had cardboard petals," adds Jax.

"But the little girl had a problem," says Ander. "She wanted to bring them home to her mom, but there were too many to carry."

"So she took off her hat and placed the flowers inside it," I say.

Jillian grins. "Now she had the perfect way to carry the puzzle flowers home to her mom. The end."

I reach for the red button on the table and press it. The timer flashes *two minutes, fifty-three seconds.*

"Jax, good thinking. That one was close."

"How did you even think to do that anyway?" asks Mare.

"Well, most of the problems here don't need to be solved in the obvious way. Remember that concrete room, the one with all the items that needed to be covered in paper? Well, this was like that."

"Glad to see you figured that out," Seraphina replies. "Nicely done."

"And impressive that the rest of you caught on," says Gregor. "But last year's winning team was twenty seconds faster."

"Great," I say.

"No worries yet," he replies. "But it will not serve you well to be overconfident. Let's move on, shall we?"

After lunch, we return to the training facility, but I wish we had stopped at the first two tasks. When we try to predict if an orange will float and prove our hypothesis, we can't agree on if it will float or not. We eventually decide it is a trick question so we say it will float, but then we peel the orange and test it in the water . . . and it sinks. We totally should have left the peel on.

The rest of our tasks are easier, but Gregor says they definitely won't be this easy come competition day. I just hope that when we walk into that room, we get one that we can figure out—quick.

THE WATERFALL

WE WALK BACK from breakfast the next morning and Seraphina and Gregor are waiting for us in front of our tree suite, sitting on the steps. "Good morning, my Crimson Kids. Are you ready to get your creative juices flowing and come up with a way to solve this task that only the five of you can?"

"Yup," says Ander. "We're ready."

"Okay then. Your job is to hang out in the Inspiration Room and let your brains unwind however they will. The best ideas break free when you're not trying too hard. So relax and have fun. Meet in the backyard clubhouse in thirty minutes. We'll check in with you then."

Jillian grins. "I know where I'm going for inspiration."

"Jillian, the craft area is in the Work Room."

"But all that stuff inspires me. Can't I think in there?"

Gregor nods. "If you like."

"I'm going to the Harmony Room," says Ander.

"Me too," says Jax.

"Well, I'm going in the nap room," says Mare.

Seraphina laughs. "It's not a nap room, Mare."

"Just kidding. I would never sleep when we're supposed to be thinking."

"Yeah, right," I say. "I'll go in there too, to make sure you don't."

We walk up the steps of the tree suite, steadying ourselves across the wobbly bridge, and climb up the rock wall to the door. I wish I could stop at the floating playground, hang out on the flying carpet, and think there for a while. But instead I head upstairs to the quiet area of the Inspiration Room with Mare. I mean, *someone* has to make sure she doesn't sleep. I flop onto a pillow facing one side of the waterfall and she heads to the other.

The waterfall that separates us never stops moving. The water drops, but no matter how far down it falls, a few seconds later, it appears right back on top again, ready to fall again. That's kind of how I feel about this whole Piedmont Challenge. Just when we solve one task and reach the very top, we take a step off the ledge and fall to the bottom. The only way to get back up to the top is to solve another task.

I settle against the pillow and stare at the stones surrounding the waterfall. They're arranged in a perfect pattern. It must have taken someone a long time to fit them together like that. The ideas on the red board float around my brain like a puzzle. They don't fit together at all. I'm not even sure they're the right pieces. I close my eyes and soon an idea pops into my head, but it's swirling in a jumbled clump. So I take several deeps breaths and try to unjumble it.

We need to think of something that has already been invented and find a way to make it do something even more life-changing. What invention can we use? The task says that many inventions have already changed the world. Okay, we know that—there are a lot of amazing inventions. But there has to be one that can be made better. What can we invent that will change the world more than it already has? An aero-scooter would have been a good one, or an aero-car. People used to use just regular scooters and cars—until someone reimagined those.

I stay huddled up in the quiet area, but not one great idea comes to me, nothing unjumbles. I peek around the waterfall and see Mare with a book on her lap, but her eyes are closed. Of course. I glance at the other end of the room and see the boys and Jillian hanging out in the harmony area playing with the drum sets. When thirty minutes is up, the door to the Inspiration Room swings open, and I walk through it feeling like a failure. I trudge down the stairs behind my teammates, while they chatter about naps and drums and crafts, hoping their time in the Inspiration Room was more inspiring than mine.

When we get to our backyard clubhouse, Seraphina jumps up from her log chair. She's now wearing her platform heels. I swear, she must wear them as slippers. "Hi, guys! How did it go in the Inspiration Room? Any great ideas?"

"Yes!" says Jillian. "After I left the Work Room, Ander and Jax and I played with the instruments. I played the tambourine and the xylophone. It was so fun. I was thinking that since we're good at doing skits, we should do another one this time when we present our solution to the judges. The task states that we have to sing anyway. Maybe we can add instruments this time too."

I picture us singing in a choir, wearing robes and clanging bells. "I don't know. Maybe."

The red board records her idea.

Ander jumps up on the log. "Jillian's right. We're good at performing. That's what made our team memorable at the National Finals. I definitely think we should do another skit. We can make even better props this time using stuff from the craft area."

"I think we should do a skit this time too," I say. "Definitely. But I was in the quiet room, and I'm sorry, I don't know what's wrong with me. It's like all my great ideas have dried up."

Seraphina smiles. "I'm sure they didn't dry up. Something will come to you. What about you, Mare? Did any ideas come to you in the Inspiration Room?"

She folds her arms across her chest. "Nope."

"Alright. What about you, Jax?"

"When I was in the harmony area, nothing really came to me. I don't know if we should do a skit again."

"But we ran into this problem last time," says Jillian. "A skit is the best way to present whatever our solution is. What other way is there?"

"Maybe something more like everyone else."

I look at Jax. "Why would we want to be like everyone else?"

"Yeah, Big Guy, why?" asks Ander. "We'll never win that way. Remember what Seraphina said last time. We want to be memorable if we're going to win."

"What's so great about winning anyway?" asks Mare.

Ander's arms flail. "What's so great about winning? What a stupid question! First of all, the Ancestor App will get built, and second, we'll get to go on the Swirl and Spark Tour."

"All over the world!" Jillian squeals. "With two other teams! We'll be together for like a whole year. It would be so amazing!"

Mare glares at Ander. "First of all, my question was not stupid."

Ander sits back down. "Sorry."

All I can think about is the Ancestor App. "Don't you want everyone to be able to talk to their relatives like we did? Grandma Kitty thinks it's really important. Her mother died when she was only thirteen years old. She still misses her a lot. And even though she can't talk to her anymore, with the Ancestor App she could learn things about her and then maybe she wouldn't miss her so much."

"I know why winning is important and why the Ancestor App would be important to people. I want it to be built too. But what about the Swirl and Spark Tour? Do you really want to leave home for a whole year?" asks Mare.

"I don't," says Jax quickly and sits up straight, like he has been waiting for someone to ask him that question all day.

"Well, it's not like it's for a whole year straight," I explain. "We would go to one place, like France maybe, for a few days, and then come back home for a while before we go to another place, right Gregor?"

Ander looks at me like I'm five years old. "Did you learn any geography in Human History at all?"

I shrug. "Yeah. Some."

"Do you know how far away all those places are?"

"Ander's right, Kia," says Gregor. "If you win this competition, you'll leave on the Swirl and Spark Tour for a full year. We would not come home during that time."

"But what about our parents?" I ask.

"They would be allowed to visit you two times during the tour. Once in England and once in Japan."

"What? That's it?"

"That's it."

My stomach twists in a knot. I didn't think it would be like that. A whole year away from my family—away from Grandma Kitty?

"Is this why some of you are having a hard time coming up with ways to solve this task?" asks Seraphina. "Are you afraid to win?"

"I'm not!" Jillian insists. "It would be fabulous, an adventure of a lifetime. We'd definitely be famous then. We'll probably be treated like royalty."

"Or sports stars!" says Ander. "I'm not afraid to win. Nope. Not me. It would be just like being on the road playing hockey for the Buffalo Sabres."

"Well, not exactly," says Gregor. "You would be showcasing your invention and meeting with children at their schools . . . talking to them about how you solve your tasks so creatively and giving them tasks to solve as well."

"Well, that's okay," says Ander. "I can do that."

I pick at the skin around my nail. "I could do that too," I say. "But what about PIPS? We all planned on going to the Piedmont Inventors Prep School after we get home from Québec."

"You would still be allowed to enroll. You would take your place there the following year as eighth graders."

"So our whole seventh grade year would be spent on the tour?" I ask.

"I don't know if I can leave my mom alone for a whole year," says Mare. "My brother lives with my dad now, and my sister moved to New York City for her first job. She would live in our house all alone."

I've never seen Mare look so sad.

"What about you, Jax?" asks Seraphina.

His face turns beet red. No, fire engine red. "I'm not sure."

"Why, Jax?" says Jillian. "It would be so fun!"

He wipes his hands on his shorts. "I may want to enter the military."

"Jax, if you want to be placed on the military track, none of this is for you," says Gregor.

"I know. I talked to my dad about it when we came back from Camp Piedmont. At the end of this competition, we all have the choice of going to PIPS or being programmed into the category we performed best in. I think I would be placed in New Technology. One of the career choices for that program is to work for the military in a government position."

"So even if we don't win here, you might not enroll at PIPS with the rest of us anyway?" I ask.

He looks at the ground. "I don't know."

My head pounds. This can't be happening. I finally have four best friends, but if Jax gets programmed into New Technology, I would be down to three.

We sit in silence for a long time. Finally, Seraphina says, "Okay, guys, I think you should take a break. Do you want to play on the floating playground?"

None of us answers. Bouncing on the floating clouds doesn't sound fun at all.

"I think a break out in nature would be best," Gregor suggests. "Perhaps a walk down to the Creativity Pool would help—take your minds off the task."

"I don't feel like swimming," I say.

"Me neither," says Ander.

"You don't have to swim. Just walk over there together. Preceptor's orders."

We know we don't have a choice so we head down the path, passing the German tree suite and the Texas tree suite. They all look the same from the outside, all shimmery-silver. I wonder what they're like inside though. I wonder how they're doing on their solutions. Probably better than us. I mean, we've got nothing. We don't even have an idea yet, and I don't even know if my whole team wants to win. And if they don't, that means they won't even try to figure out this task. This is worse than bad. It's like falling off the waterfall and getting stuck in mud.

THE CREATIVITY POOL

WHEN WE GET to the pool, about ten other kids are already there, swimming and splashing and laughing under the hot afternoon sun. Becca and the kids from the Texas team are trying to cross the pool on the problem-solving bars. They must be pretty weak because none of them are able to cross. Maelle, Danielle, and Zoe from the French team are diving from the Think Pad while Stephan and Gwyndol are swinging from the Idea Swings, competing to see who can jump the farthest into the water. I'm not sure much thinking or brainstorming is going on here, and even though I want to be back at our tree suite figuring out a way to solve this task, this stuff looks really fun!

Ander climbs onto the pool ledge. "Let's go in!"

"But we don't have our bathing suits," Jillian reminds him.

"Who cares? Neither does the Texas team."

"But I brought my fabulous polka-dotted suit from our trip to NYC. I want to wear it!"

"Go ahead, but I'm not waiting." He takes off his socks and sneakers and jumps into the pool.

The kids from the French team swim toward us. Zoe yells, "Come in! Don't worry about your suits. The water is so nice."

I look at the rest of my team and shrug. "Will Seraphina and Gregor be mad if we get our team shirts wet?"

Mare takes off her sneakers and socks. "Who cares? We have like a million matching shirts."

Jillian looks like she's about to cry.

Ander splashes her, soaking her shorts. "Come on, Jillian. You'll miss all this."

"Ander!" she screams.

"What?" He grins. "You're wet now, anyway." Jillian huffs but jumps in eventually, and together we race for the Think Pad.

"Hey guys," says Becca. "I can't believe none of the other teams are here. This pool is crazy cool!"

For the rest of the afternoon, we swing on the Idea Swings and dive a million times from the Think Pad. The sparkles float all around us, and that's when it hits me. These are just like the air purification sparkles at Camp Piedmont. They must purify and chlorinate the water!

Gwyndol emerges from underwater. "I have found a secret drawer underneath this Thinking Pad. There are floating toys to throw. Perhaps we shall be able to play with them?"

"I'll help," Ander calls.

"Me too!"

We dive underneath and see the drawer Gwyn is talking

about. He pulls it open easily, and there they are, small blobs that look like they're made of rubber. We tug at them hard, and after a few tries, they release from the drawer and float to the surface. I come up for air and take a deep breath, wiping the water from my eyes. When the blobs reach the surface, they quickly spread out around the pool, each expanding into thin circular mats.

"They're turning into lily pads," Jillian exclaims.

The French kids look at her in confusion.

"You know, the things that float in a pond. Frogs leap on them."

Ander grabs a hold of one. "Maybe we can leap on them too!"

While the Texas team and the French team look on, he climbs up. It wobbles at first but he steadies himself. Spray comes shooting out of the mat and he shields his eyes. I freak out at first, thinking he's definitely getting poisoned, when a voice from a speaker calls out, "Sunscreen is being applied."

Ander looks at his arms and legs glistening with oil. "It has built in sunscreen? Cool! Come on, guys, let's leap on these things like frogs."

"All of us?" I ask.

"Sure, there's a lot of them."

Soon we're each balancing on a lily pad, covered in sunscreen, falling off, getting soaked, and getting right back on. Ander and Gwyndol leap to the empty ones. We follow them, jumping from one to the next, sometimes falling off, sometimes not. My shirt is soaked and heavy, but I don't care. This is for sure the most fun I've ever had in my life.

Sometime later, Maelle floats over to me. "I'm so tired from all this jumping. I must lay down."

"Me too."

Before long, Danielle, Zoe, and Becca join us and we float in a clump on our backs. I shield my eyes from the sun and peek at Mare and Jillian still jumping with the boys. But then I close them, letting the warmth of the September sun wash over me. The next time I open them, everyone else is lying on their lily pads too, and now it's all fifteen of us, resting and floating like frogs in a pond—with no worries in the world.

I almost feel hopeful about the Piedmont Task. Maybe I was worrying too much about it. We solved a big task before—after our first one got smashed. We can definitely do it again. Maybe Jax and Mare will change their minds about wanting to win. Maybe today was so much fun that Mare won't worry about her mom so much and Jax will forget about his idea to enroll in New Technology. I'm still a little scared to think that I wouldn't see my family for that long, but after today, with all these kids and cool inventions, maybe I'll be okay without them.

The French girls sit up, and I open my eyes. "Goodbye, everyone," Danielle says. "We must go now. Our preceptors are waiting for us."

"Me too," says Becca. "The others are leaving, and I have no idea how to get back to our tree suite without them. I get lost all the time."

I float over to the rest of my team. "Do you guys want to try the problem-solving bars? See if we can cross them?"

"Sure," says Jax.

We swim over and climb up the ladder, but when we get to the top, it looks different than before. Each bar is ten feet apart. How in the heck do we get across?

"What do we do, leap for it? We'll just fall into the

water," says Mare.

"Yeah, we'll never get across," says Jax.

"I bet I can do it." Ander jumps up to the first rung, his feet dangling ten feet from the water. If he stretches for the next one, his arm won't even reach halfway across. Instead, he swings with both arms, waving his legs wildly, and lunges for it. He falls quickly to the water and lands with a splash.

He pops to the surface and wipes the water from his eyes. "How close was I?"

"Not close at all," calls Mare.

He slaps his hand on the top of the water. "Ugh!"

"Let me try," she says. She jumps up to the rung and swings just like Ander did. She's way more graceful than he was, but no closer to the next bar. She falls into the water right next to him.

"Maybe you should try, Jax," I suggest. "Your arms are the longest."

He steps up to the rung and doesn't even need to jump. He grabs onto it with one hand and reaches for the next rung. He gets closer to it than Ander and Mare, but still misses by a mile and crashes into the water with a huge splash.

Jillian looks at me. "It's hopeless."

"We may as well jump in anyway." She shrugs, and we each give the problem-solving bars a try. But just like the rest of our teammates, we aren't even close to solving them. I come up to the surface and wipe my bangs away from my eyes.

"KK, you didn't even come close. I think your arms need to grow about three feet if you're going to have any chance," says Ander.

I splash him with as much water as I can. He laughs and pushes me under. I come back up and push him right back. I may have shorter arms than him, but they're definitely stronger. Finally, we all get out of the water, dripping and tired, and sit on the ledge of the pool so we can dry off at least a little bit. I decide I may as well take advantage of the fun we had today and confront Mare and Jax.

"You know guys, if we did end up winning and got to go on the tour, I bet there would be really fun things for us to do together—just like this."

"Yeah, can you imagine how tricked out the aero-bus would be then?" asks Ander.

Jax nods. "Yeah, today was awesome. I think I'd like being on the tour."

Mare looks down into the pool. "Me too."

"Would your mom really be all alone if you went, Mare?"

She glares at me. "Yeah, I told you she would be."

I bite my thumb nail. "Well, what about your grandparents, or anyone else? Maybe they would spend more time with her."

"I don't know. Maybe. But why are you so worried about it?"

"Because I feel bad about your mom. I would have a hard time leaving, too, if I thought my mom would be all alone. Besides, I think you guys won't try to win if you don't want to go."

Ander looks at me like that was the dumbest thing I could have said. "Of course they'll try."

"Oh really? If you're playing hockey and you don't want to win the game, why would you even play?"

Ander shakes his head. "First of all, I always want to

win, but even if I didn't, I would play because I like playing."

"You think I'm not going to try?" Mare asks. "Our chances of winning stink, but I'm still going to try. Don't you know me at all? I wouldn't do that to all of you."

Jax shakes his head. "I wouldn't do that either."

Now I feel awful, but I don't think they understand. "I'm afraid to go on the tour too, you know. It's just that the Ancestor App is really important. I want to give it a fair chance to win."

We sit there in silence for a long time. Finally, Jax says, "I want to go on the tour, but I really want to be programmed into New Technology too."

"You don't want to go to PIPS anymore?" asks Mare.

"I don't think so."

I sit there on the pool ledge, stunned. I guess I thought that after Québec, we'd all be going to PIPS together.

"I'm sorry," he says.

"Why?" asks Ander. "No one should tell you what to do."

"That's funny," I say. "Everyone gets told what to do. That's what getting programmed is. If the school thinks you're good at math, you're forced to study only math."

"Except us," says Jillian.

"That's why I wanted to win the Piedmont Challenge so much. They know that the kids who win are good at a lot of categories. That's why we're allowed to enroll at PIPS if we want to and focus on different things. It stinks that most kids don't get that choice."

Ander looks at Jax. "Are you sure you'd be happy studying just New Technology?"

"Sure. Because New Technology includes so many things I like."

I think about that for a second. He's right. It has some things I like too. But so do all the other categories.

Jillian wrings out her dripping hair. "You could be programmed into New Technology *and* go on the tour. You know, enroll the year after."

"Yeah, I guess I could do that."

"That means we have to win," I say. "If we don't, Jax will be separated from us in a few weeks."

"From me too, maybe," says Jillian.

"What do you mean, you too?"

"I've been thinking that I might want to enroll in Art Forms—if I can."

"What is happening?"

"Kia, you're all about thinking up inventions and stuff. All of you guys are. But this whole time I've been wishing I could sneak into the Work Room and design costumes. And the best part of this competition for me is acting out our skit. If we didn't have that, I'm not sure I would be very into it. But I'm going to try as hard as I can to win because I don't know if I'd get programmed into Art Forms anyway, and I do want to go on the tour with all of you."

Ander nods. "I will too."

"Me too," I say.

"I will too," says Jax. "I didn't realize I'd be separated from you guys so soon."

"I'll try hard too," says Mare. "My mom has always wanted to go to England. This might be her chance to get there. And I bet the rest of my family and her friends would keep her company while I'm gone."

I smile at Mare.

Ander leaps up. "Okay then, it looks like we have a competition to win, right?"

"But a task to solve first!" I reply, looking at my wristband.

Be Curious. Be Creative. Be Collaborative. Be Colorful. Be Courageous.

Maybe that's what we were forgetting earlier today during brainstorming when not all of us were committed to winning. But now we are, so we better get going. The Global Championships are in just nine days!

THE REINVENTORS

THE NEXT DAY we gather in our clubhouse, calling out ideas for our skit. Since our first one made us memorable in the National Finals, hopefully this one will make us memorable at Globals too. But we get stuck trying to figure out what it could be about. "Maybe we should read through the task again," I say, and I walk over to the tree where the task is still pinned to the bark. My teammates gather around me to listen. "The world is full of life-changing inventions. Your task is to take an invention commonly used by people today and re-imagine it. It must continue its current function but also yield a new, life-changing function. Your task solution must be created using skills from all six categories, take no more than twelve minutes to present, and include lyrics to a song."

Ander shakes his head. "This is so frustrating. We don't even have time to think up new characters or write a new story."

"Maybe we don't have to," I say. "What if we make our skit a sequel to the one that goes with the Ancestor App?"

Ander nods. "That's good. I like that. I can be Freddie Dinkleweed again."

"Me too," says Jillian. "Madam Sparkles will once again make an appearance in Crimson Catropolis!"

"I'm fine with that," says Jax.

Mare shrugs as if she doesn't care one bit about this whole thing. "Me too."

"Really?" I ask.

"Really. Do you still think I'm going to be a pain about every decision we make?"

"Sorry, it's a habit." I pace in the grass and my brain starts swirling, like I can feel an idea coming on. "Okay, so the task states that we have to re-imagine an invention, right?"

"Right," says Jax.

"Well, you know how in our first skit, the little girl wonders what she'll be like when she grows up, and she goes to Crimson Catropolis to figure it out? What if in this skit, she's called back to Crimson Catroplis to help the residents who live there make sense of a random box they've found? Inside the box is an old-fashioned object. She has to help them figure out a way to turn it into something better."

"Oh, that's good," says Jillian. "I like that idea."

"Then we'll need to re-imagine an invention that fits inside a box," Ander replies. "How do we do that? Let me think. Let me think."

"What if we make a list of things that have already been invented?" suggests Jax.

Mare leans against a tree. "There's the pillow. That's

already been invented."

I shake my head. Of course Mare would think of a pillow.

Jillian smiles. "There's also paint and paintbrushes and sewing machines."

"And hockey skates," says Ander.

"Well," says Jax. "There's also electricity but that's hard to put inside a box."

"There's also the aero-car," I say. "Which is already a re-imagined version of the original car, but that definitely won't fit inside a box."

"What about a clothes washer?" asks Jillian. "We could invent something new, like a hyper clothes cleaner, that washes clothes as fast as a person could snap their fingers."

"That would be cool," says Jax. "A washing machine was life-changing when it was first invented. But do any of you know how to make an instant cleaning machine that fits in a box?"

I shake my head and sigh. "This stinks because I have a list of sixty-seven inventions that I've thought up, but those are all my original inventions. None of them are old inventions that I've made new. What a waste. We could have used one of those."

"None of those sixty-seven inventions were based on something already invented?" asks Mare.

I think for a second. "Well, maybe the Underwater Bubble Bike."

Mare stares at me. "Of course that's based on an old invention—the bicycle."

"Yeah, and that won't fit easily into a box either."

"That *would* be a life-changing invention," says Jax.

"I know," I say. "I think so too! But I'm not sure how to

build it anyway."

Ander tosses a rock into the air and then catches it. "Maybe we need to use the Inspiration Room or Work Room for ideas."

"I'm on it!" Mare calls, already sprinting to the front of our tree suite. The rest of us follow and spend the rest of the day running in and out of the tree suite, using the books and technology for research, the music to get inspired, and the quiet area to think. We scour the craft area for something that will spark an idea, rummaging through the drawers of fabric, duct tape, and lots of random items. We hang out in our clubhouse too, letting the fresh air fill our lungs while we think, and none of it feels like work or like we're trying to solve a task. It feels like we're all hanging out like regular friends. But we still don't have an invention to build, and I just wish something would pop into my head.

Later, we're lying on the pillows in the quiet area of the Inspiration Room. Well, all of us except Ander. He's sitting up, staring at a blank corner of the room.

"What are you looking at?" I ask.

"I'm imagining that I've reinvented the eyeball."

"Seriously?" ask Mare.

"I wish I could reinvent the eyeball. Instead of just giving people vision, it could connect with aliens somehow. Each Earth person would have their own alien partner, who acts as their protector. Since aliens have a better vantage point of Earth, they can see everything all around us. And since they can see through their Earth partner's eyes, they could warn them if they are about to walk into a dangerous cave or about to talk to a dangerous person."

"Are you for real?" asks Mare.

I sit up on my knees. "That would be so cool! And you'd

get this warning signal that your aero-scooter is about to fly into a bird because the alien is seeing exactly what you're seeing—and more."

"And if you're lost," says Jillian, "the alien could tell people where you are, because they could see everything and know where you are.

"If an alien was *protecting* me," says Mare. "I would want it to do things for me."

"Like what?" I ask.

"Like look into my mind and know that I'm in a bad mood. It would tell people not to bother me."

I nod. "On second thought, I'd want mine to tell me not to bite my nails."

"I would want mine to take pictures of everything I see," says Jillian. "Like a camera, only better."

"Actually," says Ander. "I would make mine my assistant too. If I wanted a new game for my watch, it would send it to me. Wouldn't that be cool?"

"I don't know about the alien part, but the rest of it wouldn't be impossible," says Jax.

We stare at him, and Ander jumps to his feet. "What do you mean?"

"Using GPS satellites instead of aliens."

Mare sits right up. "How?"

"There are millions of satellites all around the Earth now and they're really close to the atmosphere. That means they can locate objects more accurately. Like with these watches. Seraphina and Gregor can locate us within a few inches, right?"

I think about that for a second. "Right."

"If we were to connect individual people with satellites, and program some warning signals into them, a person could be alerted when they veered off course with their aero-scooter, or walked into the street when a car was coming, or even if you were about to bump into someone."

"What do you mean if we were about to bump into someone?"

"Well, to keep order on the sidewalks, the program could be set up so that everyone always walks on the right side of the sidewalk and doesn't walk too close to the person in front of them. If they did, they would be alerted."

"But hearing all these beeps go off all the time would be so annoying," says Jillian.

"What if they were silent so only the person heard them?"

"Like your own personal communicator."

"Wait!" says Ander. "What if it was programmed using something like virtual reality goggles too?"

"I don't know what you mean?" I say.

"What if each person had a virtual reality assistant that worked by satellite, like you said, Jax. It could do all that stuff and more too, like tell you that you have one hour left to finish your homework, or you have four minutes to leave your house so that you'll be to school on time."

"That would be amazing!" Jillian squeals.

Jax smiles. "If we programmed it correctly, it could do that. It could probably store games too, ones that you could access by punching numbers like we do on the air screen. But if we did that we'd need to restrict them because it would be fine if people talked on the phone while they are walking but not while they are flying. Or it would be fine to play games while sitting on a park bench but not while you're walking down the street.

I bite my thumb nail. "You're talking about this like we

could really do all of it."

Jax shrugs. "I think we could. We could probably program it to sense emotions too and maybe even sense the emotion of people you're approaching. Then, like Mare said, you could get a warning that the person sitting next to you is tired or upset and wants to be left alone."

Jillian's eyes get huge.

"Seriously, Big Guy?" says Ander.

"Why not? We have the satellites to pinpoint individual location. We have the technology to use virtual reality. And we also have the ability to write a computer program. All we have to do is mix it all together using a small computer chip."

"If we *were* able to make this for each person, how would we be able to attach it to them?" asks Mare. "We can't glue it to them."

"I'm not sure," says Jax. "Maybe we make a badge or something."

"But in order for the satellite to see what we see, doesn't it have to see exactly what we see?" I ask.

Jax nods. "Oh yeah."

"I got it!" Jillian says. "We could put it on a really cool pair of glasses!"

Ander grins. "That could be our re-imagined invention! Glasses improve vision, but if we add a programming chip or something to each one, we'd turn regular glasses into super satellite glasses or something!"

"Satellite Spectacles!" I say. "That's an old-fashioned word for glasses."

Jillian makes a weird face. "Spectacles?"

"Of course," I say. "That's another name for glasses!" My brain keeps swirling. "Glasses fit inside a box too, so this invention would work in our skit!"

Jillian squeals. "This is perfect!"

"Only if we get them to work," says Mare.

Ander walks in circle around all of us. "What do you think, guys? Should we try? Do you think we can? Would this be an incredible invention?"

"It would be incredible," says Mare. "But I'm not even sure where we would start."

I smile. "That didn't stop us with the Ancestor App."

So we scatter around the Work Room, gathering the materials and information we need. We race in and out of the tree suite, some of us working outside and some of us working inside. But while Jillian and I are in the Craft Area, looking for a box and a pair of glasses, Ander, Mare, and Jax barge in.

"Guess who was just here?" says Mare. "Outside."

I close a drawer and turn around. "Who?"

"Witch Girl. I mean Martina."

"What did she want?" asks Jillian.

"She invited us to hang out at the pool later," says Mare.

"Seriously?" I ask. "Did you tell her no?"

"I was about to, but Ander said yes."

"What was I supposed to say?"

"How about, 'We'd rather swim in a sewer full of alligators than swim with you and your team of nasty boys,'" says Mare.

Ander shrugs. "I think we're supposed to meet all kinds of people here at Globals. You know, experience all this place has to offer."

"Why can't we experience it with the French team or even the Pennsylvania or Idaho team?" I ask. "We haven't hung out with them at all."

"How bad can it be, KK?"

"Really bad, besides, we have so much work to do."

"It's fine, Kia," says Jillian. "We can go for a little while—after we create our Satellite Spectacle box."

"Speaking of that," says Jax. "When we were researching on the air screen, we found something. We found that an invention similar to the Satellite Spectacles was attempted before in 2013. But it must have failed, and I'm not sure why. This sounds like a pretty complicated invention."

"Yeah, but once we figure it out, the Satellite Spectacles are going to be way better than those were supposed to be, anyway," says Mare.

Ander nods to Jillian and me. "So we'll meet you guys in a little while before we go to the pool."

"Fine," I say, and Jillian and I continue our search. She shuffles around looking for paint and duct tape so we can decide how to decorate the box if we can find one.

Later, we walk outside to the clubhouse where Mare and the boys are sitting on the ground huddled around the air screen.

"Hey guys" says Jillian. "Did you find anything?"

Ander looks over his shoulder. "This is hard. We're trying to find a way to connect the glasses with the satellites."

"We realized that we'll need to sync the glasses up with the satellites every day," says Mare. "So we thought we could use the box as a syncing station. We'll just need to find a way to turn on the syncing mechanism and make the glasses and the satellites sync together."

"Okay, we'll help you, but first we want to tell you what we did. We found the perfect box that the glasses can go in, but it's metal. We want to paint it with all our favorite colors—you know, swirl them all together, sort of like colorful clouds."

"Yeah," I continue. "We thought that would make sense since the glasses will be syncing with the satellites that are stationed up in the sky."

"Cool, but can you help us with this? Because if there isn't a way to sync with the satellites, this invention won't work at all."

She's right, so Jillian and I help with the search and try to make sense of the information we find, mostly scientific words I've never heard of before. My head pounds trying to figure out what goes with what and I can feel myself wilting. My teammates look like they're wilting too. So we agree we need lunch and head over to le Cantine.

"Do we really have to meet Martina at the pool?" I ask. Even though I'd rather swim with frogs than research using the air screen for another million hours, we're finally making progress on this task, and I don't want to stop. Besides, why would any of us want to swim with Martina?

Jillian shrugs. "It'll be fine. And I'll get to wear my new bathing suit."

"Maybe it won't be so bad," says Ander. "We can race her team across the lily pads."

"Yeah, I guess that would be harmless." I reply. "It's not like they're going to drown us or anything."

THE IDEA SWINGS

WE GET TO the pool and Martina is swinging on the Idea Swings alone. The boys on her team are trying to cross the problem-solving bars—and failing. She sees us and grins.

"Wow, New Yorkers, you came. I thought you'd be too busy being interviewed or something."

"Nope," says Mare. "No interviews this afternoon. Probably after dinner and then again before we go to bed, but for now we're free to hang out with you."

Martina looks like she doesn't know how to answer her. But finally she says, "Yeah, well, you better swim while you have time, then."

I can't figure out the look on Martina's face. She looks like she doesn't like what Mare said, but she also looks sad. I don't know why I care, I mean she is Witch Girl. Whatever. I jump into the pool, and Jillian follows me, where we sit on either side of her on the Idea Swings. I'm not going to be friends with her or anything, but she's the one who invited us here, so I'm just curious. That's all. Mare jumps in too but hangs out along the edge of the pool.

"Come on, Jax," says Ander. "Let's go jump on the Thinking Pad."

I pump my legs to get the swing going. Martina and Jillian do the same but none of us say anything. It's sort of awkward, and I hate it being so silent. I don't really know what to say to Martina though. All we have in common is this competition, but it's not like I want to ask her about her team's project.

"So did you know any of your teammates before you went to Camp Piedmont?"

"Nope. We all came from different parts of Michigan."

"What part are you from?" I ask.

"Kalamazoo."

"Oh. Is it nice there?"

"I guess so. I've never been anywhere else, well except for New York once. My grandpa lives there."

"Oh. We're from Crimson Heights," I say.

"Yeah, I know. Everyone knows you're from Crimson Heights."

I feel my face turn red. "Oh, right."

"My team thinks you guys are weird."

Jillian looks at her. "What's weird about all of us?"

"It's a big coincidence that you all came from the same school."

"Well, it just happened like that. We go to a really good school."

"Then why hasn't anyone from your school ever won before?"

"How do you know that?" I ask.

"It was all over the news. Remember?"

My face heats up even more. "Oh yeah."

"I'm sure you've considered that the competition was fixed though, right?"

"What do you mean, *fixed*?" I can't believe she's even suggesting it.

"Like the judges in New York picked all of you or changed the results so that you'd all win."

"Why would they do that?" I ask.

"I don't know. I'm just saying. It's really the boys on my team who told me about the theory. They heard it from a lot of other kids here at Globals. But when I heard them say it, it made me wonder, that's all. I mean, haven't you wondered about that? Wondered if all of you *really* scored the highest in New York?"

"We did," says Jillian.

"Okay, if you say so. Like I said . . . it was the boys who brought the idea up. It wasn't me who thought it."

The truth is . . . I have wondered the same thing. Kind of a lot. I've wondered how it could be that all five of us came from the same school, when no one from Crimson had ever won before. But I never thought that somebody messed with the results. I pump my legs harder on the swings. The Idea Swings are supposed to give us great ideas for the competition, but the only idea I'm thinking about is that someone—or all of us—didn't score the highest in New York, that somehow one of us—or all of us—don't belong here. That someone changed our scores.

The boys yell for us and we swim to the Thinking Pad. The boys on Martina's team are jumping with them. Mare swims over too and we jump for a while, but all I keep thinking about is why Martina wanted to hang out in the first place—and about what she said.

"Come on, guys," Mare says when we're all jumped out. "I'm starving. Let's go to dinner."

We climb out of the pool, and Martina stares at us. "You're leaving now? Okay."

"Yeah, I guess we're going to eat," I say.

"Don't worry about what I said before. Not everyone thinks the New York results were fixed. I just was telling you so you'd know what some people are saying."

Jillian and I exchange glances. "Um, okay, thanks."

Later that night as I try to fall asleep in my sleeping egg, I think more about what Martina said on the. Could she be right? Could the results of the New York Piedmont Challenge really have been changed? But why? Who would do that? I turn over on my other side and listen to Jillian and Mare breathing in the same rhythm. What Martina said was horrible. But then I realize Principal Bermuda *could* have done it, and I think of an even more horrible thought. If the results were changed, which one of us doesn't belong here? Is it Jillian or Jax? Ander or Mare? Is it me?

I toss and turn trying to think about something else instead. Like Grandma Kitty. I haven't talked with her for a few days and I suddenly miss her a lot. I have so much to tell her about, like the Creativity Pool, our new invention idea, the French team, and these tree suites. She'll definitely want to hear about all of it. I keep trying to push the stupid thing Martina said further out of my brain, but it keeps shoving its way back. So I guess there's only one thing I can do. Starting tomorrow morning, I'll find out if it's true. I'll find out which of us doesn't belong here.

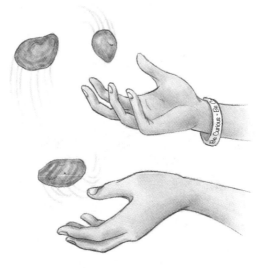

THE PEBBLES

IN THE MORNING, we walk over to le Cantine for breakfast. On the way, I consider which of my teammates could be a weak link, who didn't really win the Piedmont Challenge. What if it's Mare? What if it's Jillian? Or even Jax? But, oh no, what if it's Ander? The Piedmont Challenge tests who's the best in all the categories, and I don't know for sure if Ander is really good at all of them. I mean maybe he is, but he's Ander. There's just no telling with him.

What if it is him? What if he really isn't supposed to be here? He does want to take a lot of breaks. He doesn't work all that hard—and he jumps up on stuff when he has an idea. Not that that's a bad thing, though. Oh, I don't know. He's my best friend on the team. How can he not belong here? But what if it's true? Shouldn't I tell him that it could be a possibility? Should I tell them all? And what about Jillian? She heard what Martina said. I wonder if she's wondering the same thing about me. If it was me, I would want to know.

My head hurts as I think about how I would tell Ander something as awful as that. I decide I can't tell him. I need to know for sure first. But how do I find out for sure? There has to be someone I can ask. Someone who knows.

"KK, are you there?" Ander is snapping his fingers in front of my face. "What's up with you? I've been talking to you for like a minute. Did you hear anything I said?"

"What? No. I'm sorry, I was thinking about something else."

"Well, I asked you if you want me to teach you how to juggle when we get back. I've been practicing every night in our tree suite, and I want to show you how awesome I am."

"Sure."

"Okay, come on. Let's finish breakfast and then I'll race you there!"

After breakfast, we start to race back, but then we end up walking and talking instead. Ander spouts random facts about the history of juggling, the science behind it, and the mathematical probability that I'll be able to juggle three balls on the first try, the second try, and the tenth try. I really hope it's not Ander that doesn't belong here. I don't care one bit about juggling, but I would miss the way he talks about it if he wasn't around.

We gather around the table in the Work Room to work on our project, the Satellite Spectacles Box. The five of us work together to add a tiny satellite antenna to the frames. Then we attach a cable to the inside of the box that will hook onto the glasses. When activated, it will turn on the power and sync the computer chip in the glasses to the satellites.

Next, we cover the box with duct tape, using all our favorite colors—yellow, pink, green, light blue, and dark blue, but leave the hole on the front for an activation button. Then we paint over the duct tape using a combination of the same colors, making a swirling cloud-like pattern over the whole thing.

While the box dries, we flop onto the pillows to figure out what else we need to do. "The Satellite Spectacles are the most important thing," says Jax. "We need to keep working on the program for those."

"Don't worry. We'll figure it out," I say, even though I'm not sure how.

"Then what else?" says Ander.

"We need paperwork showing how we're using all six categories in our solution," says Mare. "And we need another script."

"And a song too," I say.

"Don't forget the costumes," says Jillian. "We have to fix up the ones we have. Can I work on that?"

None of us dares to tell her no. She races back to the craft area in search of our costume container.

"I want to get the computer program figured out before we start another project," says Mare. "I'm going to the tech area."

"I'll help you," Jax offers. "I want to get that part finished too."

"Maybe Ander and I should stay here to work on the script so we can all begin learning our lines."

Mare nods. "Okay, sounds good. See you guys later."

When the rest of my teammates leave, I grab a notebook from the Work Room and open up to a new page. I stare at it on and off while Ander takes pebbles from the waterfall, trying to juggle them while he "thinks." Most of them end up flying across the room. Finally, I can't ignore him anymore. "Can you focus please?"

"I am focused."

"No, you're not. You're playing with pebbles."

"So? That doesn't mean I'm not focused."

"We're never going to get this script written if we don't come up with some good lines. We could use more help too, but Jillian is going to take forever in the craft area. How long does it take for her to fix our costumes? It's not like they're changing so much, and what are Jax and Mare going to do anyway?"

Ander stares at me. "KK, what's wrong?"

"Nothing."

"Why are you freaking out?"

"I can't think of anything, and our script has to be perfect because if it isn't, no one will understand our invention. It won't make sense and we'll get an awful score and we won't win."

He stares at me, longer this time, and then walks out of the Inspiration Room.

"Are you leaving me here to work on it myself?"

He turns around and grins. "Nope, come on. We're going someplace else. This room stinks. It's way too quiet. Besides, all that water is making me have to pee."

I grab my notebook and follow him. I'm not sure where we're going but we head down the stairs and out of the tree suite. We make our way along the brick path, away from colony square and the Creativity Pool, away from everyone.

"So what's actually wrong? Something's bugging you. I can tell."

I consider keeping it in, not telling him what Martina

said to me. I don't want him to be upset too. But all this thinking about which one of us doesn't belong here is all I can think about.

We walk for a while, past the New Mexico tree suite. Just beyond it, we find a dirt path that leads into the forest. We turn onto it and keep walking, mostly in silence.

"Well?"

"Why do you think something's wrong?"

"Well, earlier, when we thought we might have to build a box, you asked Mare how she knew for sure how to get the right dimensions, if she would use any equations to figure it out. You asked her if she's ever read any books about building or designing things."

I look down at the floor remembering Mare's face when she said, "Just because you don't take a course in something, Kia, doesn't mean you don't know how to do it."

"And when we were walking past the Swirl and Spark training facility, you asked Jillian how hard she studied for her tasks before the Piedmont Challenge. You wanted her to tell you exactly how many hours."

Jillian looked at me like she didn't even know me.

"And at breakfast you asked Jax if he was any good at Human history, and you asked me how I usually score in Art Forms."

Suddenly I feel bad for grilling my teammates.

"So, what's the deal, KK?"

I look up at Ander, who has climbed onto a giant boulder halfway buried in the ground. I climb onto it too, and we both sit down.

"Martina said something to me and Jillian yesterday."

"What did she say?"

"She said there are some people who have been

wondering if all five of us really deserved to win the Piedmont Challenge."

"What do you mean? What people?"

"She didn't tell me. She said *she* doesn't think it, but some people do and she wanted us to know."

"Know what? That it's weird that all five of us came from the same school? Well, it is weird, but who cares?"

I bite my pinky nail. "I do."

"What do you mean?"

"I want to be sure we all really won."

"We did all really win! Master Freeman called our names. One at a time. You first. Then me. Then Mare. Then Jax. Then Jillian. That's how it happened. We all got called up on the stage. And the big screens were there too so all the other kids in NY state saw us. We definitely won, KK. We did."

"I remember all that, Ander. How could I forget it? It was the best day in my whole life. But think about it. Look what Principal Bermuda did to Gregor."

"So?"

"What if he did something to make us all win?"

"He wouldn't do that."

"Are you sure?"

He looks at me, right in my eyes. Then suddenly his eyes get huge, like he finally realized what I've been wondering for a long time. "He could have done that, couldn't he?"

"He's a really bad man, Ander."

"But why would he do that?"

"We've already seen what a big deal he's trying to make of our team. Maybe *he* wants to be the famous one."

"I don't know, KK."

"What if he messed with our task scores?"

Ander's face goes blank. He looks like he might even cry for a second. But then it's like a switch goes off in his brain. "No way, KK! He didn't do that! We all won. We were the best five in all of New York, and now we're here at Globals, and you can't wreck it!"

"I'm not trying to wreck it!"

We sit quietly for a few moments and then he looks at me. "You believe it, don't you? You think one of us—or all of us—didn't really score the highest."

"No, I don't, it's just—"

"That's why you've been asking all of us those questions." He stands up and walks away.

"Ander, wait! I just thought—"

"Whatever, Kia."

I jog to catch up to him. "Why are you mad at me? I just want to make sure."

"But why? I thought you wanted to win?"

"I do want to win."

"Then why are you trying to figure all this out?"

"Because if Martina's right, it's like we're cheating by being here." I hate saying those words aloud. I hate that it could even be true.

Ander doesn't look at me, and he doesn't say anything else either. I want to stay here. I want to be at this competition. I want to win. And I really want the Ancestor App to be built. But if we didn't earn our place, we can't compete. It wouldn't be right.

I take a deep breath. "Maybe we should see what the rest of our team thinks."

He gasps like I just slapped him across the face.

"Ander, don't you want to know if we earned our place here fair and square?"

"I already know we did."

"I think we should ask Mare and Jax and Jillian."

"Why? So then they'll wonder too?"

He breaks into a run down the path. I chase after him, but this time he's way faster than me, and he runs out of sight.

I get back to the tree suite after Ander and find the rest of our team waiting by the front steps.

"Where were you guys?" asks Jillian. "We were just checking your location on our watches and going to look for you."

Ander points behind us. "We walked that way to find a place to write the script. It didn't work though." He looks at me, and I'm not sure if he wants me to tell them or not.

"Well, it's my fault actually because I'm having trouble concentrating."

Mare wrinkles up her face in a scowl. "Why?" she asks. "What's wrong with you? You never have trouble focusing on our tasks." The rest of them stare at me like I'm an alien.

"I've been thinking about something."

"What?" asks Jillian, with a worried expression on her face.

"You probably already know, Jillian. You were there when she said it."

"When who said what?"

"Martina."

"What did she say?"

"It must not have been horrible if Jillian doesn't remember," says Mare.

"It was."

Jillian looks confused, but then she seems to figure it out. "Oh! You mean what she said about our team?"

"Yeah."

"What did she say about our team?" Mare demands.

"She said that some people think the Piedmont Challenge in New York was fixed—that the five of us couldn't have really won."

"But we did," says Jax.

"Who is she saying said it?" asks Mare.

"She said some people, like the boys on her team."

"I was there when she said it Kia," says Jillian. "She's just trying to mess with us. No one really thinks it. Maybe her team does, but it's just because they're jerks, that's all."

"That's what I said!" Ander replies.

Jillian shrugs. "Who cares what she thinks anyway?"

"I do," says Mare. "I don't want people talking about us, saying we didn't really win."

I look at Ander, and I feel like I'm betraying him. "And I want to know if it's true or not."

"Me too," says Mare. "And then we go squash them like bugs for starting rumors."

"You guys, no!" Ander holds his hands up for quiet. "We can't. If it is true then we can't be here at Globals. We'll all have to leave. What about the Ancestor App, KK? It'll never get built, and we may not even be able to go to PIPS! Did you think about that? Huh?"

"No."

"See?" says Ander. "Let's just forget about it. It's probably not even true anyway."

My teammates and I stand in silence for a few minutes. Ander shoves his hands in his pockets. Mare lets out a loud breath, and I bite my pointer finger. It seems none of us can decide what to do.

BONFIRE SPARKS

AS THE SUN dips behind a cloud, we hear a loud siren—a screeching, ear-splitting siren—coming from the Creativity Pool. "What the—?" shouts Ander, and we take off after the sound. The uneven bricks beneath our feet make it hard to sprint but we run as fast as we can anyway. We round the bend, pass the Canadian and England tree suites, and catch up to our friends from France. They see us running and slow down to let us catch up.

"What's happening?" I call to Maelle.

"I do not know," she replies. The sound gets louder and louder, but as we approach the square the siren starts to sound like musical chimes. Soon, kids from all of the trees suites are surrounding the sparkling pool.

Tiny silver packages fall from the sky around its perimeter. We inch closer. Each package is marked with a team name, and we scurry to find the one that's meant for us. We search along one side, looking up at package after package, and eventually turn the corner. Finally, near the ladder of the problem-solving bars, Jax spots it and catches it before it lands.

We head to a bench where it's quiet and crowd around him as he unties the ribbon and pulls off the cover to the box. Inside are two small notes.

> *Greetings, New York Team,*
> *You are cordially invited to attend the Piedmont Bonfire this evening at 9:00 p.m. This is a Piedmont tradition. Please write down any fears, concerns, or apprehensions you may have in regard to this competition and bring them with you this evening. We will extinguish them before the night is over. It should be a night to remember— one that will renew your positive, creative energy!*
> *Think More. Work Hard. Dream Big.*
> *Andora Appleonia*

The second note read:

> *When completing your task, you must now incorporate this object into your solution. It must be visible at all times.*

Underneath the notes, partially hidden under a sliver of tissue paper, is a small metal object—a red letter C with a silver number 5 in the center. Jillian hands it to me and I turn it over. I pass it along to Jax, and then to Ander and Mare. Mare shrugs. "It looks like a symbol for the Crimson Five."

"Whoa," says Ander. "They made a symbol just for us."

"But why would Andora want it to be part of our task solution?"

Jillian shrugs. "Maybe she made up a nickname for all

the teams and wants them visible for everyone to see."

"That's weird," I say. "Why wouldn't they want it to be a symbol of the USA?"

"Probably because there is more than one team from each country here," says Jax.

"Yeah, that's probably it," says Mare. "It'll be easy to add it to our solution."

As we walk back to our tree suite, Jillian practically floats. "This bonfire is going to amazing!"

Mare grins. "We'll finally get to hang out with some cute guys." She looks at Ander and Jax. "Oh sorry, guys, no offense." She giggles her Mare giggle and shrugs.

Ander grins right back. "I know you secretly think I'm the guy of your dreams, and you're just checking out the other guys as a consolation prize, so I don't take offense at all."

"So are you saying you're a prize—an object to be won by girls?"

"No, I just mean—"

"What are you two even talking about?" I ask. "We have more important things to worry about, like the script. Can we just hurry up and get back to work?"

"Wow, Kia," says Mare. "I thought you had writer's block and couldn't write the script?"

That's when I remember what Martina said about our team.

"So are we going to try to figure out if what Martina said is true?" asks Jillian.

My team stares at me. I stare at the ground. I'm so confused. All the wormy pieces in my brain are tangled. I don't know what to do.

"Let's just keep working," says Jax.

"Okay," I say, "and when we're not working, let's figure out if it's true—like at the bonfire tonight."

"Fine, but how?" asks Ander.

"Don't worry. I have an idea."

The bonfire is three stories high with twenty-foot-long boards surrounding it, almost like a teepee. The flames rage into the dark night, and even though they could burn me to ashes if I stood too close, I'm not afraid. I need to stay close to my team and the rest of the kids here, so I can make my move.

"Come on, Mare," I say. "The boys from the Idaho team are right over there. Let's go talk to them."

"Oh my god, yes, Kia!" says Mare. "Good call! Come on, Jillian."

I knew my plan was going to work. "Ander and Jax, stay here. We'll be right back."

We walk over to the boys with USA written across the front of their shirts and Idaho printed up the sleeve. Mare marches right up to one with black curly hair and another with blond hair and glasses.

"Hi," she says.

They look startled, but they both smile. "Hi."

Jillian is about to introduce herself, I can tell. But I don't have time for that. "Hi, I'm Kia. We're also from the United States, as you can see from our shirts. So . . . we have a question for you."

Mare looks at me like I have no idea what I'm doing, but of course I do.

The blond boy looks embarrassed for some reason. "Okay, what's your question?"

"Well, have you heard any rumors about our team?"

Mare leans close and whispers. "What are you doing?"

I whisper back. "Trust me. I know what I'm doing."

"Rumors?" he asks.

"Yeah, like about the competition, about you know, about our team competing here—"

Suddenly my words get mixed up in my head. I don't know how to ask him what I want to know. My face feels hot.

"No," the boy says. "Like what?"

Mare is glaring at me, and Jillian's mouth is hanging open. Mare says something to them, but I'm not really sure what it is because it all happens so fast. Then Mare and Jillian drag me back to Ander and Jax.

"What was that?" Mare demands.

"Yeah, Kia," says Jillian. "What were you doing?"

"I'm trying to find out if what Martina said is true."

"What happened?" asks Ander.

"She asked the boys from the Idaho team if they had heard any rumors about our team."

"Really, KK?"

"I know, I'm sorry. I couldn't help it. I just thought that if there really was a rumor, they would have heard it and maybe they would tell us."

"But we can't let the other teams think we shouldn't be here," says Jillian.

Mare shakes her head. "Yeah, and now those Idaho boys think we're weird."

"So?"

"*So?*" She rolls her eyes at me.

Whatever. I don't care if Mare is annoyed with me. But I guess it was stupid to think the Idaho boys would just come right out and tell us what they've heard. It's just that . . . I don't know what else to do.

I watch the flames crackle in the bonfire. All the teams around us are laughing and talking with other kids. I wish I felt like laughing and talking with them too. Before long, the Piedmont chimes fill the Piedmont square.

"Good evening!" Andora's voice crackles through the speakers. "The time has arrived for our Piedmont Bonfire Ritual. Prepare your fears, concerns, or apprehensions."

We reach into our pockets and pull out the papers we've brought with us. I slowly unfold mine and stare at the words. There are only two.

The truth.

That's the only fear, concern, or apprehension I have about this competition now. I guess I could have written I'm afraid the Ancestor App won't get built or I'm concerned that we won't figure out a way to make the Satellite Spectacles work. I also could have written that I'm apprehensive about talking to Mare because I'm always apprehensive about talking to Mare. But the truth is that none of it matters if we didn't rightfully earn our place in this competition. So I only have this one fear right now. I'm afraid that what Martina said is true.

I crumple my paper in my hands.

"Now we ask you to take several deep breaths, and as you do, imagine yourselves successfully solving your task without any of your fears, concerns, or apprehensions standing in your way. When the bells chime once again, throw your fears, concerns, and apprehensions into the Piedmont Bonfire where they will be vanquished for good!"

I breathe deeply and imagine that I'm holding Martina's rumor in my hand. I crumple it even smaller, and as the chimes ring out, I toss it into the fire. Pieces of paper fly all around me, and within seconds they shrivel up into nothing but ash.

The bonfire rages on three stories above me, but soon the chimes fade into the Piedmont theme song. The bonfire is extinguished, and the teepee is transformed into a giant hot spring geyser! We step back in awe as blue, pink, yellow, green, and purple steam rise from the center.

"And now," Andora continues, "all that remains is your positive creative energy! Use it wisely, for now as you solve your task, the possibilities are endless!"

I stare at the geyser. Andora's right. The possibilities *are* endless. The good we could do with the Ancestor App and the Satellite Spectacles is endless. That's why we need to stay in this competition. But I want to win fair and square, and there's only one way to know for sure—one person to ask.

"KK, are you coming?"

I see the rest of my team leaving and skip to catch up with Ander.

"What's wrong?" he asks me. "You were staring into space."

"I was? Oh sorry."

"That bonfire was so cool, wasn't it? And then that geyser! How did they do that? That was awesome!"

"Yeah, it was. The Piedmont people can do anything."

As we walk back to the tree suite, Ander keeps talking. I keep nodding and answering but I'm actually trying to formulate my plan. I need to make a phone call without anyone hearing me. I can't make the call from inside. The tree suite isn't that big, and my teammates will hear me, for sure. I could make it from our clubhouse, but what if someone from another team overhears? There are a million kids wandering around tonight, so that definitely won't work. I need to think about this. I also need to plan out what I'll say when I do call. I definitely need to catch him off guard. He won't expect me to ask, and when I hear his response, I'll know for sure.

The first thing I need is his phone number. I wish I could remember it from when we tracked him on the Ancestor App, but that's no big deal. I just need to find an air screen.

There's one near our sleeping eggs, but that's too risky. Mare and Jillian might catch me. I'll just use one in the Work Room.

I follow the girls into the tree chamber and get ready for bed. When I'm sure they're asleep, I slide out of my sleeping egg and tiptoe out of our room. The Work Room isn't too far, but it *is* on the floor below. I really hope these stairs don't creak because if they do, I'm caught.

I take my first step down the stairs and I realize I worried about the wrong thing. The stairs don't creak. They light up. The yellow board lights up underneath my foot and the words "Be Courageous" flash around it. Crap. I forgot about our team mantra steps. I continue down the steps and they each light up. At least the preceptor rooms are on the first floor. There's no way they can see the lights from there.

I step off the bottom step as lightly as I can and sneak down the hall like a spy in search of secret information. Once I get inside the Work Room, I flip on the light. I have no choice. I can't see anything without it. I walk over to the far wall and grab the first air screen I see. I type in "Blake Bermuda" and before long, his greasy hair and phone number appear. I memorize the digits as quickly as I can and shut down the screen. Now that I have his number, all I have to do is call him.

I sneak out of the Work Room and repeat the phone number over and over as I sneak back up the steps. I crack open the door to our tree chamber and Jillian and Mare are standing right there with their arms folded across their chests.

"Oh! You scared me."

"What are you doing?" asks Mare.

"I was just getting a drink of water."

"Downstairs?"

"How do you know I went downstairs?"

"You're avoiding the question."

I try to think of a good excuse, but I guess I'm really *not* a quick thinker all the time. So I decide to be honest instead.

"I found a way to find out for sure if what Martina said is true. I got Principal Bermuda's phone number, and I'm going to call him."

"Are you an idiot?" asks Mare.

"I'm going to ask him if he messed with the results."

"I repeat: Are you an idiot?"

"No."

"Well you have to be if you think it's okay to call him."

"What else are we supposed to do?"

"I don't know," says Mare, "but not that."

"Don't you guys want to know for sure?"

"Duh, Kia, yes. But what if we have to leave here? If we find out our scores from the Piedmont Challenge were changed, then they'll ship us back on the aero-bus. We'll look like idiots, and they'll send other kids here to solve our task—or there'll be no New York team at all. Is that what you want?"

"No! But, oh, I don't know! Why did Martina have to be such a jerk? Why did she have to say it in the first place?"

"I don't know, but I'm going back to bed, and so are you. And you're not calling him, got it?"

Jillian yawns. "Don't call him, okay, Kia? Please?"

I climb back into my egg bed. "Fine, I won't call him."

I lie there wide awake and realize they are probably right. Calling Principal Bermuda is a dumb idea. I just wish I knew for sure if we placed in the top five, because right now I feel like a fake winner of the Piedmont Challenge.

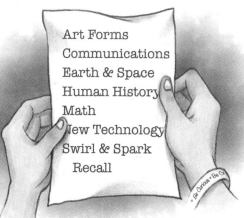

Art Forms
Communications
Earth & Space
Human History
Math
New Technology
Swirl & Spark
Recall

THE PIEDMONT CHALLENGE TASKS

WE SIT AROUND a table in the clubhouse staring at our metal box. The morning air is crisp, and instead of thinking of the box, I think of home and riding my aero-scooter. My best ideas always come to me while I ride. That's where I do my best thinking and where I can always figure things out. But here in Québec I'm not able to ride. I have to think on the ground—sitting at this table, staring at this box.

My teammates and I had a breakthrough, and we should be able to finish up this task. We found a way to tap into the satellites. We also found a way to create a virtual reality for each individual person. And we found a way to create a program that will tell the glasses what to do.

But now we're stuck trying to figure out how to put everything into the computer chip that we attach to the glasses. I guess we're not as smart as I thought.

"This is hopeless, Seraphina," I say. "I don't know how to

figure this out. I'm pretty much only good at Math anyway."

She looks at me, surprised. "Since when?"

"Don't look at me," says Ander. "My best category is Human history."

"Me either," says Jillian. "Mine is Earth and Space." I try to imagine Jillian reading Chemistry files like my mom. Nope. I can't picture it.

"Hmm," says Seraphina. "What about you guys? Mare? Jax? Are you guys stuck too?"

"I don't know," Mare replies.

Jax gets red in the face.

Seraphina's face gets serious. "What do you think your best categories are?"

"Math," says Mare.

"New Technology, I think," says Jax.

"Then we need *you* to figure this out, Jax," says Jillian.

"I'm trying," he says.

Seraphina shakes her head. "You guys do know that just because you're proficient in a certain category doesn't mean you're the only one who has the skills to use that category, right?"

"Yeah," says Ander.

"Well, you're not acting like it. Even if Jax is the best of all of you in New Technology, that doesn't mean he's the only one who can figure out how to implement the basic principles of machine programming and building."

"Well, he always figures this stuff out," says Ander.

"And why do you think that is?"

"Because he understands it."

"Maybe," she replies. "But maybe it's because he works until he unravels the problem."

"Nope. I think he's smart at that kind of stuff."

Jax's face turns even more red. Seraphina sits on the edge of the table. "I'm sure he is. But I'm also sure that all of you are too. Besides, have you ever noticed how often Jax is at his computer working?"

None of us answer.

"I'm guessing it's because he knows the rest of you are relying on him. Think back to Camp Piedmont. You told me how you all came up with the concept for the Ancestor App. It started with one idea—Ander's idea that he thought up after playing around with technology. Kia, you knew enough about technology to know that the idea Ander had could be made into something bigger. Then, you called in Jax and Mare and Jillian to help you put it all together. You *all* put the pieces together. Don't you see what I'm saying? Don't be so quick to think that you're not good in a certain category."

I sit up on my knees. "But what if we aren't?"

"You are."

"But maybe we really aren't."

"Kia, why would you say that?"

I look at my team. Ander shrugs.

"Why are you all looking so strange?"

Mare leans forward. "The girl on the Michigan team said that there are rumors going around about our team."

"Like what?"

"She said some kids are saying that the Piedmont Challenge was fixed. That we didn't all score the highest in New York."

Seraphina laughs. "Seriously? Well, I know for a fact that isn't true."

"See, KK, I knew it."

"We didn't believe it at first either," says Jillian. "But

then we all started to wonder."

"Is that why you're having a hard time finishing your solution? Are you distracted by this rumor?"

"Maybe a little," says Jax.

"Well, I'm telling you that there is no truth to that rumor. The Piedmont Challenge was not fixed. Each of you scored highest in New York."

My teammates smile. They all looked relieved. But just because she said so, doesn't mean it's *really* true.

Seraphina crosses her legs and swings her strappy purple sandals. "So . . . I'm thinking maybe you'd like to know what categories you each scored the highest in."

"Really?" I ask. Of course I want to know!

"Knowledge is power, and I think it will help you to solve the rest of your task. Who's first?"

"Me!" says Ander.

"Why am I not surprised? Okay, Ander, you first. You're incorrect in thinking you scored highest in Human history. You actually scored the highest in two categories: Human history and Communications."

"I did?"

"Yes, apparently you know a lot about history, and you also perform well persuading people to do what you want, in both verbal and non-verbal ways."

Ander nods, looking happy with his result.

"What about me?" asks Jillian.

"Jillian, you also are incorrect. Although Earth and Space is a strength, I'm not sure why you thought that would be your strongest category. Art Forms was, without a doubt, your strongest category."

"Yes!" Obviously that's what she was hoping for all along.

"And Mare, same deal. Math is not your top category."

"It's not? What is then?"

"Earth and Space *and* Math."

"Earth and Space too?"

"Now, Jax, everyone thinks that New Technology is yours. I'm here to tell you that it's not, which clearly proves my point. There's a difference between being naturally suited for a skill and being genuinely interested enough to become suited for a skill. Your highest category is actually Math."

He doesn't look that disappointed, which surprises me because he wants to get programmed into New Technology.

"And finally, Kia. You thought Math? Well, your math scores were exceptional and it was very close, but it appears as though even when you factor in the triple points, Swirl and Spark Recall was your best category. I don't know what you did to solve that task, but it was the highest in the state."

I don't know what to feel about that. I think of my mermaid song and the belt I wrapped around my legs so that I could swim on the floor and sing about swimming with my new friends all summer. I guess I didn't look like an idiot after all.

"So what that means is that you may be good in things that you may not have thought. Or maybe you *are* strongest in things you think you are. Regardless, you can be good at something if you want to be and work hard enough at it. So, go on. Go figure out how to make these Satellite Spectacles. I know you can."

After a few hours in the Work Room, we return to the metal box and stare at the pair of glasses. "Okay," I say. "What's the situation with this stuff?"

"Mare and I found the instructions on the air screen to create a virtual reality simulator, so someone can work on that."

"I will," says Ander.

"Me too," volunteers Jillian.

Mare nods. "I'll work on syncing the glasses to the satellite."

"I'll write the program," says Jax. "Kia, do you want to help me?"

"Sure. There's probably a lot of math. I'll try to help you figure it out."

So, now we know what we have to do, it's a start at least. The hard part is *doing* all the stuff we need to do to build these Satellite Spectacles—with just six days left.

THE CRIMSON SYMBOL

WE SPEND THE next few days inside the Work Room, creating the programmable chip that will attach to the Satellite Spectacles. We also write the script and song, and make up the dance to go with it. But this time we rotate so that each of us has a chance to work each task. That way we'll all understand how the box and the spectacles work. The skit is important, but our invention that turns regular eye glasses into a virtual reality assistant—well that's gigantic, and we all want to be a part of making it. Not only is it an accessory that will eliminate watches, phones, and cameras, but it'll keep people safe, organized, and on the right path as they walk on the ground or fly through the air!

When we're almost sure the programming chip is functioning, we attach it to glasses with superglue. Soon we'll attach the chip on the glasses to a cable inside the box so that it can be synched and matched up with the satellites. But first we carry it outside because the Work Room is making us feel claustrophobic.

Jillian pulls her hair into a braid. "So after the glasses are synched up with the satellites, they should be ready to test, right?"

"Yes," says Jax. "We've programmed them for Kia, since she's the one who'll be using them in the skit."

"This is going to be awesome. When can we try it?" I ask.

"Soon," says Mare. "We just need to turn the C5 symbol into an activation button. And that should be easy. We just have to attach it to these wires, and then we're ready to start syncing."

Ander tosses the C5 symbol into the air and catches it. "Here's the symbol."

"Okay," says Mare. "Let's do it."

I smile. "So the C5 symbol will be more than just a decoration that we have to display at all times. It'll make the activation process work too. I bet we get extra creativity points for that."

I hold the box in place, admiring the five colors all swirled together, while Mare grabs the soldering tool. I was just hoping we'd place in the top three at Globals so that the Ancestor App could be built—so Grandma Kitty and everyone else can talk to people they miss. But now that we're designing the Satellite Spectacles, they could become real too! We'll make life better for people all over the world just by wearing them! Our team could send two amazing inventions into the world. Wait until Grandma Kitty hears about this one.

"Come here, Ander," calls Mare. "Help me solder this wire to the back of the symbol. You hold, I'll solder."

"Why can't I hold the solder tool?"

"Because you're Ander. Besides, have you ever used a soldering tool?"

"Nope."

"Okay, then watch. I'll show you how to do it. Just hold the symbol close to the box, right over this hole. We're going to attach a wire from the inside of the box to the back of it."

I lean in close to watch. Mare holds a piece of wire near the tip of the solder tool and squeezes the handle. The heat slowly melts the wire. She uses the melted wire to attach the electrical wire to the metal on the back of the symbol. The metal will soon harden, and they will be connected. That way, when the symbol is pushed, the wire will turn the box on and activate syncing.

"That's really cool," says Jillian.

"I think you got it, Mare," says Jax. "We just have to let it cool off and harden."

"Then can we try it?" asks Ander.

"Yeah, I think so," says Jax.

"I feel like we're missing something with this task," I say. "The competition is just a few days away. Can we go through our checklist again, just to be sure?"

"Again?" asks Mare. "Okay, but I think after this we'll be done. We're almost ready to start rehearsing our skit."

Jillian skips over to the tree and looks at the paper pinned to it. We gather around to follow as she reads aloud:

"The world is full of life-changing inventions. Your task is to take an invention commonly used by people today and re-imagine it. It must continue its current function but also yield a new, life-changing function. Your task solution must be created using skills from all six categories, take no more than twelve minutes to present, and include lyrics to a song."

I read through our list.

"Invention must involve something commonly used today. Check."

"Invention must continue its current function. Check."

"Invention must perform a new, life-changing function. Check."

"Solution must use skills from all six categories. Check."

"Solution must include song lyrics. Check."

"Presentation must be under 12 minutes."

"Okay, so we're not sure if our presentation will be under twelve minutes—yet. We need to rehearse first. So let's rehearse when we're done testing the object."

"Finally," says Jillian. "It's time for Madam Sparkles to make her encore!"

Ander jumps onto the log. "And Freddie Dinkleweed as well?"

"Of course, Dahling, of course."

"Do you guys want to practice our lines while we wait?"

"Sure," says Ander, and he runs to a different spot by a different log. We sit down with him and do our circle read, with our scripts for backup, two times. Then, on the third go through, we set our scripts down. We speak our lines a little slower this time, but we get through them without even looking. We sing our new song too, which sounds a little shaky, but it's good enough.

Ander jumps up. "Let's see if the Satellite Spectacle Box is ready to be tested."

We rush to the table and Jax inspects the solder joint. "It

looks good to me."

"Okay, this is it. It has to work. So what should we do first?" I ask.

Mare steps forward. "All we have to do is attach the chip on the glasses to the syncing cable. The cable is already attached to the activation button."

Jax opens the box and attaches the glasses to the cable. "Okay, done."

"Now we close the box, push the button to turn it on, and then it will sync, right?" asks Ander.

"Yes," says Mare. "Then it should start syncing. When it's done, the tiny square on the chip of the glasses should light up. That's how we'll know it worked."

"Okay, here it goes." Ander presses the C5 button on the box. A light illuminates around the button, and a small hum escapes from inside. I watch for something else to happen. Anything. Anything at all.

"How long is it supposed to take?" Jillian asks.

But then the box shuts off. Jax lifts the top of it slowly. The glasses are inside but the square isn't lit up.

"I don't think it worked," says Jillian.

I give her the side-eye.

"Sorry. I'm just wondering if it should have worked by now."

Obviously it should have worked by now. Jax's face is red, but not embarrassed red. Like frustrated red. Mad red.

"I don't know why it didn't work. It was supposed to!" He stares at the box like the answer is going to jump out at him.

"It's okay," I say. "We'll figure it out."

I wish I knew how to help. Maybe my math skills can fix whatever the problem is. The problem is, I don't know what math skills to use.

Ander walks around the table. "Maybe it's the symbol button. Maybe it didn't activate it right."

"What if we take the symbol off and try it again without it?" Mare suggests.

"But according to Andora's rule, it needs to be visible during our presentation," I say.

"It's not the C5 button," says Jax. "That just turns it on and begins the activation process—and it did do that. The problem is with the instructions, the programming. It instructed the chip on the glasses to *start* syncing but I don't think it told it to *keep* syncing until it was done."

"Why?" asks Jillian.

"I'm not sure," says Jax. "I'll check."

"Okay, Big Guy, you do that. I'll go look for some snacks."

"No!" I say. "We can't make Jax do all the work. That's what the Michigan team does. We can't be like them."

"We'll all help you," says Mare. "We all need to know how to make sure it works anyway."

"Okay," says Ander. "But then we need snacks."

Soon after, when we're sure the program is right, we try again. "The glasses are attached," says Mare. "Go ahead and push the button."

Ander does. We watch the box and wait. And wait and wait.

"Great," says Mare. "What do we do now?"

"I knew this was impossible," says Jillian.

A few seconds pass and suddenly the button lights up and a humming sound comes from the box—louder and longer than the last time—and then it stops.

I open the box. "The square is lit! Does that mean it

worked? Did the glasses sync?"

"It worked!" yells Ander

Jax grins bigger than I've ever seen him grin.

"Don't be so excited yet. Now we need to see if the virtual reality part works." Mare disconnects the glasses from the cable, pulls them out of the box, and hands them to me. When I put them on, a yellow virtual smiley face pops out in front of my face, floats there for a few seconds, and then disappears. "Whoa! A yellow smiley face just popped up in front of me!"

Jax laughs. "Good, it's working."

"What do I do now?"

"Tap the right side of the glasses once. That will allow you to take a picture."

"Okay." I tap it once.

"Now hold your hands out like a frame. Place them around the item that you want to take a picture of."

I turn and hold my hands up so that I can see Jillian and Mare. They pose and smile.

"Now blink once and keep your eyes closed for two seconds. That will take the picture."

I do as Jax says and then open my eyes. The picture I took flashes in front of my face like a ghost—and then disappears. "It was here," I say. "But where did it go?"

"It's filed away until you want to see it again."

"That's amazing!" says Jillian. "But what if we want to see the picture too?"

"There's an invisible air screen in front of Kia at all times. All she has to do is push any button to make it appear. Try it, Kia."

I push an invisible button in front of me.

"So now you should see a keypad. On it is a button that

looks like a photo album. Touch that and you'll see a list of your pictures. Touch the one you want to show, then touch it again to make it turn around. It will appear in front of you so everyone else can see it. When you're done, touch the picture again."

I do as Jax says, and the picture I just took appears in front of me. Jillian, Mare, and Ander lean in to see it.

"That's incredible!" says Jillian. "Not only are the glasses a fabulous accessory, but they take pictures too!"

"And with the air screen, the glasses can show the time and make calls too," says Mare.

"It also has buttons to access your homework and your practice schedule, doesn't it?" asks Ander.

"Yes, and let's say you need to be at home by four o'clock, the glasses will already know that. So they'll remind you to hop on your aero-scooter by a certain time," says Jax.

"We were going to add a countdown timer. Is that in there?" asks Ander.

"Yes, numbers will count down like a hologram in front of your face to remind you."

"This is crazy!" I say. "Okay, what else?"

"If you're walking down the path along the tree suites and you're about to bump into someone because you aren't paying attention, the glasses will inform you that you're about to enter someone else's space."

Ander grins. "Yeah, the words, *entering private space* will float in front of you!"

I take the glasses off. "This is amazing! These glasses might even be better than the Ancestor App!"

"Yeah," says Ander. "It's too bad the judges can't see what you're seeing when you have them on though."

"Aww," says Mare. "Our presentation would be so much

better if they could—if the whole audience could see too."

We stand there in silence for a few seconds, probably all wondering the same thing. "Wait guys, could we do that? Could we put it up on a screen somehow?"

We exchange glances trying to decide if there's a way to do it. Finally Ander breaks a random twig in half. "We were almost done with everything too."

Jillian sighs. "We need to find a way, huh?"

Jax nods. "I think the judges would understand the capabilities of the glasses better if they could see them on the screen."

I bite my thumb nail. "I guess we better get back to work."

THE CRIMSON CURSE

AFTER HEARING ABOUT our Satellite Spectacle success, Seraphina and Gregor insist that we head to the Creativity Pool for some fun. My teammates dive in right away, in search of the lily pads, but I sit by the edge of the water instead. Being here reminds me of what Martina said last week. If it's true, I have no right to swim here. I have no right to be here at all—even with an amazing Satellite Spectacles. Sure, Seraphina told us we won the Piedmont Challenge fairly, but how does she *know* Principal Bermuda didn't change the results? She also told us what our highest category scores were, but that doesn't mean anything either. It doesn't mean we scored the highest in the whole state of New York. Besides, mine was Swirl and Spark Recall. That's not even a real category.

Seraphina comes over and sits down next to me,

sticking her purple polished toes into the water. "Hey Kia."

"Hey."

"What's wrong?"

"Nothing."

"You're not getting nervous for the competition, are you?"

"No, I'm not nervous. I don't get that nervous."

She laughs. "Yes, I forgot. So what is it then? You don't usually hang out by yourself."

"Can I ask you a question?"

"Sure."

"Do you think it's a coincidence that we all came from the same school? I mean everyone thought our school was cursed because no one had ever won before, and I know you said not to worry about that, and the rest of my team doesn't seem worried anymore."

"Okay, Kia. First of all . . . breathe."

I take a breath.

"That's better. So the rest of your team doesn't seem worried. But you are."

"Seraphina, Principal Bermuda is evil. He can make people do bad things. What if he got someone to switch our test scores, like the way he made Gregor smash our Ghost Gallery? What if he did that? It would mean one of us, or all of us, didn't even score the highest. Then we really don't belong here. The kids that *did* score highest belong here. I mean, if it was me, I'd want to know."

"Do you think that the five of you don't deserve to be here, that you're not every bit as smart as the rest of the kids, that your ideas aren't every bit as creative?"

"Well, I don't know. I know we just thought up another really good invention, but we weren't even able to figure out the problem-solving bars in the pool."

She laughs. "Kia, what your team created at Camp Piedmont and what you've just created here in Québec is incredible."

"Yeah, but I just keep thinking about what Martina said. Besides, no one at Crimson had ever won before, then suddenly this year Crimson has five winners."

"I know all of that."

"So can you help me find a way to know for sure, and not let the others know? I don't want to wreck this for all of them, but it feels wrong to be here if we cheated. I want more than anything to be here and to finish our task and everything. I guess I just wish I could know for sure if he did something bad to get us here."

"And who do you think would know for sure?"

I shrug.

"Do you think Andora would?"

"Yeah, but what if he fooled her too?"

"Andora is a smart person."

"Yeah, I know."

"And she's a good person. She would never allow cheating."

"But what if she didn't know?"

"Andora has a way of knowing things that we don't about this competition, even stuff about Principal Bermuda."

"Really?"

"Yes, and do you want to know something else? I had a talk with her about your team before I even met you."

"You did?"

"Yes, all the preceptors met with her to discuss the children they would be working with. Most of our talk involved the rules of the competition, but some of it was about something else."

"What was it about?"

"She said to me, 'Seraphina, there will likely come a time when one or more of the children will question the validity of the results. They will wonder how it's possible that all five of them advanced, considering they came from the same school—and that no student from Crimson Heights had ever done so in the competition before. It will be your job to reassure them. The manner in which they have become a team is unique, and as such, we have challenged the results. Be assured that each one of your children from Crimson has earned their rightful place here. If the time comes when one of them questions the validity of their presence here, it will be up to you to put their mind at ease.'"

"So Kia, you can relax. You and your teammates placed in the top five at the Piedmont Challenge—fair and square."

"So you're saying our scores definitely weren't changed?"

Seraphina shakes her head. "They were not changed."

"But Andora didn't exactly *say* they weren't changed."

"She didn't have to, Kia. When Andora says something, you can trust that she knows what she's talking about."

Seraphina hugs me, and deep down inside I believe her.

"You know, Kia, every once in a while, a person will be part of something special—something bigger than they ever imagined. I think the experience you're having in this year's Piedmont Challenge is *your something special*. You need to embrace the something special that has happened to you."

"How do I do that?"

"Continue to question things you don't understand, and

be curious, just like you have been about this. But also know that you have a purpose, and I'm guessing it's a pretty big purpose. Look inside yourself to see what you have to offer the world. Don't doubt yourself. Believe in yourself because that's when you'll make great things happen."

I don't know what to say. But I know there's nothing else I can do about the big coincidence at this year's Piedmont Challenge—nothing except win this competition and show everyone, including Martina, that our team deserves to be here.

See the World More Clearly With Satellite Specs! New York, USA

THE WARRIORS

ON THE LAST day before the Opening Ceremony, we walk with Seraphina and Gregor to the Creativity Pool for morning yoga. Seraphina thinks it will relax us before the competition, but I don't think Gregor is happy about it. He lays down his rubber mat on the grass like the rest of us, but while Seraphina leads us in a routine, he keeps checking his watch for updates of the competition schedule.

We bend and stretch, doing poses called downward dog, cat cow, and warrior one. They seem like weird names to me, but Seraphina is all serious about it, so I get serious too.

I think of Grandma Kitty doing her exercises in her yard. She would definitely like this. When we're finished, we lay on our backs and breathe real deep. Seraphina tells us to visualize the competition tomorrow—picture ourselves performing the skit for the judges, and picture ourselves solving the Swirl and Spark Recall task successfully together.

Finally, she sits up and jumps to her feet. "Okay, my Crimson Kids, great job! I bet you'll feel relaxed and energized all day but like warriors ready to compete at the Piedmont Global Championships."

My heart swells ten times its normal size when she says that.

"I love yoga," says Jillian. "Can we do it again tomorrow?"

"Probably not. It's Opening Ceremony day, remember?"

Jillian laughs. "Oh, right. I forgot."

Oh my god, how could she forget that?

"Today is going to be busy. We have rehearsals all day and costume-making all night."

"Costume-making?" asks Jillian.

"We already made our costumes," Ander says.

"Not competition costumes," says Seraphina. "Opening Ceremony costumes!"

"Really?" I ask.

"Yes, each team has been assigned an era of costumes to wear from their own country. Gregor and I have chosen what you'll wear within that era and therefore what you'll be making tonight."

Jillian's eyes are huge. "We make them?"

"Yes!" says Seraphina.

"What are they?" asks Jax.

"Will they be just as great as the ones we wore to the National Finals at Camp Piedmont?" I ask.

Gregor smiles. "I think you'll be pleased with your attire—if you can find a way to make them in one day's time."

"One day?" asks Jillian. "Why didn't you tell us sooner?"

"Each team is given the same amount of time. You may begin tonight after dinner and you'll have until the Opening Ceremony tomorrow night to work on them."

"What are the costumes?" asks Mare. "Do we have to wear something like those Martha Washington dresses again?"

"Can my shoes be more comfortable than the buckle ones we wore to the gala?" asks Ander. "Those hurt my feet."

Gregor shakes his head. "I assure you, Ander, the comfort of your feet will not be an issue."

"Good, because Freddie Dinkleweed needs to be in top form."

Seraphina laughs. "Yes, Ander, we know. You'll find out after dinner tonight. For now we need to focus on rehearsals."

Gregor points to the brick path. "Please jog back to your tree suite and change. We'll expect you in the Imagination Centre, room eighteen, in thirty minutes."

We race back to the treehouse and Ander barely beats me to the wiggly bridge. I pass him and leap to the rock wall first. But he's better at climbing than me, and he reaches the door first.

"I hate that rock wall," I say. "It always slows me down."

"I'd say your feet slow you down—and your hands, and your legs. But don't worry, KK, I'll coach you sometime."

"Yeah, okay."

We have twenty minutes before we have to meet Gregor and Seraphina so we stop at the floating playground before going upstairs to change. We grab the bean-bag blobs and try to start bouncing. But this time, instead of bouncing us to the top of the clouds, they bounce us around the room, in between the swirling ladder, behind the yellow pole, and around the spinning slide. Soon we crash into to each other like old-fashioned carnival bumper cars.

The door to the tree suite opens. "I see you're all ready to rehearse." Gregor stands in the doorway, looking stern as ever. I keep forgetting that even though he's not as bad as we thought he was, he still is pretty strict. He still is Gregor.

"We're just about ready," Ander calls. "Just getting our creative energy flowing before we change."

"You're such a suck up," says Mare.

"You can thank me later." He grins, and we hop off our blobs.

Gregor points to the stairs. "Perhaps you should get your creative energy out of those sweaty clothes. I suggest you hurry."

"But can't we ride with you on the aero-cart?" he asks.

"No. I have supplies to transport and you need your exercise. You know what they say."

I stand up straight. "It takes a fit brain and fit body to be at your creative best."

"That's right, Kia. I will see you all at the Imagination Centre."

We reach room eighteen, a space similar to the gala room but smaller. The ceiling is high and the walls are covered with pretty tiles. It's dark, too. I don't think people at this university like light very much. Mare grabs our costume bags and tosses one to each of us. We head to the bathrooms to change and emerge a few minutes later as residents of Crimson Catropolis once again.

I skip out in my yellow overall shorts with pigtails in my hair. I'm getting used to this costume, I've worn it so much. Ander jumps out of the bathroom across the hall, wearing his black baseball pants, funky shirt and vest, and crazy jester hat—and none of it is inside out. Jax strolls out behind him, like always, flaring his black cape and tipping his top hat. Jillian twirls out next throwing her silver boa over her shoulder, and Mare follows behind while she's still tying on her choker necklace.

It's only been a little over a week since the Showcase Festival, but I almost forgot how much I love our costumes, especially now that Jillian fixed them up. It'll be the first time Gregor and Seraphina see our skit with all of it put together: the dance, the box, the Satellite Spectacles—everything.

We've decorated a table with a map. It shows people all over the world wearing the Satellite Spectacles—with smiling faces, air screens, camera icons, and commands like *car approaching, homework assignment due,* and *mom's birthday* floating around them. The box, which holds the Satellite Spectacles, is right in the center. Our team sign hangs from the front of the table with letters cut from colorful duct tape:

See the World More Clearly With Satellite Specs!
New York, USA

"Okay, my Crimson Kids," says Seraphina. "I think it would be best if two of you stand on the ends of the table to start and three of you stand behind it. When the judges tell you to begin, you can simply lift the table together and carry it to the presentation area."

"So, Seraphina," says Mare.

"Yes?"

"I've been thinking."

"Okay."

"I think we should have something going on while we

carry the table, so it's not so awkward while the judges wait for us to start. What do you think?"

"I think that's a great idea. What do you want to say?"

"Remember last time, at the National Finals, we chanted part of our song? What if we make up something like that, like one of the chorus lines?"

So we figure out which chorus line to use, and soon we're ready to start. The opening scene begins with everyone scurrying around preparing for my second visit to Crimson Catropolis.

Little Girl stays hidden behind the table.

Jillian—Madam Sparkles—flits around talking to everyone who will listen, while Jax—the Gatekeeper—paces. Ander— Freddie Dinkleweed—entertains them with his juggling, and Mare—the Teenager—files her nails while wondering what is taking me—Little Girl—so long to arrive.

On cue, Little Girl skips out from behind the table. Freddie Dinkleweed dances a jig. "She's here! She's here!"

Madam Sparkles claps her hands. "Oh wonderful, Dahling. You made it back to Crimson Catropolis!"

"Yes, I did!" Little Girl exclaims. "I got Freddie's message. What is it? What is so important?"

The Gatekeeper walks slowly to her. "You were summoned here for one very important reason."

Teenager Mare smirks. "Yeah. You have a job to do."

"Me? What kind of job can I do?"

"A very important one indeed," says the Gatekeeper.

"But I'm only small. I don't think I can do a really big important job."

"Oh, Dahling. That couldn't be further from the truth. Here

in Crimson Catropolis, anything and everything is possible no matter how big you are, no matter how small."

"Really?" asks Little Girl.

"Really, Small One," says Freddie. "Or no matter how different you are at all."

"You just need a dash of confidence, and I just so happen to have some to share." Madam Sparkles pulls her silver boa from her neck and drapes it around Little Girl and back off again.

Little Girl spins around. "Is that my confidence?" she asks.

"Right-o, that's it!" says Freddie. "That's it indeed!"

Little Girl looks at her arms and legs and hands. "Now that I have confidence, I think I'm ready to hear what my job is."

"Are you sure?" asks Teenager Mare.

"Yes, I'm sure. I'm sure I can do whatever job you need me to do. I'm in Crimson Catropolis, and I have my confidence, so I can do anything."

The Gatekeeper walks to her side. "Then yes, you can, Little One. Yes, you can."

"What do you need me to do?"

The Gatekeeper flares his cape. "We need you use your imagination."

Little Girl gasps. "Use my imagination?"

"Yes," the others reply. "By opening this box and telling us what you see."

Little Girl tilts her head. "But why do you need me to do that?"

The Gatekeeper steps toward her. "Ah, Little One, that is easy. Because when people use their imagination, they see things no one else can. We've looked inside this box, but all we see is a pair of eyeglasses, used to improve a person's vision. It seems that we need you to remind us what else they might be used for."

"So you need me to tell you what I see inside the box?"

"Yes, Little One. Do you think you can do that? Can you tell us what you see in this box?"

Little girl nods and tries to open the box. But it will not open . . . until she pushes the magic button—the C5 button. And when she does, it illuminates, and the box hums. When the humming stops, she opens it. She peeks inside and gasps. She carefully lifts the glasses out of the box and place them on her face. As soon as she does, a smile breaks free. She spins around and around and while she does, the screen behind them swirls to life. And that's when the audience sees what she sees . . .

A world of endless possibilities—a virtual personal assistant powered by satellites and an ever-present air screen, helping her to see more around her than she could see on her own . . . like the dangerous place she's about to enter because it doesn't appear that scary. But the audience also sees the spectacles guiding her in practical ways . . . like turning off her game capabilities while she's flying her aero-scooter, reminding her to study for a test, and allowing her to take pictures with just the blink of an eye.

Little Girl takes off the Satellite Spectacles and holds them close to her. "That's it. That's what I see when I hold these glasses. A safe, organized world where people are good to each other because they see things they couldn't see before."

The Gatekeeper walks toward her. "What did you see? What did you find in the box?"

"Ohhhh, I saw too many things to list."

"But how do you see so many things?" asks Freddie. "With only one pair of glasses."

"Oh no, these are not just regular glasses. They are spectacles."

"What does a pair of spectacles do?" asks Madam Sparkles.

"They are like a friend . . . a friend who protects me and guides me and never leaves my side. They help me to see the world more clearly."

"Do you think it's possible that we could see the world more clearly with these spectacles too?" asks the Gatekeeper.

"Yes," says Little Girl. "I know you could." She motions toward the box. "The world, these spectacles, and this box are all you need to see it."

AFTER OUR finale song and dance, Seraphina and Gregor stand up and clap. They grin, and I can't tell whose smile is bigger. And that's saying a lot for Gregor.

"Oh my gosh, oh my gosh, you guys, that was beyond amazing!" says Seraphina.

"Indeed it was," says Gregor. "That was . . . how should I put it? A solution worthy of your team!"

We bask in their compliments, but not for long. Our skit may have been amazing the first time, but when we practice again, it's not great. It's not a solution worthy of anything. It's a mess. The button sticks so the box doesn't turn on, the program glitches so the glasses don't communicate with the big screen, and our dance is awful because we forget where to stand.

"It's fine," says Seraphina. "Try it again."

So we try it again, but this time, the box turns on but the air screen buttons don't appear. How are we supposed make people see things around the world more clearly if our invention glitches right in front of them?

"This is bad," I say. "What's wrong with it? It worked before!"

But no one answers me.

"Try it one more time. I know it'll work. We saw it with our own two eyes, didn't we Gregor?"

He stands there with his hands on his hips. "Yes, we did.

But the judges need to see it work also."

So we huddle around the table and check the programming. We go over our dance positions, say our lines in our heads, and double-check the C5 button. "I think it'll work this time," says Jax. "Can we practice it again?"

"I'm afraid you don't have time to practice the whole thing," says Seraphina. "We need to store this all away before the building is locked."

"But the competition is tomorrow!" I say.

"We don't have a choice," says Seraphina. "We can't be here after six o'clock."

I look at my watch. It's 5:55 p.m.

"We'll have just enough time to gather our things."

This is horrible. "Can we at least try the Satellite Spectacles once more—real quick?"

And so we do. Twice. They work the first time but not the second. Those are not good odds. But at exactly six o'clock, we pack up and leave the room, sulking as Gregor locks the door.

Seraphina flashes us a small smile. "It's fine, my Crimson Kids. You always do spectacular when it counts. You may need to activate the spectacles more than once during the performance, that's all. That wouldn't be that bad."

Yes, it would.

"Now run over to dinner. We'll meet you in the tree suite afterwards to start your Opening Ceremony costumes."

"Okay. Yay," says Jillian.

We leave the Imagination Centre and my stomach twists in a knot. The next time we'll be here is for the Opening Ceremony. And I don't feel like a warrior. I don't feel ready at all.

THE COSTUME CHALLENGE

WE WALK TO le Cantine for dinner. Maelle, Danielle, and Zoe stop by our table just as we're finishing our chicken lasagna.

"I am sorry we missed you at the pool the other day," says Maelle. "We were so excited to get our pretty package that we ran off very fast before we could say hello. And then at the big fire also we looked everywhere for you, but we couldn't find you."

"That's okay," I say. "I'm glad you found us this time."

"Speaking of the team packages," says Ander. "What's your team symbol?"

"What do you mean by team symbol?"

"You know, like the thing you need to display on your solution for the judges, the thing that symbolizes your team?"

"I am so sorry," says Maelle. "I still do not understand."

Ander keeps trying to explain. "Didn't your team get a metal symbol in your package? Like ours is a C with a 5 for the Crimson Five."

"No, we did not get any such symbol."

"You didn't?" I ask. "Maybe you just didn't see it. But you need it for the competition."

"But I am certain there was nothing else in our package. Even Gwyndol tipped it upside down to be very sure. I think he was looking for something else to be there. Like maybe chocolate!"

"Hmm," says Mare. "I wonder if any of the other teams are missing symbols too."

Ander stands up. "I got this." He walks over to a boy from Canada. "Hey, random question . . . Remember when our teams got packages at the Creativity Pool? The ones that invited us to the bonfire?"

The boy replies, "Yeah."

"What was inside your team's package?"

The boy looks at the rest of us, and then back at Ander. "The invitation to the bonfire."

"Was there anything else?"

"No, why?"

"Are you sure there wasn't anything else in there? I mean, I was just thinking maybe we were supposed to get something else, like chocolate or something, and I wanted to be sure we didn't miss out."

The boy laughs. "Oh, okay. I was wondering the same thing. I tipped it over just to be sure. I was happy about the bonfire and all, but I really was hoping there was something else."

"Yeah, us too. Okay, thanks. I just wanted to be sure."

We scatter around the dining hall and each ask someone

from different teams. Their answers are all identical to Maelle's and the Canadian boy's.

"What do you think it means?" I ask.

"I don't know," says Jillian, "but I have a feeling we're the only ones who got it."

"Why would we be the only ones?" asks Mare.

I shake my head. I have no idea. But we don't have time to worry about it. We hustle back to our tree suite to begin work on our costumes for the Opening Ceremony. When we arrive, Seraphina and Gregor are leaning against the swirly ladder at the floating playground.

"Yay! You're here! Your costumes are going to be fantastic," says Seraphina. "You're each going to wear an outfit represented by a different period of time in American history during the 1900s."

"Okay," says Ander. "What am I going to be?"

"You're going to represent the disco era of the 1970s."

He grins. "Nice."

"What about me?" asks Mare.

"You're going to represent the 1980s, and Jillian, you're going to represent the flapper period of the 1920s.

Mare nods. Jillian looks like she just won the lottery.

"What about me?" I ask.

"Kia, you'll represent the sock hops of the 1950s, and Jax, you'll represent the hippie period of the 1960s.

"That's awesome," I say. "What are you two wearing?"

"I'm going dressed as a gangster from the 1930s, and Seraphina is representing grand ballroom dancing of the 1910s."

"You'll have full access to the Inspiration Room and the Work Room. We've also placed an invention inside that you're free to use—and will totally love. It was thought up by the team from Canada last year. It's called the Costume Copier and has an air screen attached to it. All you do is look up a piece of clothing on the air screen, feed fabric into the Costume Copier tray, push the button, and the piece of clothing you selected will slide out the bottom, kind of like an old-fashioned copy machine for paper."

"Seriously?" asks Jillian. "That's amazing!"

Ander grins. "Can we start?"

"Not so fast," says Gregor. "You're only allowed to use the Costume Copier for the main part of your costume. Not the accessories. If you want any of those you'll need to make them yourselves. The copier is extremely expensive."

"And," Seraphina adds, "the copier cannot make the clothing in the exact size you need so you'll have to tailor them by hand also."

"No problem!" shouts Jillian. "Let's go!"

We head to the Work Room and use the air screen to figure out costumes we can copy. We take turns listening to music from our decades for inspiration. We laugh mostly at the music from the seventies though, especially when Ander dances.

I need to wear a poodle skirt—one that flairs out past my knees. I choose yellow, make one on the Costume Copier, and hold it up to me. It's huge! So I get to work cutting, trying to make it smaller. Soon it's nine o'clock, and we have to stop for the night. The rest will have to wait until tomorrow. The boys head into their tree chamber, and the girls and I head into ours.

"Okay," says Jillian as we sit in our sleeping eggs, "we don't have much time tomorrow,

and the accessories will totally be the best parts of our costumes, so let's make them tonight."

When we're sure the boys are asleep, we sneak back into the Work Room for more supplies—fabric, felt, sequins, a pair of light blue gloves, glue, and Velcro—and carry them back to our tree chamber.

"Kia, you're a girl from the fifties, so you need to wear a scarf around your neck to match your poodle skirt. But you also need a poodle to put on the skirt."

"My skirt is yellow, so I'll cut this yellow silky fabric to make my scarf the right size."

"Perfect."

"And then I can draw a poodle right on this felt."

"That's perfect too. Then all you'll have to do is cut it out and glue it to the Velcro and attach it to your skirt tomorrow."

"Got it." I grab the scissors and cut out my scarf. Then I find a pencil and get to work sketching a poodle. Meanwhile, Mare cuts scraps of fabric to tie her hair with and cuts the fingers off the pair of gloves.

"Why are you cutting those off?" I ask.

Jillian answers before Mare can. "All the girls in the eighties wore fingerless gloves. It was a thing back then."

Jillian gets back to work on her pink sequined flapper headband, and I cut out my poodle. But by eleven o'clock I can't keep my eyes open anymore. "Come on," I say. "We better go to bed. The competition is tomorrow, and we need sleep."

I look over at Jillian and Mare, but they're both already sleeping with their materials still scattered all over their sleeping eggs. I move the craft supplies to our cubbies, climb back into my bed, and watch the germ-eating eggs sanitize the room for a second time. The Opening Ceremonies are tomorrow, and our families will be here! I've only been away two weeks this time, but I miss my family more than I thought I would—especially Grandma Kitty.

It's weird, I haven't heard from her in a few days. She hasn't sent me any messages. I think I'll send her one on my watch before I go to sleep.

Hi GK! I miss you so much. I can't wait to see you so I can show you every single thing! Like the sparkling pool and our tree suite and definitely our new invention. It's a surprise and you're going to freak out when you see it! I'll give you a hint. If it gets made for real you'll be able to ride your aero-scooter without even navigating the birds! I'm getting nervous to compete, but I know as soon as I see you, I won't be nervous anymore. xoxo

I slide deep under my blankets. Grandma Kitty is going to love this place. Wait until she sees the tree suites, the floating playground, the Satellite Spectacles . . .

THE PHONE CALL

I WAKE UP in my sleeping egg way earlier than I have to. I look at my watch to check for messages. Nothing. I could get up and beat the bathroom hogs to the shower, but I can't bring myself out of bed for some reason, and then I realize why. Grandma Kitty still hasn't answered me. That's really weird. Even late at night, she always answers me. Always. And now it's been hours. I don't know what's taking her so long, but I roll out of bed and I head to the shower anyway. Maybe I'll get her message while I'm getting ready.

When I get back to my cubby, I see a message on my watch—from my mom. I'm happy to hear from her and everything, but I still wonder about Grandma Kitty. What the heck is she doing that's taking her so long to message me back?

Mom: Hi Kia, tonight's the big night! I bet you're really excited. We can't wait to see you at the Opening Ceremony.

Me: Hi Mom! I am, but do you know where Grandma Kitty is? I sent her a message and she hasn't answered me yet.

Mom: I'm sure she will. You know Grandma Kitty.

Me: Yeah, she always answers me, and she hasn't in like twelve hours.

Mom: Don't worry about your grandma.

I decide to call my mom and talk to her instead. I don't want to wake Jillian and Mare up, so I go outside and sit on the ground.

"Mom, why hasn't she called me? Or sent me a message back?"

"Hi Honey, she has a cold, that's probably why. Now don't you need to go to breakfast with your team?"

"Not yet. If Grandma Kitty has a cold, she can still message me. But she hasn't sent me any 'good luck' messages or 'you're going to be so fabulous' messages or 'I can't wait to see all the inventions' messages."

"Kia, you don't need to be worrying about Grandma Kitty, and now I need to finish up some work so we can leave on time later today."

"Well, is she flying with you, or is she taking her new scooter? She promised me she'd practice and take me on a ride through Québec after the competition."

"No, she's not driving with us."

"Then she is flying her scooter!"

"No, she's not flying her scooter."

"Oh, then how will she get here?"

She pauses for way too long.

"Mom?"

"Kia, I didn't want to tell you this over the phone, but your grandma won't be able to come tonight."

"Wait, what? Why not?"

"Grandma Kitty's in the hospital, Honey."

"The hospital? What happened?"

"She had a crash. She crashed while she was riding her new aero-scooter."

"Oh no! Is she okay?"

"The doctors are working very hard to make her better, but she's going to be in the hospital for a while. I'm so sorry. I know how badly you wanted her to be at your competition."

My voice catches in my throat. "She's not coming tomorrow either?"

"No, she's not."

"But what's wrong with her? Is it her leg or something? Can't they just give her a cast?"

"It's not her leg. The injuries affected her brain. She has some swelling that the doctors are trying to fix."

"But the doctors have to let her come. She wouldn't miss this, Mom! Not for anything."

"No, she wouldn't, not if she could help it."

"Then I want to talk to her."

"Kia, you can't right now. She's sleeping. That's what her brain needs to get better."

"Well, can I talk to her when she wakes up, at least before we compete?"

"I don't think so, Honey. She's going to be sleeping for a while."

"Awhile!" I choke back a sob. "Is she going to be okay, Mom?" I suddenly realize that she must be hurt pretty badly.

"She is a tough lady, Kia, and you know how stubborn she is. If anyone can get through an injury like this, she can. Now I don't want you to worry about her. The doctors are watching her very closely, and Dad and I will still be there for the Opening Ceremony tonight. Malin and Ryne will be too."

Why can't they just wake her up?

"I want to talk to her."

"You know she would talk to you if she could."

I blink back my tears. "But I wanted her to come here. It's the Global Championships. I wanted to show her our tree suite and the Creativity Pool and our new invention."

"She wanted to see all of that too—so much."

The tears sting my eyes. "Can I see her when I get home at least?"

"Of course, Honey. She would like that. Now tell me about the competition. Are you ready for it? Are you excited for the Opening Ceremony?"

"I was."

"Grandma Kitty would want you to be excited and enjoy every second of your Piedmont experience, so you can tell her about it when she wakes up. Promise me you'll still do that."

I don't want to promise. I just want Grandma Kitty to be okay.

"Kia?"

"I'll try."

"I love you, Kia, and so does Grandma Kitty. You know that. And I'll see you tonight, okay?"

"Okay."

I end the call, but I don't get up. I picture Grandma Kitty lying in a hospital bed with no sparkles in her hair. This is all my fault. I told her to practice riding on her scooter while I was gone. I wanted her to ride it here, but I never should have asked her to do that. She's a grandma. She's old. She supposed to ride in a car—an aero-*car*, not an aero-*scooter*. And now she's hurt—all because of me.

The door to the tree suite opens, and Ander climbs down the rock wall. He scrambles across the wiggly bridge and jumps down next to me. "Hey, KK. What are you doing out here? I've been looking all over for you."

I don't say anything.

"What's wrong?" His blue eyes open wide. "Are you okay?"

I bite my lip to keep from crying. "My grandma was in an accident."

"What kind of accident?"

"An aero-scooter accident."

"Is she going to be okay?"

"I don't know."

"Is she in the hospital?"

I nod.

"Then she'll be okay."

"I hope so."

He takes a marble out of his pocket and looks at it. "She will."

"But now she can't come tonight."

He turns the marble over and stares at it. "That stinks."

"Ander, it's my fault. I was the one who told her to ride it here."

"But you didn't mean for her to get into an accident."

"But she did, and now everything is wrecked."

He puts the marble back into his pocket, and we sit in silence.

"Ander?"

"Yeah?"

"I don't think I want to go on the Swirl and Spark Tour anymore."

"Why not?"

"Because I can't leave my grandma for that long. It's a whole year, and she needs me. She needs me right now, and I can't even help her because I'm here!"

"But, KK, the doctors are taking care of her."

"But they don't know how important she is. She's not a normal grandma. She's really important, and if anything happens to her it will be all my fault. So can you just tell our team that if they don't want to go on the tour anymore, I don't mind, because we can still go to PIPS, and that's really what I wanted anyway."

"No, I'm not telling them that. You really do want to go on the tour. We all do!"

"Well, just tell them I can't. I can't leave my grandma for that long."

I jump up.

"Where are you going?"

I take off and run. I hear Ander call after me, but I yell for him to leave me alone. I run past the other American tree suites. I run past the Canadian tree suite. I run while the morning sun blinds me, but I don't even care. I don't care about any of this anymore.

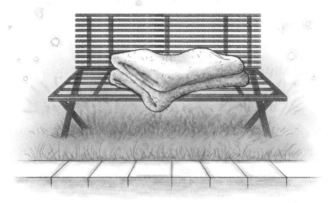

THE BEACH TOWEL

I RUN TO the end of the brick path, past two kids from Mexico and a boy from Switzerland. I run until I can't breathe anymore and stop on a bench near the Creativity Pool. The pool and the grassy square are empty and quiet. It's just me and the shimmering pool.

I try not to cry. I try to breathe normally and to be brave. I try to tell myself that Grandma Kitty is going to be okay and that it's no big deal that she isn't coming tonight. No big deal. It's just a ceremony, probably like the one at Camp Piedmont.

But this is the Opening Ceremony for the Piedmont Global Championships. And she won't be here. She won't see us march in. She won't see me before the competition. She won't grab my hand. Her bracelets won't jingle next to my wristband while she tells me that I can do this. She won't tell me that our team is amazing and together we can

212

do anything. She won't tell me that we can place in the top three and get picked to go on the Swirl and Spark Tour. She won't say any of that. She won't say, "Mark my words."

The tears stream down my face faster than I can wipe them away. I try to use my sleeve, but it's too short. Oh, what difference does it make, anyway? I bury my head in my knees. I just want to go home.

A colorful beach towel lands on my head.

Startled, I pull it off and shield my eyes from the sun. Martina is staring at me. "Do you want to use my towel?"

If I could crawl under the bench, I would.

"It's okay. Take it. I was just going to swing on the Idea Swings before breakfast, but I have to sit down here for a minute anyway, you know, to take off my shoes."

I look at her shoes. They're flip flops. It doesn't take much to take them off. She's looking right at me, waiting, so I slide over and put the towel on my lap. "Thanks."

She presses her lips together. "Are you okay?"

"I'm fine."

"You don't look fine, no offense."

I wipe my eyes and hand the towel back to her.

"Are you upset about the competition?"

Why can't she just go away? She made me doubt our team and think that we didn't win fair and square. I don't want to talk to her about the competition, or about anything.

"Like, did something happen to your solution or something?"

"No."

"Did you get in a fight with your teammates?"

"No."

"Why are you crying then?"

"What do you care?"

"I care."

I stare at her for a second. "If you really want to know, it's about my grandma. She's in the hospital and can't come here to watch us compete. But why would you even care? You tried to tell us that we cheated, that the competition was fixed. But guess what? It wasn't, so you don't have to keep trying to hang around us and act like you want to talk to us, because you don't. I know you just want to intimidate us."

She looks at the ground. "So your grandma isn't coming?"

She acts like she didn't even hear what I said.

"No."

"What's wrong with her?"

"I don't *know* exactly. I just know she crashed her aero-scooter, and I know she's really upset that she can't come because she would do anything to be here."

Martina nods like she cares, but I'm not letting her fool me.

"Are you close to your grandma?

"Why?"

"I was just wondering because I was close with my grandma too, but she died, and my grandpa moved away after that. We used to be close, but we're not anymore."

My stomach drops. I'm such an idiot. I never even pictured Martina with a family—with grandparents and everything. She might be a jerk to me, but she still has feelings. She probably misses them both a lot. "I'm sorry your grandma died."

"It's okay. I'm sorry your grandma's in the hospital."

"Thanks. I'm sorry you're not close with your grandpa

anymore, either."

"It's probably because he moved away."

I shift my weight on the bench. "Where did he go?"

"New York."

"New York City?"

"No." She turns away and says quietly, "He lives in Crimson Heights."

"Did you say Crimson Heights?"

"Yes."

"That's where I live."

She slides her foot in and out of her flip flop. "I know. He's a principal there."

It takes me a second to realize what that could mean. "Hold on a second. He's a principal?"

"Yes." She gets up from the bench. "I have to go."

"Wait a second. What's his name?"

She walks away and doesn't answer.

I catch up to her. "Martina, what's his name?"

She finally blurts out, "Blake Bermuda."

"Your grandfather is Principal Bermuda?" *How is Principal Bermuda her grandfather?*

She tries to outrun me, but I chase her through the grassy square. "Martina, wait!"

I catch her and grab onto her arm. She tries to pull away, but I hang on, and we stumble to the ground.

"What did you do that for?" she shouts, brushing the grass from her knee.

"I'm sorry, but you wouldn't stop. What do you mean, our principal is your grandfather?"

"What's to know? He is, that's all."

"Why didn't you tell us?"

"What difference does it make? He's your principal. He

cares more about your team than me. I'm just Martina, the only girl in Michigan to win the Piedmont Challenge—no big deal. Not like the five fabulous kids from Crimson—from his school—who won the Piedmont Challenge in New York."

I stare at her for a second, and I don't know what to say.

"Can I go now? My teammates are probably waiting for me to go to breakfast."

I look at the Michigan tree suite in front of me. I think of the four boys that she's been working with and living with all this time. I realize she probably has her own side of the tree suite, with the boys all bunked together on the other.

"Martina, wait."

But she doesn't wait. She walks inside her metal tree-house, the one that looks identical to ours on the outside. But the metal on hers doesn't seem to sparkle like ours. It just looks cold.

I stand up, dust the grass from my knees, and race back to my tree suite. Mare and Jillian are probably wondering where I am, or maybe they're just hogging the bathroom like usual. I stop to send them a message from my watch and see that they *are* looking for me—that Ander did talk to them. I tell them I'll be back soon and walk the rest of the way along the brick path.

I get it now. That's why Martina hates our team so much. Even at Camp Piedmont she hated us—from the very first day in line at Piedmont Chamber. She said we were *that team* from New York.

Our team must seem like it has everything. We've been getting all this attention from her grandpa, and she hasn't gotten any from him at all. He's been doing media blasts and putting us all over the news. I wonder how much of it she's been seeing. All this time, I wonder if she's been watching, wondering why he's making such a big deal about us and never once even talking about her. She's his own granddaughter, and he never told us—or anyone—that she won the Piedmont Challenge too.

No wonder she hates us so much.

I think about Grandma Kitty, how proud she's always been of me. I've always known that. I wonder how it would feel if she left me and went on to cheer for some other kids, acted like she wasn't my grandma anymore. But Grandma Kitty would never do that. She's always been there for me, and now I need to be there for her too. I have to tell my teammates about Martina. They are never going to believe it.

I walk past the Canadian tree suite. I need to tell my teammates everything else too. I need to tell them that I don't want to go on the Swirl and Spark Tour. I shouldn't have asked Ander to do it for me. Seraphina always tells us to be courageous, and I'm just being a coward by having him tell them. So I'll go back and explain it all myself. But my brain is swirling in a million directions, and now all I can think about is Martina, Principal Bermuda, and those four teammates of hers. Change of plan! I'm not going back to my tree suite, not yet.

I turn around and sprint back in the direction I came from. This time I just need to reach Martina.

I'm not sure what I'll do when I get to her tree suite. I haven't figured that part out yet. But I know I have to talk to her, or, at least, I have to try. When I get there, she's sitting on the front step, playing on her watch. She sees me and folds her arms across her chest. "What are you doing here?"

"I'm not sure," I say.

She looks at me and wrinkles her forehead.

"Can I sit here for a second?"

She shrugs.

We don't say anything for a long minute. Finally, I ask, "What's it like being on a team with four boys?"

She looks at me like I said something horrible. "It's awesome. I wouldn't want it any other way."

"That's good."

"Yeah, I don't have to share my room or the bathroom with anyone. It's perfect."

"Yeah, Mare and Jillian definitely take over our bathroom." *But I don't mind. I would hate being in my room alone.*

"Where are all the boys now?"

"They went to breakfast."

"Why didn't you go with them?"

"I wasn't hungry."

We sit there quietly for another long minute. Finally, I say, "I'm sorry that Principal Bermuda—I mean your grandpa—has been making such a big deal about all of us. I don't know why he is. And I don't know why he wouldn't have made a big deal about you too. I mean, he's *related* to you."

"I don't care anymore. I'm used to it."

"If it helps a little, we don't like him making such a big deal about us."

She shrugs. "It does."

"We're no different from any other team here. We just happen to be from the same school. But who cares about that anyway? All the schools in the whole state are exactly the same. We all study the exact same things. We all get numbers. We all dress the same. I don't really know why they give our schools names anyway. They may as well just number them too."

"I never thought about that before. It's the same for us in Michigan."

"So I don't know why Principal Bermuda acts like it's his doing that got us here. Because it's really not."

Martina looks at me. "I'm sorry I was such a jerk to your team. I'm sorry I made up that rumor about the results being fixed. No one was saying that. It was just me."

I know I should still be mad at her, but I'm not. "It's okay."

"No, it's not. I was jealous of all of you. First, I get stuck on a team with all those stupid boys who never include me in anything, and then I find out that five kids from my grandpa's school all win. And then he never even calls to say, 'Good job,' or 'I'm proud of you,' or anything. And then I see all of you getting along and laughing and having fun. I guess I just wanted to be on your team instead of mine."

My stomach twists. "But you said you liked your team."

"I lied."

"Oh. So what's wrong with them? Are they mean, or are they just annoying? Because Mare can be really hard to get along with, but she's not actually mean. Like when we all wanted to do a play to show our task solution and she didn't. At first we thought she was just being a brat to get her way. But then we talked to her and realized that she was really scared to perform in front of people."

"Seriously? I watched you guys at the Showcase Festival. She was really good. You all were."

"Thanks."

"I don't think the boys on my team are afraid of anything—except maybe Simpson. He acts like he's afraid of everyone."

"Are you nice to the boys?" I ask, and as soon as I do, I know I shouldn't have. Martina glares as me. But then she smiles a little.

"Not as nice as I could be, I guess."

I laugh. "It's hard for me to be nice to Mare sometimes too."

"Your team just seems so perfect."

"Well we aren't. It took us forever to even solve the Human Pretzel."

"You did that too?"

"Yes! And we were horrible at it the first time."

"We still can't solve that one."

"Try it again. Maybe you'll be better at it now."

"I don't know if the boys would want to."

"Maybe they'll do it just because they want to hang out with you."

"With me?"

"Well, yeah, you're a team, remember?"

"Yeah, we're supposed to be."

"Remember what Master Freeman said? 'The teams who form the greatest bonds have the greatest success,' or something like that."

"I don't remember him saying that. I guess I've been so mad at everything I've tuned most people out."

"I say try the Human Pretzel again. It's really fun."

"Okay, I will. Isn't your team looking for you?"

"Yeah, I should go back. I have to talk to them anyway."

"About what?"

"I'm going to tell them that even if we win, I don't want to go on the Swirl and Spark Tour."

"Why not?"

"Because my grandma's sick. I can't leave her for that

long."

"You could still talk to her through air screens though, or on the phone."

"It wouldn't be the same."

"You're crazy, Kia. If I had a chance to spend a whole year with teammates like yours, I would go. You're lucky. You have a grandma that cares about you. If my grandpa wanted to talk to me, even through an air screen, I'd be happy. I'd tell him all about my world-wide travels with my friends."

"I don't know. All I ever really wanted was to go to PIPS. If we skip the Swirl and Spark Tour, I can. That would make my grandma really proud. Maybe your team will make it, and then Principal Bermuda will realize what an idiot he's been. He'll be really proud of you then."

"I don't know. Maybe."

I stand up from the step. "Good luck in the competition, Martina. Maybe I'll see you at the dining hall. And thanks for making me feel better about my grandma."

She smiles. "You too, Kia. Thanks—for everything."

I make my way back to my tree suite, but my head is spinning. I don't know what to think of first. I have so much to tell my teammates, and we have our costumes to finish, and oh my god, the Opening Ceremony is tonight.

THE SILVER SWITCH

I CAN HEAR my teammates talking in the clubhouse. I walk around to find them gathered under the tree, working on their costumes.

"Kia! We heard about your grandma," says Jillian. "We're so sorry. Is she going to be okay?"

"I hope so," I say. "She crashed her aero-scooter."

"Ander told us," says Jax. "That's awful."

"Good morning, my Crimson Kids!" Seraphina appears with a box. "I have breakfast! Scrambled apples and oatmeal. Since you wouldn't go to the dining hall, I brought the dining hall to you."

I look at my team. "You guys didn't go to breakfast."

"Not without you, KK."

I can't believe my team would miss breakfast for me.

"Kia," says Seraphina. "I'm sorry about your grandma's accident. I really hope she's going to be okay."

"Me too."

"Go ahead and eat. I'm going back inside to gather the rest of your materials. We need to finish these costumes, pronto."

When she leaves, I motion for my team to come closer. "I have something big to tell you guys."

"What is it?" asks Jillian.

"It's big, really big, and you're never going to believe it."

My teammates drop their materials and gather around me.

"It's something about Principal Bermuda."

"Ugh, I don't want to hear anything else about Principal Backstabber."

"But you have to hear this, Mare."

"Fine, what?"

"He's Martina's grandfather."

"What?" Jillian replies. "No!"

"Witch Girl is Principal Backstabber's granddaughter?" says Mare in disbelief.

"No way!" says Ander.

"Where did you hear that?" asks Jax.

"She told me."

"She's totally making that up," says Mare.

"No, she's not. I talked to her about it myself. She's not lying, and that's why she hates us—or used to hate us. Because he never even congratulated her or told anyone she won the Piedmont Challenge."

"That's really low of him," says Ander.

Jax shakes his head. "Just when we thought he couldn't get any lower."

Seraphina arrives with more supplies, and we tell her about Martina. Her mouth hangs open. "That's unbelievable. I wonder if she'll ever reach out to him and tell him that she was here, that she made it all the way to Globals too."

"I don't think so. I think she hates him now just like we do."

We get back to work, but none of us say anything. I guess my teammates are as stunned by the news as I am. I pick up some yellow thread and a needle and make the first stitch on my poodle skirt, sewing the Velcro on the left side, near the hem. Then I take the felt poodle that I made last night and stick it right on top. Meanwhile, Jax works on his hippy shirt and Ander works on his bell-bottom pants.

Mare cuts into the neckline of her 80s sweatshirt. "Hey Kia, Ander said you don't want to go on the Swirl and Spark Tour."

I bite my nail. "Um, yeah, I'm thinking maybe going on the Swirl and Spark Tour isn't a great idea anymore. I mean, not all of us wanted to go in the beginning, like you, Mare, remember? And Jax, you weren't really sure either. So if we win, maybe we should just say no and let another team take our place."

"But why?" asks Jillian. "It would be so fabulous to travel the world together! Why are you changing your mind now?"

"Because my grandma's hurt, and she needs me. I can't leave her for a whole year."

Mare shakes her head. "But I thought your grandma was all about the Piedmont Challenge. Don't you think she would want you to go if we won?"

I shrug.

"Why are we talking about this now?" asks Jax. "We haven't even competed yet."

"Because!" says Mare. "If all of us don't really want to win, then we won't try our hardest. Isn't that what you said, Kia, when you tried to convince me to go?"

I look at my fingernail nubs. "Yeah, but it's different now that my grandma is in the hospital."

"So you'd bail on all of us now? After all this?"

I don't know what to say to her. I'd want to go with my team, but I'd want to go to PIPS too. At least then I could see my grandma once in a while. It's only eight hours away, not the other side of the world. I don't want to let everyone down, but no matter what I choose, someone will be mad at me. "I don't know!" I blurt out and run out of the clubhouse.

Seraphina follows me to the front of the tree suite, and I suddenly feel stupid again for storming off. "I have to go inside and get something. Can you wait for me on the front step?" She doesn't wait for my answer, but instead scurries up the metal tree suite steps with her heels tapping along the way. Soon she reappears and sits beside me.

I can feel her staring at me. "What do you think it will be like at PIPS, Kia?"

I sit up straight. "I think it'll be awesome. We'll get to build our inventions—the Ancestor App and the Satellite Spectacles."

"Could any of the other kids at PIPS build them—or are you the only ones? Since you thought up the ideas?"

I shake my head and laugh. "No, we don't even know how to build stuff yet. They would teach us."

"That's true. What about the Underwater Bubble Bike?"

"You know about that?"

"And your sixty-six other inventions."

"How do you know about those?"

She smirks. "I have my ways."

"Okay, so yeah. Hopefully we can build those too, why?"

"Kia, don't you understand? You're smart and so are your teammates. But so are the hundreds of kids who are here. Any of you, and all of you, can go to PIPS and learn how to build the inventions you've thought up."

"So you don't think we should bother going to PIPS?"

"I didn't say that. What I'm wondering though, is if you were lucky enough to place in the top three tomorrow, and have the opportunity to go on the tour, would that be a good choice for you?"

"I don't know. Maybe."

"What do you think the point of the Swirl and Spark Tour is?"

"To show kids our cool inventions."

"No, it's not."

"It's not?"

"It's true you would show them your cool inventions, but your role would be to *inspire* kids to do what you've done—to think more, work hard, and dream big."

"But anyone could do that."

"Could they? What do you think kids would rather see? A demonstration of an invention by kids in lab coats, or a play showing them a real-life entertaining scenario of an invention in action?"

My stomach flips over. I picture kids all over the world watching us do our plays.

"Your team is special, Kia. What you've done together is special. You are the ones who thought to demonstrate your invention in the form of a play. By yourselves you're great, but together you're spectacular. You could be the ones who inspire other kids to be spectacular too."

I suddenly feel important. Like I could do important

things.

"But I know you have your grandma to consider, so you should think about what you really want. If PIPS is really what you want, right now, and that's your choice, then no one will be mad if that's what you decide."

I picture Grandma Kitty lying in her hospital bed. I hate that picture in my head.

"You know, Kia. When we spoke as a whole team about the results of the Piedmont Challenge, there was something I didn't tell you. I didn't want you to know, unless it was absolutely necessary, but maybe now is a good time."

That sounds strange. "What is it?"

"I told you that you scored the highest in Swirl and Spark Recall, and that right after that your next highest score was Math."

"I remember, and I was kind of bummed out because Swirl and Spark Recall isn't even a category."

"Maybe not, but that doesn't mean it isn't of great importance. I may have told you that you scored very high in that task, but that was not the whole story."

"It wasn't?"

"Not exactly. In the Swirl and Spark Recall category, students are awarded triple points to their score. That way students who are creative will be awarded appropriately for being . . . well—creative."

"That makes sense."

"Many children, even with their score being tripled, don't score very high in that task. On the other hand, some children score very high in that task because their score is tripled."

I nod. "I get it."

"But for you it was different."

"It was?"

"Yes, it was. Your score in the Swirl and Spark Recall task was the highest in all of New York State—even without being tripled."

"It was?"

Seraphina smiles. "Yes. You didn't need it to be tripled in order for you to win."

"I scored *that* high?"

"In solving that task, you did something that none of the other children in the state did. You understood, whether you knew it at the time or not, the essence of the Piedmont Challenge."

"What do you mean, the *essence* of the Piedmont Challenge?"

"You solved the task using all six categories—in the most creative and thought-provoking way possible."

"I did?"

"I bet you could tell me how you did it—how you used skills from all six categories to solve that task."

I think about that for a second. "Let me see. I thought up a poem about mermaids and sang it. I also wore my belt, socks, and shoes like a costume."

"So you used skills from what category for that?"

"That would be Art Forms."

"What else?"

"I talked about teaching my friends the language of the water world. That would fall under Communications."

"Yes, what else?"

"I talked about water, which we study in Earth and Space, and I talked about teaching kids how to breathe under water . . . oh and squids are in there too! The kids play soccer with them."

Seraphina laughs. "Of course!"

"So sports would fall under Human history, right?"

"Right."

"I also said something about submarines and friendship, so I guess those would fall under Human history too."

"They would. What about Math and New Technology?"

"Well, I talked about giving my million new friends water gliders so they can swim with me, so I guess I'd have to calculate how many fins they need so that would show Math skills . . . and water gliders are an invention that make humans able to swim deep down in the ocean. That's New Technology!"

Seraphina tucks her foot underneath her. "Wow, you did use skills from all six categories. What was the question you had to answer?"

"'If you could be anything else besides yourself, what would you be and why?'"

"And what did you say?"

"I said I would be a mermaid, so I could swim with my new friends all summer—and I acted it out and sang."

Her eyes get big. "No wonder you won this." She opens her hand and a shiny metal light switch shimmers in the sunlight. "I was going to give this to you after the completion of the entire Piedmont Competition, but I want you to have it now. On behalf of the Piedmont Organization, this is for you, Kia. This Silver Switch represents your superb ability to access information from all six categories and turn on your creative thoughts with ease . . . like the flip of a switch."

I take the small metal switch from her hand. Seraphina's smiling her big purple lipstick smile. "Congratulations."

I bite my lip. "I won this?"

"You did. See those tiny stars engraved on it?"

I rub my finger over the surface and a smile breaks free. "They sparkle."

"Just like you."

I flip up the switch. "It even turns on."

"Well, of course!"

I close my hand around it. "I can't believe I won this. But why did you give it to me now though?"

"You'll have a big decision to make if your team places in the top three in this competition. I thought you should have all the facts as you consider what's important to you."

She leans in to hug me. "Congratulations, Kia. Being awarded the Silver Switch is a very big deal."

"Thanks, Seraphina. I'm really happy I have it, but is it okay if we don't tell the rest of the team I got it? I don't want them to feel bad or anything."

"That's entirely up to you, but I promise I won't tell them."

"Thanks."

"I'm going to go check on the others. I'll leave you alone for a few minutes, but we need you back soon to finish up your costume. You don't want to wear a poodle skirt with no poodle, do you?"

I shake my head.

"Oh, and Kia, one more thing. Have you thought at all about your balloon message? Maybe that will help."

My balloon message? I forgot all about that.

Our true dreams are sometimes different than what we wish for. Have the courage to make your true dream come true.

I try to think of what my true dream is. It's always been

to win the Piedmont Challenge so I could go to PIPS and build my sixty-seven inventions. I think back to the Piedmont Challenge—and all the tasks I solved in each category. I think back to the day I solved the Swirl and Spark Recall task, when I was just trying to answer the judge's question as honestly and creatively as I could.

"If you could be anyone else besides yourself, who would you be and why?"

My mind jumps all over the place before an idea comes to me. I rush to ask, "Can I use props in my answer?"

"Yes, as long as you do not move outside the taped off area."

"Can I sing part of my answer?"

"Yes."

I reach for my shoes. The straps are tricky, but I manage to get them off. I set them down, take off my knee socks, and unfasten my belt. I tug it from the loops of my skirt, wrap it twice around my legs, and then buckle it back together. I pull one sock over each arm. I lay on the floor sideways and I prop myself up on my elbow. A tune from a TV commercial pops into my head . . . If I can just change the words—

Ding!

"If I could be anything, I would be a mermaid. I would invite human kids to spend their summer vacation with me. First, I'd speak to them in the language of the water world, which of course is made up of songs like this:

"Summer break is here at last and you need something new,
Let me show you where I live and all that we can do.
I'll teach you how to use your mind to breathe first out then in,
And give you water gliders, that work just like real fins.

We'll dive deep down into the sea and find a sunken ship,
Or play some soccer with the squids and take a submarine trip."

When I'm done singing, I slide across the floor like I'm swimming and hold up my shoes. "Then, I'd present the human kids these water gliders. They'd put them on and together we'd explore all summer. I'd have a million new friends, and that's why I'd choose to be a mermaid if I could."

I stare at the sparkly silver switch in my hand. So what is my true dream? I can't be a mermaid, teaching humans to swim underwater with me, so I guess that's out. But then I jump to my feet and stick the switch in my pocket. Why am I trying to figure this out now? We haven't even placed in the top three yet. We haven't even competed yet! What is wrong with me? My team is counting on me. Besides, the only way Satellite Spectacles will be built is if we win. So many people are counting on us—people like Grandma Kitty, who wouldn't have crashed if she had been wearing them. So even though people don't know about it yet, we have to try our hardest for them.

I run behind the tree suite to my team and plop myself inside the log area. "Okay, guys. I'm sorry I was such a jerk before. I'm going to try my hardest when we compete because the Satellite Spectacles have to win. We can figure the rest out later."

My teammates look relieved. "Okay, good," says Ander. "Now, can you help me with this purple shirt? It's perfect for my disco outfit, but it doesn't fit."

I take the shirt and hold it up to him. "We could pin it, I guess. No one would notice the pins under the jacket.

But wait, where's my poodle skirt? I still need to attach the poodle!"

Mare holds it up. "I did it for you."

"You did?"

She smiles her Mare smile. "Well, actually, I did it for the poodle."

THE FLAGS

WE STAND TOGETHER outside le Stadium de Creativite. The campus is buzzing with sounds of hundreds of kids and their preceptors waiting to get inside the back entrance. I smooth out my poodle skirt and pull my ponytail tight.

"Be careful, Kia!" shouts Jillian. "You'll squish your bow!"

I adjust the scarf around my neck and make sure the knot is on the side. "I am being careful, Jillian."

She scratches her forehead underneath her sparkly headband. "Gosh, this thing is itchy!"

"I thought you always said, 'Glamour may be painful, but it's a necessity'?"

"I never said that, but that's good, Kia. I'm stealing it from you."

Ander saunters over to us, wearing his leisure suit from the 1970s. "Like the purple shirt?"

"Definitely," I say. "You can't even see the pins."

"And how about my man, Jax, here? Nice wig, huh?" Jax stands tall wearing a striped poncho, a long wig, and a headband tied around his head. I stifle a laugh and tell him how awesome he looks.

Mare smirks. "I could totally rock the 80s style." Her hair is teased so big I hardly recognize her, and her sweatshirt, ripped at the neck, is hanging off one shoulder. "Like my fingerless gloves?"

"I love your whole outfit, and Seraphina, I love your dress!" says Jillian. "You look so pretty."

Ander extends his arm to Seraphina. "I agree. Do you need an escort, Madam?"

Seraphina laughs. "Ander, you're from the 1970s. You weren't even a thought in 1910."

Gregor strolls over to us in a pin-striped gangster suit, white-and-black shiny shoes, and a fedora. He tips the fedora and says, "Now, these shoes, my friends, are called chaps. Watch and learn." He spins on his heel and bows.

Ander steps back. "Whoa, Gregor, I'm impressed!"

"Now, listen up everyone," says Seraphina. "When the Opening Ceremony procession begins, all the teams from around the world will be walking into the stadium single file. You're going to be walking with the other kids from the United States. You'll march in order of the time period you were assigned. The Pennsylvania team will go first, dressed in costumes depicting the 1700s. They will carry the American flag. Next will be the Idaho team dressed from the 1800's. You'll follow them in your costumes from the 1900s. The Texas team will follow you dressed like people who lived in the 2000's, and the Michigan team will bring up the rear wearing costumes of the future, the 2100s."

Jillian's eyes get big. "I didn't know we were *all* dressing in a different time period. This is beyond fabulous."

While we wait for the doors to open, Maelle rushes over to me. "Kia! I was hoping to see you, to wish you luck!"

"Thanks! You too."

"I know our chances are not very good. There are so very many teams competing tomorrow. But I really hope that if our team does not win, then yours does."

"You do?"

"Yes, because then we will see each other again. If we win, we can see you when we visit the United States of America. And if you win, we can see you when you visit us in France!"

"You're right!"

"So I will be wishing for your team to do well."

"Okay, I'll be wishing for that also."

She hurries back to her team as the doors open. We inch our way into the tunnel of le Stadium de Creativite, and there must be a million people inside. We search for the other American teams and find the Michigan team first. My teammates glance at me. I feel like I made some progress with Martina this morning, but I'm not sure the rest of them are ready to forgive her. She smiles and says, "Wow, you guys look really good. What century are you?"

"We're the Twentieth Century," says Jillian. "1901 through 2000."

"That's so cool. We're from 2101 and up."

"How did you know what costumes to make, since that's in the future?" I ask.

"We had to brainstorm."

"How did that go?" asks Mare. "Did you make Simpson over there do it for you?"

We look at Simpson standing with the other boys.

Strange, he's not off by himself this time. They look like a team of the future wearing colorful, shimmery space suits.

I shoot Mare a dirty look, but she just shrugs.

"No, we actually all worked together. We didn't want Simpson to do all the work. He's done enough. I helped the boys make their costumes after we did the Human Pretzel. That was Kia's suggestion."

Her teammates walk over to us, and one of them says, "Are you guys the ones who play the Human Pretzel? That was kind of cool. We did crappy the first few times, but we got it after a while."

My teammates look at me. I'm as shocked as they are.

"Maybe after the competition, before we all go home, we can mix up all the US teams and try it together," says Martina.

Mare shrugs. "Yeah, okay."

I smile at Martina. "I love your costume, by the way. You look like you might live on the moon!"

"My preceptor helped me find these old-fashioned hoola hoops. I used duct tape to hold them in place around my skirt. I feel like I could fly."

Seraphina gathers us together. "Okay, listen up again, everyone! You'll enter the stadium in a procession, but Master Freeman won't be announcing your country. This isn't very formal, it's more of a celebration this time—a celebration of all your amazing ideas and of all of your hard work. So when the line starts moving, just follow the person in front of you. But stay with your teams, so we can keep track of all of you."

Jax gets in line behind the last boy from Idaho. Mare steps in next, then Jillian, then Ander, then me. I guess I don't mind going last. I like seeing my teammates in front of me, leading the way.

We walk into the music-filled stadium, which feels more like a concert than a ceremony. Ander turns around. "We're here, KK. We're really here. We made it to the Global Championships!" I smile and lean out to look ahead. The teams in front of us in the center of the stadium have created a swirl formation, almost like a carnival lollipop. Colorful flags from every country dot the stadium floor. And that's when it really hits me that kids who've traveled here from all over the world are competing against us. We are definitely not guaranteed to place in the top three. Not even close.

We take our place at the end of the swirl and sit down. Ander is on one side of me and Becca from Texas is on the other. She looks nervous. I smile at her so she'll know that all of this will be fine—that we won't mess up our Global Solutions tomorrow and that we'll solve the Swirl and Spark task easily, but I'm really not sure of that either. We could all totally choke.

Master Freeman walks up to a podium and I shove that thought out of my head. Grandma Kitty always tells me that worrying is just imagining the worst outcome. I definitely don't want to imagine the worst outcome.

"Welcome to the 2071 Piedmont Global Championships!" A spotlight shines on him, and the whole place erupts. I look around at the thousands of people gathered. My parents are here somewhere. My sister is here. My brother is here. But Grandma Kitty isn't. She's not even awake. And I feel like a Thanksgiving wishbone, pulled in two directions. Being here at Globals is a dream, but I feel like I should be at the hospital with Grandma Kitty too, because if she heard my voice, maybe she would wake up. I just hope that while I'm here, she's getting better.

"Parents, family members, teachers, judges, and members of le Universite de Creativite, we at the Piedmont Organization are honored to welcome you to our international competitive event. For the last two weeks, the world's brightest children have been working to solve the Piedmont Global Task. For the next two days, teams will present their solutions to our judging staff. They will also solve a mystery task in our Swirl and Spark Recall event. Those two scores, together with their scores from the Showcase Festival will be added together and then tallied. The winners, will be announced Saturday evening at the Global Stars Award Ceremony. Teams, we wish you the best of luck and look forward to bearing witness to your inspired ideas, boundless creativity, and unmatched imagination!"

With that, the music returns, and we march out of the stadium. When we get outside into the cool evening air, Gregor and Seraphina leave to get our competition times, and we look around for our families. Ryne taps me on the shoulder and yells, "Boo!"

"Nice costume, Kia," says Malin. I turn around to see my sister smiling. "So, I saw all the boys here. Any cute ones to tell me about?"

"Still no, Malin. I've been busy solving my tasks."

"Well, I saw cute boys in the crowd. They were probably from Mexico, Italy, Australia . . . "

My dad and mom jog over, and I hug them both. My mom checks out my costume. "Oh, Sweetie, I missed you so much. You look so pretty dressed as a 50s sock hop!"

I grin. "I made the poodle skirt myself—well, with a little help from a Costume Copier—and Mare."

"That Opening Ceremony was impressive," says Dad.

"Even more so than the one at Camp Piedmont. Seeing the flags from all over the world. That was really great."

Gregor and Seraphina drive up in the aero-cart. "Hi everybody. We have your competition times."

"Oh, what are they?" I ask.

"I'm not sure this is what you would have chosen, but you have both task assignments tomorrow. You have Swirl and Spark Recall in the morning and your Global Task Presentation in the afternoon."

"Oh man," says Ander. "No break tomorrow, huh?"

"What time do we need to wake up for Swirl and Spark Recall?" asks Mare.

"Fairly early," says Seraphina. "We need to report at nine o'clock, so as soon as we get back to our tree suite, off to bed you go!"

"Then that's our cue to leave," says Dad. "Good luck, everyone. We'll be cheering for you!"

I hug my family and jump into the aero-cart with my team. We fly back to our tree suite and get ready for bed. *How in the world am I going to fall asleep tonight?*

THE SWIRL AND SPARK CARDS

WE STAND OUTSIDE the Swirl and Spark task room, waiting like statues. I take a deep breath, like the kind Grandma Kitty always tells me to take. And then I do it again. I hear a beep coming from my watch, then more beeps coming from my teammates' watches too.

I look at mine and there's a message from Principal Bermuda.

"Good luck, team. The town of Crimson Heights is rooting for you. When you solve your tasks remember that NEW YORK is number one. Make sure you put it on top."

"Ugh," says Mare. "It's him again."

I click off my watch because I can't throw it across the room. "And now I'll be thinking about him when we're supposed to be solving our task."

Ander shakes his head. "Leave it to him to mess with

our heads right before we walk into the room."

"He can't hurt us here," says Jax. "Just forget about him."

"I just want to get this over with," says Jillian.

Me too. But I have a bad feeling about Principal Bermuda.

Our team is called by a judge with a jester hat almost like the one Ander wears in our play. Ander grins. Maybe it's a good sign. We walk silently into the room and take our places around a tall table which sits on a raised platform. The oval platform is surrounded by tables of judges, all staring at us with their computers and buzzers ready.

"Good morning, New York. Welcome to Swirl and Spark Recall. As you have been instructed, your job is to solve this task as a team. I will read the task to you, and the other judges will be looking to see that as you solve this task, none of the rules are broken. If you hear a buzzer sound, that means you have broken a rule and been assessed a penalty. Do you understand?"

We nod.

He nods back. "Your two-part task is as follows: There are many teams here at the Global Championships and you have met many children from all over the world. As you've learned about these different places, you may yearn to travel to one of them, or even yearn to travel back home. First, name the place your team would most like to travel to. You must agree on what that place is, and then, as a group, tell a story about that place. You'll also nominate one team member to begin the story.

"The procedure for completing this task is as follows: The first part, where you decide on the place, must be done in complete silence. If anyone speaks, your team will be assessed a penalty. You each have blank cards in front of you and a pencil. You will take turns suggesting places to travel to by writing one word on the card and placing it into the center, forming a pile. You may only add to the pile on your turn. You will take turns doing so in a clockwise fashion until you have all agreed on the same place. You will then do the same thing for which team member will be starting the story. Remember to choose a place you can tell a creative story about, and lead with the person you feel will get you started in the right direction. When you are satisfied that you have agreed upon a place and on a person, one teammate will ring this bell. Please be aware that the more time it takes you to ring the bell, the lower your score. When time begins, I will say go.

"When you have finished, I will check both your piles. I'm looking to see the place that is on top of the first pile, and the team member that is on top of the second. I will also check to see that all five of you have selected the same ones. Now please prepare to begin."

We pick up our cards and pencils.

"Go!"

We scribble places on our cards. Mare slides hers into the center first. It says New York. Of course it does. Mare is obsessed with New York City. Jax is beside her so he goes next. He crosses out Texas and writes New York too. Okay, I get this. We have to agree really fast so we'll all just pick New York. Ander gets it too. He crosses out Switzerland and writes New York. Jillian makes a mad face, crosses out Paris, and writes New York. Ander is bouncing in his seat. I've already crossed out Australia and written New York. I'm about to place my card on the pile, but something feels wrong. We're putting New York on the top of the pile. I think of my watch—the messages we got on our watches!

Principal Bermuda! Wait a minute . . . Is it possible he knew ahead of time that we'd have this question? If he did, then we can't use New York. That would be cheating. If the Piedmont people are tracking his messages, they'll see that he signaled us and that we used New York anyway. I know we'd get disqualified. But how do I tell my team?

They're all staring at me, pleading at me with wide open eyes. I scribble out New York and hope that they get what I'm trying to say.

Bermuda.

They stare at me like they can't believe I'm messing this up. Mare glares. I know she's wondering why I would write that. I silently plead with her. She crosses out New York and writes Bermuda. My teammates all do the same, and on their turns, they place their cards on top of the pile. Then when it gets back to me, I write *Kia* and start the second pile. I need to be the one to start our story, to explain why we're picking Bermuda. I don't think my teammates will be able to start the story I'm thinking of. They each quickly write *Kia*, and on their turns, each of them places it on top of mine. Ander reaches across the table and slams the bell.

The judge picks up our cards. "Okay, New York. It looks like your place is Bermuda and your story will begin with Kia. You have one minute to tell your story. Your story must include a beginning, middle, and end, a problem and a solution. It must also contain the name of the place you chose and the name of the person you chose."

Ding!

I sit up straight. "Once upon a time, a little girl named Kia traveled to a beautiful place full of sunshine, pink sand, and pastel-colored roof tops, where her pen pal was waiting to meet her for the first time. But as she traveled the sandy path to her house, a very bad man popped out from behind a large rock. He had a plump belly and greasy, slicked back hair." I turn to Mare so she can go next and hope that she can think of some way to continue the story.

"The man tossed a marble to the girl and told her that the marble was magical and would lead her to a place where she would be famous and have all the gold and silver in the world." Mare turns to Jax.

Jax sits up straight. "But Kia tossed the marble back to the man and said, 'I don't want to be famous or have silver or gold. I want to meet my friend.'"

Jillian continues. "The man wouldn't give up though. He stood in her way and waved the marble in front of her. Finally she said, 'Sir, you can't spoil Bermuda for me. My pen pal has told me so much about its beauty and culture. I want to learn it from her—first hand.'"

Ander continues speaking as quickly as I've ever heard him. "So you can keep your marble and offers of riches and fame. Offer it to someone else. I came to Bermuda for adventure and friendship. That's all. The End.'"

Mare smashes the bell. Done!

I let out a breath.

The judge dismisses us and we file silently out of the room. Jillian squeals. "Oh my god you guys, that was hard!"

"KK, what was up with that?" asks Ander. "We wasted all those seconds when we switched to Bermuda. We lost points for not using New York!"

"I think Principal Bermuda may have gotten the question ahead of time. I think he was trying to give us a clue when he sent us that message on our watches. He was trying to help us cheat!"

Jillian gasps. "He said be sure to put New York on top."

"I don't know about that," says Jax.

"Kia might be right," says Mare. "There is a chance he was trying to signal us. Why else would he have sent that message right before we walked in the room? If the Piedmont officials suspected he was, we would have been disqualified."

"Besides," says Jillian, "our story was pretty good."

"It was pretty good, actually," says Mare. "If we picked New York, I was just going to talk about the Statue of Liberty or something."

"I'm so mad at him," I say. "Why can't he just let us compete and leave us alone? Why can't he bug Martina's team?"

"Just forget about him, okay?" says Ander. "We solved it without his help anyway. Hopefully we didn't lose too many points from when we switched our answer. Let's go find Seraphina and Gregor and tell them how it went. They're probably wondering what's taking us so long."

FLIPPING THE SILVER SWITCH

SERAPHINA AND GREGOR are waiting when we get to the preceptor's lounge. About twenty other preceptors are sitting there too, waiting for their teams. Gregor notices us first. "Ah, there you are."

Seraphina jumps up from her chair. "How was it?"

We pull them into a corner. "We did okay," says Ander.

Seraphina folds her hands. "But . . .?"

"But we could have done a little better if we didn't have to change our answer at the last minute."

"Why did you have to do that? What was your task?"

"It had two parts," I say. "First, we had to name a place where we'd all like to go, but we couldn't talk, and we had to use cards, and then we had to tell a story about it."

"That sounds hard," Seraphina replies.

"It was," says Jillian.

"But I think we did okay," says Jax.

"I think we pulled it off, even if we did almost choke."

"What happened?"

"Okay, so can I tell them?" asks Ander. But he doesn't wait for us to respond. "Right before we went into the task room, we each got a watch message from Principal Bermuda."

Gregor shakes his head. "Him again."

"Yeah, he said that New York is the best team, and today we had to be sure to put it on top."

"That does sound like something he would say."

"Anyway, we thought he was wishing us luck and that's it, but when we got the task, we all put the New York card on top, and at the last second, Kia picked Bermuda, and since we all had to agree in as little time as we could, we all picked Bermuda then too."

"Because I think he was trying to give us the answer ahead of time, and I didn't want to get us disqualified if he was, so it was the only way I could think of to tell everyone else not to pick New York."

"I don't know if he was trying to signal you, but if he was, you surely could have been disqualified. The Piedmont Organization does monitor those things."

"But our story was good," says Jillian. "It was about Principal Bermuda."

We laugh. "Well, sort of!" I say.

"That's great because it's one third of your score. It will be added to your Showcase Festival score and then that will be added to the last task score," says Gregor.

"Yes, the Global Task—and it's just a little while away," says Seraphina. "We better head over to the Imagination Centre so you can get ready."

And just like that, we forget about Swirl and Spark

Recall and shift our focus to our skit and the Satellite Specs. We step outside into the warm breeze together and make our way through the campus. Ander and I walk side by side. He's practically bouncing on his toes. "So, KK, one more task to go. One more task to present to the judges—ever."

My stomach butterflies wake up. "I didn't think about it like that."

"It kind of stinks. I like being Freddie Dinkleweed."

"I like being Little Girl too."

"You know . . . if we place in the top three, we get to keep performing our play. Crimson Catropolis will live on and on."

"I know."

"Wouldn't that be awesome?"

"Yeah, it would."

"Even better than being at PIPS."

"I know what you're trying to do."

"What am I trying to do?"

"You want to know if I've changed my mind."

"I am good, huh?"

I smirk at him. "Yeah, you're the best."

"Well?"

"I don't know, Ander. I'm going to try my hardest—as hard as I possibly can—to win, really I am. Because I really *might* want to go on the tour. Besides, I wouldn't even know how to mess up on purpose anyway. That would be even harder than trying my best."

"When are you going to decide then?"

"Soon, I hope."

"I hope so too."

I try to put what happens *after* the competition out

of my head, to focus on competing today, but when we walk into our final task room, I'm sure I'll be looking for Grandma Kitty and I know she won't be there. I just wish she could send me a sign, something that tells me I can do this without her. I mean I know I can perform just fine, but I'm not sure I can perform like I did at Camp Piedmont. Not when she's lying in a hospital bed unable to talk to me.

We drag our props out from a small corner of the prep room and set them up for when we compete. We have an hour until we start, enough time to practice a few more times and get changed into our costumes. I inspect the syncing box, its bright colors and shiny button. The C5 symbol is slightly off center, but I don't think the judges will notice. I pick up the Satellite Spectacles and hope that they work when it's show time.

I look at the C5 button again, closer this time. I like having a symbol for us, just us. I think about what the other teams said, about none of them having a symbol, and I wonder why that is. I wish we had thought to ask more teams if they had one too. I mean, why would Andora give us one and no one else? I mean, she wouldn't. There's no favoritism in this camp.

Oh my god! She wouldn't.

But Principal Bermuda would.

"Guys, come here!" I yell and quickly gather everyone around me. "This is bad. This is really bad!" I feel myself freaking out. I can't get the words out fast enough.

"Kia, what's wrong?" asks Seraphina.

"The symbol, the C5 symbol! We can't use it!"

"Why not?" asks Mare.

"The same reason we couldn't use New York!"

My teammates look at me with blank stares, but then

they get it.

Mare puts her hands over her face. "You think Principal Bermuda sent us the symbol, don't you?"

Jax shakes his head. "This is great. Just great."

"What are you all talking about?" asks Gregor.

"We got these packages from Andora with invitations for the bonfire."

"Yes, I know."

"We also got that symbol. It was inside the box, with instructions to add it to our team solution somehow."

"We didn't hear about any symbol," says Gregor. "We thought it was just a nice symbol one of you had from back home."

"No," I say, "and none of the other teams got symbols, and we couldn't figure out why. But it makes sense now. Principal Bermuda has been trying to create buzz about our team, any way he can."

"I know he has," says Seraphina. "He knows there will be photos taken of your inventions after the Global Championships are over. He probably wants to advertise that your team wasn't just from the USA, not just from New York, but from Crimson Elementary."

"He's such a rat!" says Mare. "I hate that guy so much!"

"So we have to take the button off!" I say. "We can't have any outside help with our task. He's the one who told us to use it."

Mare walks around the room. "What are we going to do? We have to compete in like an hour."

"Less than an hour," says Gregor.

"But we can't just rip it off," says Jax. "Our syncing box will look awful and won't power up or activate without the metal symbol. We need it to trigger the action."

We pace the room. "I knew this was too good to be true. We have another really important invention to show the judges, and maybe even the whole world, and now it won't work at all. What good is our idea if we can't show it to the judges? This is our only chance. We have to make it work. We have to think of something."

Ander grabs a pen from the table and starts tapping it. "Okay, so we need to break the C5 symbol off, find another metal object, and solder it in place."

"That's all?" asks Mare. "Oh good. I thought this was going to be a problem. We have no cutting tools for metal, we have no other metal object, and we have no soldering tool. Not a problem at all."

"We packed our craft kit, remember?" says Jillian. "It has all our extra fabric and stuff. I'm sure the tools are in there too. Maybe there's even a small metal piece we could use."

"Great idea, Jillian," says Seraphina.

We scramble to the craft kit and rummage through the glue, duct tape, fabric, thread, and glitter. "Here's a cutter thing!" says Jillian. We keep looking, but there's no solder tool and no metal object.

I bite my thumb nail. "How much time do we have?"

"Forty-five minutes," says Gregor.

I think as hard as I can, but I feel myself starting to panic. There has to be something we can use. "Come on, guys, we have to think of something!"

Seraphina frowns. "We can't help you. I'm sorry. You're on your own with this."

"It's hopeless!" says Jillian.

"No, it's not," says Seraphina. "You're here for a reason. You're smart and creative—the best in New York State. That means something. You can't give up. You can do this. I know you can."

She's right. We are the best in New York. The best in New York State. *Ohmygodohmygodohmygod!*

"I have it!" I say. "I have something we can use!" I pull the silver switch out of my pocket.

"What is that?" asks Ander.

"It's a silver switch."

"Where did you get that?" asks Mare.

I look at Seraphina and smile. "A friend gave it to me."

Jax looks it over. "That would work if we had the solder tool."

"Ugh!" yells Ander. "But we don't."

"We don't need it," says Mare. "We can use this." She holds up a roll of red duct tape.

"Will that work?" I ask.

"Sure," says Jax. We just need the wire to touch the metal. We can attach the post from the switch to the wire with the duct tape."

"We can slip it over the hole we made for the C5 symbol," says Ander.

"The switch actually flips up and down too," I say. "So can we make it flip to activate?"

"Let's try," says Jax.

We gather close around the table, cutting the C5 symbol off the box, and then ripping duct tape and securing the silver switch in place. While we do, Gregor examines the C5 symbol. "Just as I thought," he says.

"What?" asks Seraphina.

"It looks like a tracking device. He was planning on tracking these kids."

"Are you serious?"

"Then he probably already has," says Jax. "He's probably

been watching us."

Gregor looks closer. "On second thought, I don't think he has. This is a very primitive picture taking device. It appears as though it has been taking pictures of your team. But in order for him to get the pictures, he needs the symbol to be in his possession so he can develop them. I'm fairly certain he was planning to use the pictures upon your return to generate even more buzz."

"Yeah," says Ander. "He was probably going to sell secret pictures of the Crimson Five to whoever wanted them."

Mare secures the last piece of duct tape. "It should work now, just like the symbol did. But this time, we have to flip the silver switch instead of pushing the C5 button."

"Do we have time to try it?" asks Jillian.

Seraphina looks at her watch. "Oh no! You need to report in ten minutes, and you're not even in your costumes. There isn't time to try it again."

Ander laughs. "We got this Seraphina. Don't worry. We just recreated our syncing box. Heading back to Crimson Catropolis, even if we do have an untested silver switch, will be a breeze."

What, is he kidding?

We grab our costume bags, race to the bathroom, and change as quickly as we can. I put my hair in pigtails and add the yellow ribbons. I look at myself in the mirror and hope that I won't forget my lines. I hope and hope and hope that the silver switch works. But most of all, I hope Grandma Kitty is okay so I can tell her all about this when I get home. I make a silent wish that I'll hear from her when all of this is over.

We roll the table full of props down the hallway. My

team has serious looks on their faces, and I know we need a pep talk. But my heart is thumping too fast to give one. My watch rattles. My teammates glare at me. "Sorry! I'll turn it off."

I look down to see who it is, and my mom's face is smiling back at me.

Why is she messaging me? She should be inside the presentation room. Maybe something worse has happened to Grandma Kitty!

Hi Baby Girl. You were probably hoping for a message from Grandma Kitty before you compete, and I'm sorry she couldn't give you one. But I'm going to tell you what she would be telling you if she could: She's going to be fine and if you go out in front of those judges and do what you do best, with that wonderful team of yours, you'll win—in all the ways that count. Mark my words.

The screen goes blank. I blink back my tears. And now I know what I have to do. I have to win for Grandma Kitty. She would want me to.

We walk into the task room, and I see Mom, Dad, Malin, and Ryne in the row behind the judges. I smile at my mom and she smiles back. I see the judges smiling too. This is weird. They don't look as stern as they usually do. Is this a trick? But then I realize that maybe it's because we've all come this far already, and that's a really far way to come.

We take our places and I skip out from behind the prop table. My nerves fade away in an instant and I belt out my lines so the back of the room can hear me. I skip and I sing and I become Little Girl again, this time a little girl who is able to use her imagination and see things in the world more clearly than anyone else. A little girl who has found a way for people to see things and people they never saw before with a little help from a re-imagined invention.

Soon, as Jax waves his cape near the table, I step toward the syncing box and flip the silver switch. The lights inside the box glow, the lights on the table glow, and the screen behind me swirls. I open the box, and there they are . . . the Satellite Specs! The audience and the judges watch and see what I see, our invention that might just change the world.

The audience's applause fills the room as we wrap up our finale song and stand there like statues, waiting to be judged, analyzed, and graded. I wish it didn't matter what the judges thought. I wish this wasn't our last Piedmont task. I wish we could do all of this for fun. I wish I could show other kids who don't get to go to Camp Piedmont or to the Global Championships how much fun it is to make stuff . . . especially the kids who think my ideas are weird, like most of the kids at Crimson.

THE BREAKNECK STAIRS

SERAPHINA BARGES INTO our tree chamber, waking us up earlier than usual. "Come on my Crimson Girls! Wake up! We're going on an adventure!"

I peek out from under my blanket. "What are we doing?"

"The Global Stars Award Ceremony isn't until tonight. You didn't think we were going to sleep all day waiting for the results, did you?"

Mare groans. "I did."

"Drink these breakfast shakes and get dressed. Gregor and I will be waiting out front."

We get ready as fast as we can and pile into the aero-cart. The boys sit in the back seat, and the girls and I squish into the middle one. "Can you at least tell us where we're going?" asks Ander.

"Young Ander, you are all about to experience the

culture of Old Québec!"

Jillian squeals. "Yay!"

I rub my ear.

"Sorry, Kia. I'm just so excited! We're going to speak French, aren't we, Seraphina?"

"We'll see," she says. "We'll see."

We fly over the tree tops and away from le Universite de Creativite. Never in all my dreams did I imagine I would be flying around a country like this, with all my friends. Ander leans up to my seat. Hey KK, look. There's a road down there. I bet if I raced you, I'd win!"

I turn around. "Only if you were on a turbo scooter."

We soon land on the streets of Old Québec, a historic area clustered around the city's harbor on the banks of the St. Lawrence River. The old stone buildings and the narrow winding streets look like they've been here for a million years. Gregor drives the aero-cart up to the Notre-Dame de Québec Basilica, and as we stand there in front of it, I feel like I've been transported to another world.

"Come on," says Seraphina. "Let's go in." We step inside the church, and I can't believe my eyes. It's made of gold and must be at least a thousand stories high!

"I wish we had more time," says Gregor. "We could tour the crypt. It's the resting place of more than nine hundred archbishops, cardinals, and governors."

"You mean there's nine hundred dead bodies in here?" asks Ander.

"That's so creepy," says Mare.

I laugh. "I bet we could look them all up on the Ancestor App and talk to them."

"That would be so cool!" says Ander.

We spend a while in the church, and after that we head

to a place called the Quartier Petit-Champlain, the oldest shopping district in North America.

"But I don't want to shop," says Ander.

"I do!" says Mare.

"Me too," says Jillian.

"Me too," says Seraphina. "But we're not shopping. We're just wandering."

We pass antique shops, gift shops, and sweet-smelling cafés and soon we come to Escalier Casse-Cou. "What's this?" I ask.

"This," says Gregor, "is where you will see a fantastic view of Old Québec. It's otherwise known as the Breakneck Stairs because the steps are so steep. Follow me."

"Great," says Mare. "Can't we take an elevator?"

"We could take the funicular to the top, but you know what they say," says Gregor.

"We know," says Mare. "A physically fit body leads to a creative mind, blah, blah, blah."

We trudge up the steps and my legs begin to ache.

"I feel like we're walking up the steps in Piedmont Chamber back at camp," says Jillian.

When we finally reach the top, we look down over a railing at all the people and all the stone buildings. It feels like we traveled back in time.

"This is how I picture Europe looking," says Jax.

"Me too," says Mare. "I never pictured Canada looking like this though. I like it."

"I like towering above everyone else. I feel like the king of a castle," says Ander.

Mare punches him in the arm. "But in reality you're a jester, remember?"

Ander shrugs. "Freddie Dinkleweed, at your service!"

Seraphina gathers us together and takes pictures of us until we tell her we can't smile any more. "Okay, okay," she finally says. "Anyone hungry?"

"I am," says Ander.

"Me too," says Jax.

"Let's head back down the stairs and look for someplace cute to eat."

"It doesn't even have to be cute," says Ander. "Anything with hamburgers or pizza is fine with me."

"Don't you want to try Québec food?" asks Jillian.

"What's Québec food?" asks Jax.

"You'll see," says Seraphina.

We walk back down, which is obviously way better than climbing up, and wander into a small café. Gregor and Seraphina guide us through the menu. The waiter approaches us with a writing tablet and I listen closely as Seraphina and Gregor place their orders in French. I laugh when Ander orders speaking in English using a French accent. Jillian, of course, does the same. Mare, Jax, and I look at each other and don't even try to speak French, even though I wish I could. The waiter tells us it's fine, that even though French is spoken in this province, people speak English here too.

Soon after, he brings us our food, including poutine—a dish of french fries, gravy, and cheese curds that Québec is known for. It practically melts in my mouth. "This is almost better than scrambled apples."

"You know," says Seraphina. "If we were in Québec in the winter, we could take dog sled rides in the snow."

"Really? That would be awesome," says Ander.

"I'd love to live here," says Jillian. "It reminds me of France."

"Me too," says Seraphina. "It's so full of culture."

"If I could go dog sledding, I'd live here too," says Ander.

"Is this what it would be like if we were on the Swirl and Spark Tour?" asks Mare.

"I think so," says Gregor. "Although we would travel by aero-bus and make many stops throughout the year, it would be like this on some of the days, for sure."

I smile. The Swirl and Spark Tour would be like a total dream.

"But we would also go to many schools. We would meet the young children and show them your inventions. Only three teams are selected, so please remember that. I don't want you to feel disappointed if you don't get first, second, or third place."

"Yeah, I know," says Jax. "We weren't even top in the country, remember? We got second."

"And there are a lot of teams here," adds Mare. "A lot."

"I'd rather think positively," says Jillian.

"Yeah," says Ander. "Me too."

I don't know what to think, so I don't think about it at all. Instead, after we're finished eating, and as we wander through the streets, I think of all the people who live in this place, a place that I had barely even heard of before this summer. It's weird. The world's a lot smaller than I thought.

We climb into the aero-cart, and the butterflies in my stomach go crazy. They must realize what's happening next—the Global Stars Award Ceremony. *Ohmygodohmygodohmygod!* Soon we'll know for sure whether we're going on the tour or not.

THE NIGHT OF GLOBAL STARS

THE LIGHTS IN le Stadium de Creativite dim around us, but
I can still see my teammates as they sit in the row with me.
Ander is on my left, and Mare is on my right. Jax is next to
Ander and Jillian is next to Mare. Seraphina and Gregor are
sitting in the seats behind us. We're wearing matching shirts
again, but this one is my favorite of all. It has a picture of
the American flag on the front; the words "New York" on the
back, the words "The Crimson Five" down one sleeve, and
best of all, "Kia" is scrolled in swirly letters across the other
sleeve. It's nice to be part of a team, and it's really nice to
have people know my name too.

Seraphina leans forward and whispers, "This is it!"

I turn around and smile. Gregor pulls her back and says
something to her. I'm not sure what. Mare nudges me. She
puts her hand out, but I don't know what she wants me to do.

"We're supposed to hold hands, right? Like we did at the National Finals."

"Oh, yeah." I take her hand and grab Ander's too. We sit there in a row, all five of us connected, ready to hear what happens to us next.

If we don't place in the top three, our inventions won't get built. Not the Ancestor App or the Satellite Spectacles. Only six inventions, two from each team, will have that honor. That's all. But we'll still have a place at PIPS. We can choose to enroll there, or we can choose to be programmed into the category we scored the highest in. The choice is ours. I, for sure, would choose PIPS. Ander would choose PIPS too. I used to think Jillian would choose PIPS, but she loves acting and creating so much, I know now that she would choose Art Forms. And Jax might choose Math. I'm not really sure. I think Mare would pick PIPS, but her mom might not let her go there after all. So there's that. If we don't place in the top three, I'll get to go to PIPS, but not with all my friends. Some of them maybe, but not all of them. And that's not how I wish it would be.

But if we do place in the top three, both the Ancestor App and the Satellite Spectacles will be built. And when she wakes up, Grandma Kitty can talk to her mom and know all the information that she left behind. People all over the world will wear our glasses and become more aware of the world they live in. And as for us, we'll go on the Swirl and Spark Tour with Gregor and Seraphina. We could show kids all over the world how fun it is to make new things. We would still be together for a whole year and that would be a dream come true.

But I would be away from my family—from Grandma Kitty.

I'm still not sure what I want to do, but I do know one thing for sure. I want to be able to choose. And besides, somebody has to win tonight, so if I had to pick, I'd still pick us.

The Piedmont theme song thunders through the speakers. The crowd roars to life, and we squeeze tight. I look at Mare, my friend who isn't as awful as I thought. I look at Ander, my best friend who *is* as funny as I thought. I look at Jax and Jillian, my other best friends, and I can't imagine not being with them every day.

"Welcome to the Night of Global Stars!" yells Master Freeman. "We gather here on this prestigious campus of le Universite de Creativity to honor the brightest stars around the globe, every single one of you! You have brought honor to your countries by sharing your talents and twinkling light. We hope that the experiences you have gained here, and the friendships you have created, will last a lifetime."

I think of my team and all that's happened since we got to Québec. But I also think of Maelle, Danielle, and Zoe from France, and Becca from Texas. I even think of Martina.

"Our world is better when we connect with each other and better when we work together. That is the theme of this year's competition and we hope you have learned a great message in that. Keep connecting, keep growing, and keep creating. That is when you will do great things and make great things—together."

"And now, a twist to the results of this competition. I will announce the top five teams in the world. These five teams will have their inventions brought to life, not only the top three."

I look at Ander and then at Seraphina. Oh my gosh, the

top five teams! Our chances are a little better.

"The top three teams will also take part in the year-long Swirl and Spark Tour which will begin this fall. If your team is called, please come down to the stage to receive your Piedmont Globes."

He reaches to the table next to him and picks up an envelope. My butterflies flip out and I think I might throw up all over my lap. Ander squeezes my hand. I squeeze back just so I can forget about my stomach.

"In fifth place is the team from Marrakesh, Morocco!"

The team from Morocco, sitting just one aisle away from us, pops up like popcorn. The whole section around them erupts, and they race down the steps to receive their globes. It seems to take forever.

Master Freeman picks up another envelope.

Mare sits on her hands, and I elbow her.

"Oh, sorry."

"In fourth place, the team from Beijing, China!"

I exhale. The team from China races down to the stadium floor, and I bite my thumb nail. I wipe off my sweaty palms, grab hold of Ander and Mare's hands, and close my eyes.

"In third place, earning a place on the Swirl and Spark Tour . . . the team from Brittany, France."

"Oh my gosh! That's Maelle's team! They're going on the tour!"

Ander's eyes are huge.

The French team is across the stadium. I wish I could see their faces. I wish I could see how happy they are. I wish there were better odds that our team was about to be called too.

Mare leans over. "It's fine if we don't get called. It's fine."

I wish Mare would shut up.

Ander squeezes my hand and I squeeze his right back. We look at each other and not at Master Freeman's envelope. "And in second place, also earning their place on the Swirl and Spark Tour, the team from New York, United States of America."

Ohmygodohmygodohmygod!

We jump up and scurry out of our seats. The stadium is as loud as thunder, and I follow the feet in front of mine. I think they're Jillian's, but I'm not sure. We land on the stadium floor, and just like at the National Finals, Andora Appleonia is waiting there for us, but this time she hands us each a globe. A swirling colorful globe. "Congratulations, Kia Krumpet. I am honored you will be traveling with us on the Piedmont Swirl and Spark Tour. I can think of no one else who will better inspire the children around the world to think more, work hard, and dream big."

She places her hand on my shoulder, turns me around, and I realize we're posing for a picture with Master Freeman. Her voice crackles, "Smile for the television children. The world is watching and smiling at your accomplishment." My head is spinning and I cannot even believe this is happening. My family is out there in the stadium . . . and maybe, just maybe, Grandma Kitty is awake and watching too.

We stand still, all in a row, as Master Freeman announces the first place team, "Bern, Switzerland!"

Seraphina and Gregor hug us. We jump around in a circle and hug the other teams. Maelle and Danielle run to me, and we jump even more. But once the jumping subsides, we look at each other and stand still. I don't think any of us can believe what just happened.

"I now present to you the global ambassadors of the first ever Piedmont Swirl and Spark Tour!"

The fifteen of us pose together holding our globes, with our six preceptors behind us like one united squad—ready to take on the world. But are we ready? Am I ready? Is this what I really want?

Our families find us in the atrium, and Dad scoops me into a hug. Mom and Malin and Ryne wrap their arms around us and they squeeze me until I laugh. "Little Bear! Congratulations! I told you, didn't I? You have all those swirly ideas in your head. I knew those Piedmont officials would recognize talent when they saw it!"

"Good job, Kia!" says Ryne. "I knew you were going to win."

Tears are running down Mom's face. I'm not sure if it's because she's happy or because she knows what might be coming next. She pulls me close and says, "Kia, I'm so very proud of you, and I know your grandma is too."

Malin stares at me in disbelief. "Are you really leaving for a whole year?"

Seraphina calls above the crowd. "Hey everyone, follow me. Gregor is finding a place for us to talk."

We shuffle through the crowd and out of the atrium into a brightly lit room with tables and chairs. We each find a spot and she hands each family a packet of papers. "Please bear with me as I'm still a little stunned with these results! Happy, but still stunned! I know how tired everyone is— it's been a really long day, so I'll make this meeting short. These packets will give you all the details of the trip, should we agree to go. This is your choice to make as a family, but also know that we all have to be in agreement. If someone decides not to go, then we will give up our spot to another team. If we do decide to go, I promise you that your children will be in good hands. This is a tremendous educational opportunity for all of us and would be the experience of a lifetime. Your children have earned it, and both Gregor and I would be honored to accompany them on the adventure."

Gregor continues, "We need to give the Piedmont Organization our decision by noon tomorrow. So please, read through the information and make your decision by then. I'll need your signed paperwork stating your decision either way."

My mom purses her lips together. I think she's trying not to cry. I wish I could tell her not to worry because I'm not going anyway, but then I think of Grandma Kitty. She never got to go to Camp Piedmont. She never had the chance.

My parents flip through the packet, but eventually Dad slides it back into the envelope. "I think we should sleep on it. This is a very big decision, and I'm sure it will be a little clearer tomorrow."

Mom nods. "I think so too. Kia, we'll pick you up at your tree suite at ten o'clock tomorrow morning. We can talk about it over breakfast and make our decision then."

I hope my dad is right. Maybe my sleeping egg will help me decide what to do.

I pull the covers close and lie in my sleeping egg, watching the stars through the skylight. The hum of the germ-eating eggs surrounds me, trying to lull me to sleep. I can't believe we really did it. We placed in the top three—actually, the top two. I've dreamed about this for so long that it's weird it already happened. But it didn't happen the way I wanted. I wanted Grandma Kitty to see it.

My watch flashes under the blankets and I pull them over my head to see if I have a message. But instead of a message, it's a call—from Grandma Kitty! But it can't be her. She isn't awake. I answer it anyway because maybe, just maybe, she is.

I whisper so I won't wake up the girls. "Hello?"

"Is this my Sweet Tart who just won second place in the Global Championship?"

"Grandma! Oh my god! Are you okay? Are you better?"

"Goodness, I'm fine. I'm sorry I worried you."

"I've missed you so much and I really wanted to talk to you, but no one would let me."

"These doctors are so cautious. I just had a little crash on that scooter of mine, and it took me awhile to wake up. But oh, it was the freakiest thing. Those silly cables—I forgot to look out for them. But don't you worry yourself, because I won't make that mistake again. Besides, I've bought myself a sparkly suit of armor. Even if I do crash again, nothing will hurt me like that. I'm just sorry I couldn't see you compete in person, but this cute little doctor fixed me up, and this nice nurse set up my air screen, and I saw your performance in real time. I saw you receive your Piedmont globe too. Sugar Plum, I saw the whole thing!"

"Wait, you saw it! Really?"

"And not only me but the whole floor. We had a Piedmont party in my hotel room, it was just spectacular."

I laugh. "But Grandma, it's a hospital room, not a hotel room."

"Same difference."

"So, Grandma, the Ancestor App is going to be built after all. You're going to be able to learn stuff about your mom."

"And you, my Buttercup, will learn more than you ever

dreamed about the people who came before you. And do you know why that's important?"

"Why?"

"Because we're all connected to those who came before us, and we need to continue that connection—for always."

"For always."

"And as for that Satellite Spectacle thing-a-mabob . . . you and those smart teammates of yours have figured out how to make people more aware of the world around them—with fancy glasses no less. I'm so proud of you, Smartie Girl."

"Thanks, Grandma."

"Now, I spoke to your mother just a few minutes ago. She told me you have quite the decision to make."

"Yes, I do."

"Well, I'll give you a bit of advice when it comes to making decisions."

"Okay."

"Trust the light that comes from your heart. When you feel it glowing, you'll know you've made the right decision. And you must follow that light wherever it leads you—even if you're afraid—because it takes courage to follow your heart. When you do though, everything else will fall into place."

I feel my eyelids drooping. "I'm really glad you're okay, Grandma."

"I'm better than okay. My best girl just placed second in the world at the Piedmont Global Championships, even though she's first place in my book. Besides, the doctor is letting me put sparkles back in my hair tomorrow. So you know, everything is as it should be."

As it should be.

THE FAREWELL SOIRÉE

WE SIT IN the clubhouse, leaning against the tree limbs. It's been twelve hours since the Night of Global Stars, and we need to give our decisions. We have the option of giving our spot up, letting the next team in the standings take our place. But the thing is, either we all go or none of us go. Like if Mare decides not to go, or if I decide not to go, then none of us can go—even if the rest of the team decides they want to.

So much of the Night of Global Stars is a blur to me. The cheering, the screaming, the smiling, the hugging. But hearing our name called—that's definitely not a blur. We won second place again—this time in all the world. The Ancestor App *and* the Satellite Specs will be built, for sure. Our idea and prototype will be sent to PIPS, where it'll be given to a group of people who'll begin developing it. With so many stages of planning though, my teammates and I will be able to work on some of it, even if we take the year off to go on the Swirl and Spark Tour.

I'm really proud of all of us . . . me, my teammates, Seraphina, and Gregor. Together, we did all this and nothing will change that, whether we go on the Swirl and Spark Tour or not.

Seraphina crosses her legs, swinging her purple heels. "This decision is up to you, and only you, and no one will be mad if you decide the tour is not for you. It'll be a very big deal to be away from your families and friends for one whole year. It will be a very big commitment on your part, one that we don't take lightly. If you decide to say yes, you must be certain that it's what you want."

Gregor leans forward. "You each have in your hands the paperwork you and your parents have signed—that we must submit. We need to know now if each of you is still in agreement with the decision your family has made. No matter what the outcome, no matter what your teammates decide. I also need your word that if four of you have made the same decision and one of you has made a different decision, the four of you will not be angry at the one."

We nod, and Seraphina continues, "So, no hard feelings either way."

"But what about you?" Ander asks. "Do you and Gregor vote too?"

"No," says Gregor. "We're your preceptors. If your team unanimously decides to go, we will be thrilled to accompany you, and if your team decides to return to New York for programming or to enroll at PIPS right now, we'll be thrilled to hear of your adventures there too."

"Can we just get this over with?" asks Mare.

Suddenly it hits me. I had thought I would be okay with

whatever we decided. But I'm not. I want us all to want the same thing.

"Alright," says Seraphina. "Let's see what it's going to be."

"But wait!" I say. "How are you going to tell us? Like are you going to say one at a time, how each of us voted?"

"No," says Gregor. "We're simply going to tell you if we're going on the tour or not. That way, if the answer is yes, you'll know you all agreed to go, and if the answer is no, you won't have to feel blame toward anyone, in case it wasn't unanimous."

I nod. That's seems fair.

Seraphina peaks inside each of our envelopes with no expression on her face at all. She hands them to Gregor, who does the same. He looks stone-faced too. "Shall I say it or would you like to?"

She picks at her purple nail polish. "I'd like to if you don't mind."

Oh my god, just say it!

She looks at us, still with no expression, and says, "Well, my Crimson Kids. I'm not surprised at all that you agreed."

Wait, agreed to do what?

"We're going!"

I scream. "We are? We all said yes?"

"You all said yes!"

Our true dreams are sometimes different than what we wish for. Have the courage to make your true dream come true.

And that's why I voted yes. Because sure I want to go to PIPS, but my true dream is to be a mermaid, just like I told the judges at the Piedmont Challenge, swimming with my new friends all summer.

The Colony Square is a sea of kids swimming, laughing, singing, and dancing under strands of twinkling lights. Music fills the air in an endless loop of songs from all over the world. Some we know, so we belt out the words. Others are strange to us, sung in languages we don't understand, but we dance to them anyway. Rhythm is rhythm in any language, I guess.

Martina is laughing near the Creativity Pool with her teammates from Michigan and Becca from Texas. She sees me and waves me over. "I wasn't sure I'd see you before we left tomorrow. I was hoping we could exchange numbers and maybe stay in touch."

I smile. "I'd like that."

"I have something to show you."

I can't read her face. It's not happy but not sad either. She opens a message on her watch.

Martina, I don't know where to begin so I'll begin at the Piedmont Global Finals. I headed to Québec yesterday to find my students, the New York team from my school at Crimson Heights. I wanted to keep track of them, watch their every move. I wanted them to win—more than anything—because since your Grandmother died, that's all that I had in my life. I left our home in Michigan because any reminder of her was simply too painful for me. But what I found yesterday in Québec, through the people associated with the Piedmont Organization, was something I didn't expect. I found you.

I had lost track of the years, lost track of you, and all this time I could have been cheering for you. I could have been in your corner. It may be too much to ask, but if you would agree, I'd like to see you in person to congratulate you. If

you don't, I'll understand. But I owe you and your grand-
mother that much. You deserved better than I gave you. I'll
be at your aero-bus when you leave tomorrow. If you want
to talk to me, I'll be there. Grandpa Bermuda

I don't know what to say to her, so I hug her instead.
"Are you going to go?"

She smiles. "Maybe. I think so."

"He sounds really sorry. Can you send me a message on
the way back and tell me what he says?"

"Definitely!"

I head back to my team, and they're talking to the
French team. "Maelle!" I call.

She turns around. "Kia! So it's true? We are all going on
the Swirl and Spark Tour together, yes?"

"Yes! We're going too!"

Mare smirks at me in her Mare-ish way, like she can't
stand me, but she can't fool me anymore. "So we're stuck
with each other for a whole year."

I smile and put my arm around her. "With more
matching clothes and everything!"

Jillian swirls around. "This is going to be fabulous. We're
going to be world travelers together!"

Ander pats Jax on the back. "Are you ready for this, Big
Guy? Ready for another juggling tournament?"

Jax shakes his head. "I'm definitely ready to go, but no
juggling this time."

"Seriously?"

"Seriously."

Ander shrugs. "Okay, I guess I'll have to think of something else."

I laugh. Of course, he will.

"Is this really happening, KK? Are we really going to be flying all over the world together, with the kids from Switzerland and France?"

I smile at him, and my heart feels happier than I could have ever imagined.

"But what about PIPS? I was afraid you were going to choose to go there right away. I thought that was the most important thing to you," Ander says.

"I guess I was wrong. I mean, PIPS will be great and everything—someday—but this way the five of us are stuck together for a whole year before any of us has to decide where to go next."

"You're right, KK, and we didn't even need the extra duct tape."

"We better bring some on the trip anyway. You know, in case the silver switch needs fixing again, or the golden light bulb needs sticking, or—"

"Or what?"

"I'm not sure. Who knows what other tasks we'll be getting next? But the Swirl and Spark Tour is a whole year, and you know how the Piedmont people are."

Acknowledgments

Seeing my first book in published form was a dream come true for me. Now, seeing my second book out in the world too? Well, it's so much more than I ever imagined possible. My heart is full thinking about all the people who've helped to bring *Flip the Silver Switch* to life:

To my husband, Jim: You're my constant in so many ways, and all of this is more meaningful and fun because I'm able to share it with you. Thank you for your technical advisement when my inventions made no sense at all, and your last minute idea for the Satellite Spectacles. It was a game-changer for this book. But most of all, thank you for sticking with me in spite of the fact that I live in a dream-world most of the time!

To my daughter, Danielle—my right-hand girl. Thank you for listening and cheering me on through the ups and downs of writing this story and for your perfect portrayal of Seraphina in the *Spin the Golden Light Bulb* extended book trailer. It would not have been the same without you! And to my son, Adam—the one who imagines even bigger possibilities than I do. Thank you for inspiring me with your over-the-top dreams of the future, especially as I re-lived the Odyssey of the Mind World Finals and re-imagined it into the Piedmont Global Championships. They are evident on so many pages of this book.

To my mom and dad: Thank you for showing me the importance of family. The only reason I'm able to write about close family connections at all is because I've experienced them. I'm so grateful to share this journey with you. And to my mother-in-law and father-in-law who never stop asking me about my books: It means everything to me that you both care so much!

To Terri, Amy, Candy, Joanna, Kelly, Di, Sam, and Christi: Sometimes the most important members of a team are your forever friends and sisters—the ones who cheer for you during both the big and small moments of the game. I treasure you all. To Brian, Bobby, Tom, and Dave: Thank you for being rock solid role models in our family and a source of so much support to me. I appreciate you all. And to my niece, Stella, who portrays Kia Krumpet in the book trailers in such an adorable way: Thank you, Sweetie!

To my nieces and nephews: Riley, Jordan, Jason, Tori, Eva, Mackenzie, Ben, Sarah, Eli, Stella, Samantha, and Van: You've made me smile so much through the years and bits and pieces of each of you are sprinkled throughout this book. My characters would be incomplete without you!

To Maelle Cossec from Quimper, France: You felt like a daughter to me during the short time you lived with us as an exchange student. Thank you for your friendship and for sharing your culture with all of us! I told you I was going to include you as a character in my next book. Well, I finally did! And to Zoe Lelievre, our new French friend as well: It was a joy spending time with you too. Hopefully all of our paths will cross again one day!

To Joe Burns and Melyssa Mercado, my invaluable critique partners: What would I do without you? I'm so grateful for your honest feedback, brilliant insight, support of my writing—and friendship. Thank you for helping to make *Flip the Silver Switch* the story that it is. To Jordan Meechan, my beta reader: This book is so much better because of your thoughts. One day, I hope to return the favor. And to the Electric Eighteens, 2018 Debut Author Group: You've been a source of incredible support to me as I've navigated my debut year. Thank you for helping to make it a year to remember. May all of your debut days be just as spectacular!

To Dayna Anderson, my publisher. You've changed my life by believing in THE CRIMSON FIVE books. I will forever think of you as my fairy godmother. Thank you to you and the entire Amberjack Publishing team for being nothing short of stellar. I couldn't ask for a better home for my books. I'm honored to be associated with Amberjack and its amazing authors.

To Jenny Miller, my editor, and Keara Donick, my publicist: I wish I could tell you both in person how grateful I am for the work you've done on my behalf. But, as Kia would say, "Some things are too big to spit into words." You are both so incredible to work with and have made this experience a dream come true. Thank you from the bottom of my heart.

To Rebecca Angus, my agent at Golden Wheat Literary:

Writing a book is a small thing compared to the important work carried out by so many others. You and Patrick exemplify all that is good in our country. Thank you for supporting me and my writing endeavors as you gracefully navigate your life as a military spouse too. I am in awe of you.

To Gabrielle Esposito, the amazing talent behind the covers and chapter illustrations of *Spin the Golden Light Bulb* and *Flip the Silver Switch*: You've captured the world of THE CRIMSON FIVE brilliantly. It's almost eerie, as if you were able to see the images in my head while I dreamed up this story. These books would not be the same without your magic touch. Thank you so very much!

To the Odyssey of the Mind Organization for creating a program which has inspired thousands of children around the world to solve problems in the most creative ways: If it weren't for OotM, I would have never had the idea for THE CRIMSON FIVE books. I'll be forever grateful that my kids and I were a part of your program. And to the kids I've coached through the years—every single one of you brought something special to my teams, and I'm grateful to have worked with you. Thank you for giving me such fun material for this book!

A heartfelt thanks to Kara, Adam, Meg, Jake, and Julia— the kids behind THE CRIMSON FIVE characters. Thank you for being my inspiration—again—and for stepping back in time with me to create the *Spin the Golden Light Bulb* extended book trailer. You are all amazing! And thank you to the Bilodeau, Davis, Leach, and Vanill families. Sharing the OotM World Finals with all of you was spectacular and I hope I was able to reflect a bit of that experience on the pages of this book.

And finally to my readers: every child, parent, teacher, librarian, blogger, reviewer, family member, and friend. Thank you for choosing my book, especially when there are so many wonderful books in the world to choose from. It's a privilege to share my story with you. I hope that you see yourself someplace in these pages, and that whatever path you choose or goal you set for yourself, you always remember to *Think More. Work Hard. Dream Big!*

About the Author

Jackie Yeager is a middle grade author whose stories inspire children to think more, work hard, and dream big. She holds a Master's degree in Education and spent several years coaching Odyssey of the Mind, where her team once-upon-a-time competed at the World Finals. She lives in Rochester, NY with her real life prince charming and two royally amazing teens.

When she's not writing imaginative middle grade fiction or living in her own fairly-tale world, she can be found conducting creative problem solving/writing workshops for kids and blogging at www.swirlandspark.com. You can also connect with her on Twitter, Facebook, and Instagram.

Flip the Silver Switch is her second book, following the first book in the Crimson Five series, *Spin the Golden Light Bulb (2018)*.

About the Illustrator

Gabrielle Esposito is an illustrator with a passion for using art to tell stories, capture moments, and bring imaginary worlds to life. She earned her Bachelor's degree in Fine Art from the American Academy of Art in Chicago.

Her work includes illustrating *The Story of Snowy Bear and the Lost Scarf* by T.C. LiFonti and Charles "Peanut" Tillman, and the four subsequent books in the Bear series: *The Story of Pirate Bear and the Treasure Hunt*, *The Story of Beach Bear and the Sandcastle*, *The Story of Scary Bear and the Pumpkin Patch*, and *The Story of Lovie Bear and the Valentine's Day Card*.

Gabrielle lives in Chicago, accompanied by an orange-and-white cat with a big personality, and when she's not making art, she loves spending time kayaking, hiking, gardening, or wandering through museums. You can find more of her art online at gabrielleesposito.com, and connect with her on Facebook and Instagram.